"What do you expect from me, Ms. Brooks?"

Her dark sad eyes found his and he felt a catch in his throat at all the pain he saw there.

"I'd like for us to look for new evidence like you mentioned."

"Us?" He motioned from her to him with the pencil.

"Yes. I'm Blake's personal assistant and I'm very familiar with court documents. I can help you go through all the files and maybe we can catch something that no one else has."

"Don't you think you're grasping at straws?" He had to point that out.

"You didn't think so yesterday."

"Yesterday I hadn't talked to my father. You have to remember that Asa is my father."

"I realize that, but he committed a crime. And you are the law here in Willow Creek."

His stomach churned with uneasiness. The line between family and loyalty and his job was clearly blurred.

Dear Reader,

I love secret-baby books. There. I've admitted it. I enjoy all the tension and complexity the theme brings to a story. And the tumultuous emotions. I love reading them and writing them. Saying that, I also have to admit out of thirty-three published books I've only written two secret-baby books. *A Texas Family* is my third.

The idea for this book came to me a few years ago when I was in the hospital. With nothing to do but lie in bed, I watched a lot of soap operas, which I don't normally do while I'm at home writing. Of course, I got pulled into a story line. A girl had gotten pregnant when she was about fifteen or sixteen. She had carried the baby to term, but her father had given it away because he said she was too young to raise it. Years later, she comes back to her hometown a strong, mature woman determined to find the baby who had been taken from her.

As with soap operas, they go on and on, and once I was home I had to stop watching and go back to writing. But that story stayed with me and I knew I had to write my take on it, Texas-style. There are a lot of twists and turns and if you like a tearjerker, you'll love this book. So come join Jena Brooks as she goes home and meets Carson Corbett, who will risk all to help her.

Don't miss *A Texas Hero* (July 2013), the first book in my Willow Creek, Texas series. *A Texas Child* will be released in December 2013.

'Til next time, with love and thanks,

Linda Warren

PS—You can email me at Lw1508@aol.com or send me a message on Facebook, www.facebook.com/authorlindawarren, or on Twitter, www.twitter.com/texauthor, or write me at P.O. Box 5182, Bryan, TX 77805 or visit my website at www.lindawarren.net. Your mail and thoughts are deeply appreciated.

A Texas Family

———

Linda Warren

HARLEQUIN® SUPER ROMANCE®

Recycling programs
for this product may
not exist in your area.

ISBN-13: 978-0-373-71879-5

A TEXAS FAMILY

Copyright © 2013 by Linda Warren

Printed in U.S.A.

HARLEQUIN®
™ www.Harlequin.com

ABOUT THE AUTHOR

Two time RITA® Award-nominated and award-winning author Linda Warren loves her job, writing happily-ever-after books for Harlequin. Drawing upon her years of growing up on a farm/ranch in Texas, she writes about sexy heroes, feisty heroines and broken families with an emotional punch, all set against the backdrop of Texas. Her favorite pastime is sitting on her patio with her husband watching the wildlife, especially the injured ones which are coming in pairs these days: two Canada geese with broken wings, two does with broken legs and a bobcat ready to pounce on anything tasty. Learn more about Linda and her books at her website, www.lindawarren.net or on Facebook, www.facebook.com/authorlindawarren.

Books by Linda Warren

HARLEQUIN SUPERROMANCE

HARLEQUIN AMERICAN ROMANCE

*The Belles Of Texas
+The Hardin Boys
**Willow Creek, Texas

Other titles by this author available in ebook format.

Acknowledgments

I will like to thank those long-suffering friends who listened to me plotting this story over and over—I owe you chocolate.
To all those people I phoned and questioned about the law and police procedure—I owe you a strong drink.
And to Britany Wiggins for sharing her small-town Texas—I owe you a hug.
All errors are strictly mine.

Dedication

I dedicate this book to my family,
the Warrens and the Siegerts.
Without your love and support I would be lost.
And to Kathleen Scheibling, my editor,
who lifts my spirits when they are down.
Thank you!

CHAPTER ONE

REVENGE WAS SUCH an ugly word. And Jena Brooks was about to get up close and personal with ugly.

She paused at the office door of Constable Carson Corbett, straightened her deep plum suit, made sure the buttons of her cream silk blouse were fastened and tossed her shoulder-length dark hair to emphasize its layered effect.

But even with the expensive clothes, artfully applied makeup and professionally cut hair, Jena couldn't disguise who she really was—the girl from the wrong side of the tracks whose father had killed Jared Corbett in cold blood.

Because of her.

Or that was what everyone in Willow Creek, Texas, thought.

She took a deep breath and opened the door.

Carson looked up. His green eyes narrowed as he recognized her. "You have a lot of nerve coming back to Willow Creek."

She closed the door and marched to the chair in front of his desk. His harsh words grated on her sensitive nerves like a cocklebur and oddly boosted her courage.

"You won't believe the nerve I have, Mr. Corbett."

Sitting with as much grace as her trembling limbs could provide, she placed her purse on the floor and crossed her legs. Her pencil skirt shimmied up, revealing more of her legs than she'd wanted.

She stared straight at him, resisting the urge to tug at her hemline, and was surprised to catch his eyes on her legs. Briefly.

He leaned back in his leather chair, the fabric of his light blue shirt stretching taut across wide shoulders.

"Why are you here?"

"Revenge." She fired the word at him with the force of a bullet intending to annihilate his composure. But it didn't work.

His self-possession seemed firmly intact as he asked, "For what?"

"You know what."

"Sorry." He shrugged. "You'll have to fill me in."

"Do the Corbetts have a patent on that dumb expression?"

He leaned forward, his eyes never leaving hers. "Ms. Brooks, we can trade snide remarks back and forth all day, but I have work to do. So, once again, why are you in my office?"

"I came back for my child."

"And that has something to do with me?"

"You really have that blank expression down."

"That's because I don't know what the hell you're talking about." His voice rose with frustration.

"Then I'll fill you in." Her voice rose, too. "I would be talking to your father, Asa, but I heard he's had a stroke. You'll pardon me if I don't offer any consolatory words."

His face darkened.

"Just before I turned eighteen, I was pregnant with your brother's child."

"Wait." He held up a hand. "Pa always insisted it wasn't Jared's."

"Yeah, that's why after Jared's death..."

"Murder," he corrected in a chilling voice.

Her control slipped for a split second, but she would not be intimidated or stopped. Not this time.

"Asa's goons kidnapped me a week before my due date and took me to the Bar C Ranch. Minnie Voltree, the midwife, gave me something to induce labor, and six hours later I gave birth. The baby was taken away. I never saw it and don't even know if it was a boy or a girl. Your father came in and said to my face, 'A life for a life, girlie. Now you'll never pass that kid off as a Corbett. My advice to you is to get out of town as fast as you can because if I see you in Willow Creek, I'll bury you so deep your body will never be found. And your mother and sister will join you.'"

She'd spoken the words in a cool and unemotional imitation of Carson's father, but at the end her voice cracked. She hated that she couldn't control that weakness.

"That's a tall tale, Ms. Brooks, and I'm not sure why you're telling it to me. This supposedly happened years ago."

She reached into her purse and pulled out a business card. Placing it on his desk, she said, "I work for a criminal attorney in Dallas—a very good criminal attorney. He's given me the courage to fight for what's mine. I left here a broken, naïve girl, but I've come back a mature, strong woman. I want my child, and your father knows where my baby is. I intend to get that information."

"Shouldn't you be talking to the sheriff?"

She picked up her purse and stood. "Out of respect for my child and for my mother and my sister, who still live here, I'd rather do this discreetly. I'll give you two days to question your father. After that, my attorney will be contacting the proper authorities." Without another word, she walked out.

CARSON CURSED UNDER his breath, feeling as if he'd been sideswiped by a Mack truck going about ninety miles an hour. Was she telling the truth? His mind grappled with what she'd said. It didn't make sense. He'd been in the Marines at the time, so he couldn't be sure about anything. And he sure couldn't imagine his father doing something so barbaric. But then again, Asa Corbett lived by his own rules.

He picked up the card. *Blake Davenport and Associates, PC.* Jena Brooks was one determined woman, and he couldn't ignore that. He'd start by verifying some facts and take it from there.

Glancing at his watch, he got to his feet and headed for the door—time to pick up the kids. It was the end of May and the end of another school year. His kids were excited about the summer break. Trey, his son, more so than his daughter, Claire. At four, Claire was more excited about playing with her Barbie dolls or watching *SpongeBob SquarePants.*

Trey was an outdoor boy. He loved fishing, hunting, riding his horse, helping with the cows and basically just getting dirty. When he was five, Beth had died giving birth to Claire. Trey'd been sad for so long. They all had been.

Beth had been the love of Carson's life, his high school sweetheart. Living without her was an indescribable heartache. But he had two kids to raise, and he had to be strong for them every day.

He couldn't imagine someone taking one of his children. That would kill him. His thoughts turned to Ms. Brooks. He knew she'd been pregnant all those years ago. Beth had written him many times about her and about Asa's wrath that she planned to pass her bastard child off as a Corbett. Then Jared, his brother, had been murdered by Lamar Brooks, and Carson had never given the pregnancy another thought. At the time, he'd wanted the whole Brooks family to rot in hell.

When he heard of his brother's murder, he was devastated and soon made the decision to leave the Marines. His family needed him. Beth was about to give birth to their son, and he wanted to be there.

Jared's body had been found on the side of the road next to his truck. He'd been shot with a shotgun at close range. The gun belonged to Lamar Brooks. Before Lamar could be arrested, he was found dead in his own driveway. The weapon used was also a shotgun. Asa owned one, but when the sheriff ran a ballistics test, it didn't match.

Everyone thought Asa had killed Lamar to avenge the death of his son. It was never proved, though. To this day it remained the biggest crime and scandal to ever happen in Willow Creek. Now Jena Brooks was dredging it all up again.

What had happened to her baby? And was it Jared's? Whatever the answers were, he was being dragged right into the middle of it. Their peaceful town would be abuzz with rumors and half-truths. And it was up to him to sort through it all.

He didn't relish the task.

He'd just as soon never see Jena Brooks again.

JENA DROVE OVER the railroad tracks that ran through Willow Creek. She passed a trailer park and then took a right onto a gravel road. Another left and she rolled into the Brookses' driveway. She turned off the engine of her Honda Accord and stared at the run-down frame house. It once was white, but it was hard to tell that now. The boards were almost bare. Several screens were missing. To the right was an old car with grass grown up around it.

She'd spent the first eighteen years of her life here on the wrong side of the tracks, living off welfare and food stamps. Her dad was a drunk who couldn't hold down a job, and her mother was weak, putting up with a crappy way of life. They received bags of used clothes from different charities and food and toys during the holidays. It was mortifying for a young girl.

She used to dream of leaving Willow Creek and never coming back. Never again living on food stamps and welfare. And never being like her parents.

Her hands ached and she realized she had a death grip on the steering wheel. She hadn't been home in nine years, and it was a bit unnerving. As was her visit with Carson Corbett. Since he was five years older than her and Jared, she'd never formally met him, but she'd seen him often around town with his girlfriend, Beth. Jena definitely knew who he was.

He had the same dark blond hair and green eyes as Jared, except Carson was taller and more muscular, probably because of his military training.

When she'd heard of Asa's stroke from her sister, Hilary, she'd known if she was ever going to find her baby she'd have to do it quickly. If Asa died, he would take his secret with him. It had taken her nine years to get to this point, and no one was stopping her now. Not even Carson.

She got out of the car and walked through the grass

to the front door. One of the things she remembered from her childhood was that the grass always needed cutting and they didn't have a lawn mower. She and Hil used a Weedwacker to chop it down around the house to keep the mice away.

The boards creaked as she stepped up, but then, they always did. Not much had changed. Her mother's rocker still sat on the front porch, where she used to wait for her daughters to walk home from school.

She hadn't told her mom she was coming home, and she wasn't sure how she was going to react. All these years, Norma Brooks had insisted that Jena stay away from Willow Creek. She was still afraid Asa Corbett would kill her daughter.

Opening the screen door, she called, "Mama." She didn't want to frighten her.

Norma appeared from the kitchen in jeans and a print blouse, shock etched across her aging face. Her dark eyes were dull and her dark hair was almost gray at fifty years of age. Jena stood in shock, hardly believing her mother's health had deteriorated this much.

"Jena, what are you doing here?"

She closed the door and walked in. "Hi, Mama. Aren't you glad to see me?"

"Oh, Jena, my beautiful daughter." They hugged tightly, and Norma drew back, wiping away a tear. "Just look at you. All citified. I almost didn't recognize you, but you have to go. You can't stay here."

She took her mother's arm. "Mama, we have to talk."

"Okay, but not too long." Norma sank into an old worn recliner they'd gotten from Goodwill more than twenty years ago. Duct tape covered the threadbare arms.

Jena pulled a wooden chair close to her mother and

noticed a bucket near the windows. Glancing up, she saw the brown stains. The roof was leaking. She'd sent Hilary money for a new roof. What had she done with it? She couldn't think about that now.

"Mama, Asa Corbett has had a stroke. Hilary told you."

Norma frowned. "I don't remember."

Hilary had said their mother had memory lapses and was out of it a lot these days. It was unsettling to witness.

"He has. He's in a wheelchair, and he's not going to hurt anyone. It's been so long ago no one cares anymore."

No one but me.

"I don't know," Norma murmured in a faraway voice.

"Mama, I'm going to be staying a few days, and you've got nothing to worry about."

The screen door banged and Hilary breezed in with a Styrofoam takeout container in her hand. "Hey, sis, you made it."

"Yeah."

People said they looked alike, and Jena supposed they did with the same dark eyes and hair and similar facial features. But the resemblance ended there. They were totally different in personality. Hilary was a bubbly scatterbrain who talked constantly. Jena, on the other hand, was reserved and quiet. She'd been called uptight more than once. Jared was the only one who'd seen she was a warm, compassionate person in need of love. Desperate for love.

"Did you bring my dinner?" Norma asked.

"Sure did, Mama. I'll put it on the kitchen table. It's Mabel's pot roast with mashed potatoes, gravy and homemade rolls. Peach cobbler for dessert. You better eat it while it's warm." Hil hurried into the kitchen.

"Okay." Norma followed her and so did Jena.

Hil fixed a glass of iced tea and placed it and a napkin on the table.

Jena watched this, rather mystified. Her mom was a wonderful cook and was capable of making delicious meals with the little food they'd had. Why wasn't she cooking?

Jena went back into the living room, and soon Hilary joined her. "I had no idea Mama was this bad."

"Ever since Dad was murdered and Mama got you out of town so quick, she hasn't been the same. Every day she gets a little worse."

"Did she just stop cooking?"

"She left grease on the burner twice, and it caught fire. I just happened to be home or our—" she glanced around the drab room "—mansion would have burned down. I had one of the guys turn off the gas to the stove. I can turn it on if I need to, but since I work at the café I bring her food."

Hilary had worked at Mabel's Café ever since she was sixteen. There weren't many jobs in Willow Creek, a town of four hundred. Her sister would be stuck here for the rest of her life, taking care of their mother.

She reached out and hugged her. "Thank you, baby sis, for all you do."

"Aw." Hil pulled away. "You gonna make me cry."

"I know it's not easy dealing with Mama."

"It's like dealing with a child."

"I know we talked about her doctor visits. Is there nothing else he can do?"

Hil shook her head. "He said severe trauma from the

murders has altered her personality, and dementia has set in, but I know her moods. We're okay."

The bucket caught Jena's attention. "I hate to sound critical when I'm so appreciative, but what happened to the money for the roof?"

"Oh, that. Don't get upset. Wait till you see."

Jena followed her sister through the kitchen and suddenly stopped. There was a utility room off the kitchen—a bright cheery room painted a soft yellow with a white washer and dryer. One wall had a mural of a rainbow, clouds and birds.

Jena was speechless.

Growing up, they hadn't had a washer or a dryer. On Saturdays, they usually went into Dripping Springs to a Laundromat. But if they didn't have money, their mother washed their clothes in the bathtub—a backward way of life for the poor people who lived across the tracks. A stigma that would be with her for the rest of her life, as would so many other things from her childhood.

"You built a utility room?"

"Fresh, isn't it?" She pointed to the mural. "It would have cost more money to put a window in, so I painted a scene to liven up the place."

"Who built this?"

"The guys. I bought all the supplies, and they did the rest."

"What guys?"

"The ones who come into the café: Billy Jack, Clem, Bobby Joe, Bruce, Lenny and…"

"The labor was free?"

"Yes. Bruce is a carpenter, Lenny a plumber, Clem a Sheetrock guy, Billy Jack a painter and Bobby Joe a roofer. They had it up in two days."

"For free?"

Hil grinned. "I just promised to cut their piece of pie a little bigger at the café. They'll do anything for an extra piece of pie."

Jena believed they did it for Hilary. She had a way with people.

She looked at the white ceiling. "I'm assuming this has a roof on it."

"Of course."

"Then why didn't you roof the whole house?"

"Well—" she tilted her head slightly "—I ran out of money. I can get the guys to do hard labor, but I can't get them to fork over any cash. So Bobby Joe put tar on it, and he's coming back to repair that one spot that's still leaking."

"If you're happy…"

"I am." She did a dance, swung around in a quick move and did a ta-da with her hands pointed toward the washer and dryer in a typical Vanna White gesture. "I can wash clothes anytime I want. I feel empowered."

Jena laughed, something she hadn't done in a long time, but in her heart she felt guilty. She had those conveniences in Dallas and more, while her mother and sister lived in poverty. While she was here she would try to improve things as much as she could.

Arm in arm they walked into the kitchen. Their mother sat at the table, staring off into space, her food barely touched.

Hilary went to her. "Hey, Mama, why aren't you eating?"

"What? Oh." Norma looked up, her eyes blank. "I'm not hungry. You can—" She stared at Jena. "What are you doing here? You have to go. They'll hurt you. C'mon." She stood up so fast the chair went flying into the stove.

Hilary immediately hugged their mother, motioning for Jena to go into the other room. Her legs trembled, but she did what her sister asked.

"It's okay, Mama," Hil was saying. "A little nap and you'll feel much better."

"Why do I keep seeing her?"

"Because you're worried about her, but Jena is fine. Remember I told you she's coming for a visit."

"No. They'll hurt her again."

"That was in the past. Things are different now."

"I'm so cold."

"Lie down and I'll get a blanket." In a few minutes Hilary was back in the living room.

"Is she always like that?" Jena asked.

"It comes and goes. Today's a bad day. She'll wake up and be almost normal. It's strange."

"She shouldn't be left by herself."

Hilary shrugged. "I don't have much choice. I have to work, but I check on her all the time. It's not that far to the café, and the good thing is she won't leave the house. This is familiar, and if I force her outside for fresh air she gets all nervous."

"We have to talk about this, Hil."

"I'm not putting her in a home," Hilary said with a stubborn lift of her chin.

Jena didn't want to do that, either, but they'd have to have a serious conversation soon.

"Enough with the depressing thoughts." Hil jerked off her boots and socks. "I want to try on those shoes. Off with them."

Jena smiled and really looked at her sister's attire for the first time. She wore a denim skirt that flared out around her thighs, a red-and-white-check blouse and cowgirl boots with red tops. Bracelets dangled on her wrist; large silver earrings hung from her ears. She looked as if she was going square dancing.

Undoing the tiny strap around her ankles, Jena said, "Love the outfit."

"I make sure no one forgets me." Hilary slipped on the four-inch heels. "Wow." She tottered across the living room and then mimicked the walk of a runway model, tripped and fell onto the sofa, laughing. "How do you walk in these things?"

"You get used to it, and I have to dress nice for my job."

"Oh, yeah, the big attorney."

Jena didn't miss the sarcastic tone. "He's been nice to me, Hil."

"You deserve it, Jen-Jen."

She felt a warm glow at the nickname her sister had given her.

Hilary placed the shoes on the coffee table. "I saw the Accord parked at Carson's. A lot of people did and wondered who you were. I didn't say anything."

"I don't care who knows I'm back."

Hilary played with the hem of her skirt. "They'll wonder about the baby."

Hearing the fear in her sister's voice, she got up and sat by her on the sofa. "It doesn't matter. The truth is going to come out."

"What did Carson say?"

"Not much. I told him I want to see my child and he could either get the information from his father or the authorities would. I'm not afraid of them anymore."

Hilary continued to pick at the hem. "Sometimes I have nightmares about that night."

"Me, too," she murmured as her stomach cramped. "Mama and I were so worried. You didn't come home from your shift at the convenience store. Just as we were getting ready to go look for you, Roland Stubbs and Curly Sanders dragged you into the house. Your clothes were bloody. Roland said, 'Get her out of town before Asa kills her.'"

Hilary took a breath. "Then you told us what had happened, and Mama was furious. She put you to bed and borrowed Mrs. Carter's car because the sheriff had seized Dad's truck for evidence. She and I went to the Bar C. She demanded the baby, and Asa pushed her against one of those huge pillars on the porch and threatened to kill all of us. He didn't care, he said. His son was dead."

Jena wanted her to stop talking. She didn't want to remember, but in truth she thought of that horrible night vividly almost every day. And every night.

"We came home, and Mama called cousin Nan in Dallas, and she drove through the night to get you out of Willow Creek. You lay on the backseat in a blanket and cried the whole way. I cried, too."

Jena wrapped her arms around her waist to still the trembling.

"Cousin Nan said you could stay with her, and Mama gave her some money. I don't know where she got it. Funny how I remember that. Mama and I returned to Willow Creek, and I didn't realize until weeks later that you weren't coming back. I cried myself to sleep that night." Hil wiped away an errant tear. "For weeks I looked for newborn babies in Willow Creek. There weren't any, except with women who had been pregnant. Do you…don't get upset…do you think Asa might have killed it?"

Jena tensed. "Sometimes. But I don't think even Asa

could have been so cruel as to kill the baby if he thought there was a chance it was Jared's child."

"But he's crazy."

Jena stood, needing to move to stop the flood of memories.

"Jen-Jen?"

"Hmm?"

"I know you're set on finding your baby, and I would be, too, but have you thought the child would be almost nine years old now and probably with a family who loves it dearly?"

"I've thought of a million scenarios."

"It's been a long time. You have a good life in Dallas. Wouldn't it be best to leave the past in the past?"

"I have to know where my child is."

"I'm afraid you're going to get hurt again."

"Maybe, but I'm not young and scared anymore. It's illegal, even in Willow Creek, to steal someone's baby, and Asa Corbett is going to pay for what he did."

She'd come back for revenge, just as she'd told Carson. She now had access to resources for justice, and she intended to make that happen—with or without the constable's help.

CHAPTER TWO

EVERY TIME CARSON drove under the wrought-iron arch for the Bar C Ranch, his chest filled with pride, which was quickly replaced with anger for a brief second. When he'd finished his tour of duty, he was excited to see his wife and son again. And to be there for his dad, who Beth had said had sunk into deep depression since Jared's death. But that was just one of Carson's many worries.

Even before Jared was murdered, Asa had turned over the reins of the ranch to Roland Stubbs, allowing him to sign checks. That was a big mistake. Roland sold all the cattle, horses, equipment and drained the ranch bank account. All that was left was the house, barns and land.

Carson's return home was bittersweet. His dad sat brooding in his chair and didn't show much interest in the ranch or in his daughter-in-law or grandson. Beth had been dealing with a newborn and hadn't noticed anything strange going on except for the cattle trailers going in and out, which she'd thought was normal ranching business.

He'd contacted the sheriff, and Roland and Curly Sanders were soon arrested and convicted. Curly was released last year, but Roland would be in prison for some time to come. When Jena had mentioned goons, he'd had a bad feeling in his gut. Those two were ruthless enough to do anything.

He never quite understood his dad's reasoning in handing the ranch's responsibilities to Roland. He'd said it was Carson's fault for not being here. The Bar C was his legacy, and neither he nor Jared showed any respect for what he'd built. So if the ranch was in trouble Carson had only himself to blame.

But Carson accepted only so much of that blame. According to Beth, his dad was spending a lot of time with a lady he kept in Austin. That meant he'd been ignoring his business, which had allowed Roland to weasel his way into a cushy job. As long as Asa saw money rolling in, he hadn't questioned Roland or his activities.

"Dad, you better get your money ready," Trey said from the passenger seat. "I made all A's again, and it's five bucks for every A. Remember?"

"What?"

"Dad." Trey sighed. "You're not listening."

"Five bucks for every A. I got it."

"Me, too, Daddy," Claire said from her car seat in the back.

"You got it, princess." He looked in the rearview mirror at his blonde beauty. She looked just like her mother except she had green eyes like him, as did Trey.

"You don't get grades," Trey told her. "You're too little."

"Am not."

"Are, too."

Carson held up his hand. "Enough. What are you going to do with your money, Trey?"

"Buy a new fishing rod. This summer I'm gonna catch that big ol' catfish in Willow Creek."

"I don't like fishing," Claire said. Like her mother, Claire would rather stay indoors.

The large two-story French colonial-style house came into view. It had an expansive veranda with a balcony above and the stately Greek columns typical of a Southern plantation. The Corbett home had been in the family for years, and Asa had completely renovated it for his wife, a Dallas socialite. She'd stayed long enough to have two sons and then returned to the city without them. Asa refused to let her take them, according to Carson's aunt Fran. Asa's wife had died one year later in a plane crash. Carson vaguely remembered the funeral.

He drove around back to the garages. The kids jumped out and ran through the breezeway to the sunroom. Aunt Fran, his dad's sister, had a snack waiting for them. After Carson and Jared's mother had left, their aunt came to help. She was the only mother figure they'd had in their lives. When he and Jared were older, she decided to travel and see the world. She'd returned for good when Jared died. Carson didn't know what he would have done if she hadn't. She could deal with Asa better than anyone.

"Where's Pa?" He kissed his aunt's cheek.

"In the den," she replied, pouring milk into glasses. "He's sitting in there with a picture of Jared in his lap. One of these days I'm going to hide it. It's not healthy for him to stare at it all the time."

In her late fifties, Aunt Fran had a reddish tint to her short, bobbed, graying blond hair. She was strong-willed and determined, like Asa, except she was a much softer version of him.

Carson walked into the den. Asa sat in his motorized wheelchair. He could work the joystick with his right hand. A physiotherapist was working with him, and Asa could stand and shuffle a couple of steps, but his left side was weak and stiff.

In his younger years, Asa had been a formidable, well respected rancher. Governors, senators, congressmen courted Asa for favors. Many barbecues had been thrown on the Bar C to support the candidate of Asa's choice. He'd ruled Willow Creek. Nothing had been done here without his approval. That was then. Now it was disheartening to see his robustly strong dad reduced to a shell of his former self.

"Hi, Pa," he said.

Asa turned the chair to face his son. "K-ids."

"They're having a snack. They'll be here in a minute." The only bright spot in his dad's life was his grandkids. Claire would crawl into his lap and help to work his fingers for exercise. Trey would help to work his legs, and he'd read to him. It was good for his kids. It taught them how to treat the disabled and the elderly... except his dad was only sixty-five.

Carson intended to bring up Jena Brooks but decided to wait. He didn't want to upset Asa without showing him some hard evidence. He had to prove Ms. Brooks was lying, and the only way to do that was with facts.

The kids ran in, and Claire climbed up to sit in Asa's lap, looking at the photo of Jared. Trey sat at his feet, telling his grandfather about his good grades.

"I've got to go out, guys. Trey, do your homework, and, Claire, I'll help you when I get back."

"I'll help her, Dad," Trey offered.

"Thanks, son."

He got in his constable's car and headed for Minnie Voltree's house. The woman had to be in her seventies now, but the last time he'd seen her she was still spry and had all her mental faculties, as far as he could tell.

After crossing the tracks that divided the community, he turned onto a narrow dirt road that curled into a hilly wooded area. Minnie and her family lived deep in the woods, but people were still able to find her if they needed her. Since everyone, including the poor, had access to better medical care than used to be available in Willow Creek, Minnie's midwife services were rarely needed these days.

A trailer house was barely visible. Carson drove over a cattle guard and into the front yard. Chickens pecked freely in the grass. Minnie sat in a chair on the attached front porch, snapping green beans. An old redbone coonhound lay at her feet.

"Afternoon, Constable," Minnie said as he walked up the steps. The dog raised his head and then went back to sleep.

"Minnie." He tipped his hat.

"What brings you out this way?" Minnie had a blue bandanna tied around her long gray hair. Her fingers continued to snap the beans deftly.

"I'd like to ask you a few questions."

"About what?"

"Jena Brooks?"

Her fingers paused for a second. A bad sign. "Sure."

"Did you deliver her baby?"

Minnie stopped snapping and stared at him with narrowed gray eyes. "No. Last I heard she left town, after the scandal and all."

"She's back."

"You don't say." Minnie went back to her work, but her fingers were shaky. The second bad sign.

"She said you delivered her baby."

"She's lying."

"She also said Asa took the baby from her."

"That's crazy."

"Yeah, it is, but if you and Asa took her baby that means you stole it, and that's illegal."

Minnie stood abruptly, clutching the bowl. "I did not deliver Jena Brooks's baby."

"Not even for money?"

"I resent that."

He ignored her indignation. "Did my father pay you to deliver her baby and give it away?"

"I'm not answering any more questions." She stormed into the trailer and slammed the screen door. She stood just inside.

"If you want to talk to me, you know where my office is. Jena Brooks isn't going away. She believes she has a real grievance, and she's got an attorney working on her case."

No response, as he'd expected.

He drove away with a niggling in his gut. Something fishy was going on, and his dad was right in the middle of it. His first instinct was to notify the sheriff of Hays County. They had the resources and the manpower to deal with this.

As the constable in this precinct, he provided law-enforcement services for Willow Creek and the surrounding rural areas. People called 911 for major crimes, which were rare. Those calls were handled by the sheriff's department in San Marcos, and Carson would usually assist. Most people in town had his direct number and would call for minor incidents like a fight at the beer joint, trespassers or family squabbles.

They called Carson because they didn't want to draw the attention of the sheriff. They just wanted the annoy-

ance to go away. Very rarely did he have to arrest anyone. If he did, he had to transport them to the county
jail in San Marcos.

Carson would contact the sheriff about Ms. Brooks's
allegation, but he had to be cautious for his dad's sake.
Asa wasn't in good health, and sometimes he wasn't
even in his right mind. All his thoughts were focused
on Jared. He couldn't seem to let his youngest son rest
in peace. To protect his father, Carson had to work the
case.

Reaching the paved road, he stopped his vehicle.
He'd have to do a thorough investigation and ask questions of the people in Willow Creek. They would remember. If someone could place Ms. Brooks with
Roland and Curly, it would substantiate her claim.

The best person to question would be Ms. Brooks
herself. Since he was already on the other side of the
tracks, he'd do it now. He'd like to get her reaction to
what Minnie had said.

He pulled into the Brookses' driveway. He hadn't been
here in years. Lamar had killed his brother, and he'd just
as soon have nothing to do with the murderer's family.
The house was run-down, as it had been for years. It had
belonged to Norma's mother. After her death, Norma inherited it. The old lady had kept the place up, but Lamar
had never lifted a finger to fix anything. Sorry bastard!

The sound of a mower roared through the late afternoon. He got out and saw a woman pushing a mower on
the left side of the house, making a circle to the front.
At first he thought it was Hilary, but she wasn't that
curvy. It was Jena.

A completely different Jena from the morning. In
denim shorts, a tank top and sneakers, she struggled
to move through the tall grass. Her body glistened with

sweat. She trudged behind the mower until she was about four feet from him. The whirly blades scattered grass all over his boots.

She reached down and turned off the mower. "What are you doing here, Constable?" she asked, using her forearm to wipe sweat from her brow.

"I'd like to talk to you."

"Just a minute." She ran for the porch, where there was a bottle of water. Unscrewing the top, she took a big gulp. For the first time he noticed how beautiful she was, with her dark hair and eyes and olive complexion. Beth had said Jared was besotted with Jena, and he could now see why. She had a fresh innocent appeal that was hard to ignore.

Slowly, she walked back, the bottle in her hand. "What did you want to talk about?"

He leaned against his vehicle. "You not used to hard labor?"

"Not really. I work in an office."

"Ah, the lawyer." That brought him down to earth like a shattered clay pigeon and reminded him this wasn't a social call. He cleared his throat. "I paid Minnie Voltree a visit."

"And?"

"She said you're lying. That she did not deliver your baby."

"Did you actually think she'd admit to it?" Her eyes never wavered from his, and that sincere gaze was doing a number on his senses.

"I was hoping for some hard evidence to place you at the Bar C."

She pointed the bottle at him. "Then why aren't you asking Asa? He knows everything. Or is he getting special treatment because he's your father?"

"Maybe." He wasn't ashamed to admit it. "He's not well, and he's still grieving for Jared. I want real evidence before I confront him."

"Okay." She gazed off to the oak trees. "How many people know the Bar C has a basement?"

"Not many."

"How many people have been in it?"

"Even fewer."

She brought her eyes back to his. "I know exactly what it looks like. There's a stairway near the kitchen that leads to the top floor. Underneath the staircase is a door that leads to the basement."

He held up a hand. "Jared could have taken you there."

"Other than when I gave birth, I was only on the Bar C once." She held up one finger. "Jared wanted to take me horseback riding. I didn't want to go, but he insisted. As soon as we drove up to the barn, Asa galloped up and shouted to Jared, 'Get that piece of trash off my property and get your ass back home. I want to talk to you.' After that I would never go there."

For some reason he believed her—that certainly sounded like Asa. She was confident, sure and never took her eyes off him.

"Roland and Curly grabbed me as I was leaving the convenience store. Roland had a pistol, and he told me to shut up and do as I was told. I was scared—for me and my baby. Curly tied my hands with a rope, and they took me to the basement at the Bar C. With my big stomach I couldn't see the steps very well, and I tripped a couple of times. I was shaking with fear and wanted to shield my baby. When I saw Minnie, I was relieved. She told me everything would be fine, and then she gave me some stuff to drink. She said it would calm my nerves. A half bed was in a corner with sheets and towels stacked high next to it. I became woozy, and she undid the rope and helped me to lie down."

Jena screwed the cap back onto the bottle, and her hand shook slightly. He knew she was reliving that day. At that moment he knew she wasn't lying. For the first time, he was torn between family and the truth.

Like everyone else in Willow Creek, he'd never really thought about what had happened to Jena's baby. He'd listened to what his father had said about the baby's paternity and put Jena Brooks out of his mind. When he returned home from the Marines for good, the murder cases had been closed and everyone had moved on. Now...

"I woke up to labor pains ripping through my body. I was under a sheet, and my maternity jeans and shoes had been removed. Minnie gave me more stuff to drink, and it helped the pain. Then I heard the word *breech,* and another voice said, 'Let her die.' It was Asa."

Both of her hands gripped the bottle. "I felt as if my insides were being yanked out of my body. Just when I thought I couldn't bear it any longer, I heard the baby cry. I held out my arms, wanting to hold it, and I heard Asa again. 'I got it,' he said. That's when I knew they were taking my baby. I screamed and tried to get up. I was so weak I blacked out. When I woke up, I was fully clothed. I got up, intending to find my baby. Roland and Curly were there. I fought them, and Roland slapped me and told me to shut up or Asa would kill me. He told my mother the same thing. She got me out of Willow Creek that night."

"Why didn't you call the sheriff?"

"I was a teenager and scared. My father had just killed Jared Corbett. No one was going to believe me. Just like you don't believe me now."

"It's a lot to take in." The sun was going down in the west, bathing them in a soft glow, and it seemed strange talking to her, the daughter of the man who'd killed his brother. Yet, in another way he felt something he couldn't explain. It was her. He was riveted by her soft voice and heartfelt emotions.

"You said you wanted evidence I'd been at the Bar C." Her voice interrupted his troubled thoughts. "In the basement there's a rack for rods and reels on one wall. Football jerseys hang on hooks. One has *Jared* printed on the back and the other has *Carson*. A beautiful armoire and matching headboard are stored in a corner. Boxes labeled *Caroline* are stacked next to it."

"They belonged to my mother," he said, startling himself. He hadn't meant to say that out loud.

"There's a single light bulb hanging from the ceiling with a long string to turn it on and off," she continued as if he hadn't spoken. "I bled a lot during the birth, and some dripped onto the floor. Minnie tried to wipe it up with bleach. I know because I heard her tell Roland she needed more bleach to clean up the blood. I bet the stain is still on the concrete. As you go down the stairs, it would be on the far left. The bed, towels and sheets I'm sure were burned."

"I'll check it out," he said through a dry throat. He took a moment and gauged his next words. "I don't understand why you're coming back now. It's been…what? Almost nine years?"

"When I heard Asa had had a stroke, I knew this was my last chance to find my child. If he dies, his secret will die with him. I'm not afraid of him anymore, either. I just want the child who was taken from me."

"May I ask you a question?"

"What?"

"Please don't take offense, but why was my dad so sure the baby wasn't Jared's?"

"Jared said Roland filled Asa's head with nonsense, like he'd seen me out with this guy or that guy."

"And that wasn't true?"

"No. Jared was my only boyfriend, but more than that, he was my friend."

It would be callous to point out that her father had shot Jared in cold blood. They'd talked enough for today. He had a lot of thinking to do.

"Thank you for your candor, Ms. Brooks. I'll be in touch." He got in his vehicle and drove away.

Conflicting thoughts warred inside him. Could his father do something so barbaric?

He returned home, his thoughts directed inward. Aunt Fran was in the kitchen. "Supper's almost ready," she called.

"I have to check something in the basement first."

"We caught that mouse."

"I'm just checking." He took the narrow steps two at a time. It was dark now, so he moved slowly when he got to the bottom, reaching for the string. He pulled it and light flooded the basement. Everything was just as she'd described. He walked toward the left side of the room and saw it. A large dark spot—her blood.

Oh, God. A pain shot through him. She wasn't lying. She'd given birth in this basement. What had his father done with the child?

JENA PUSHED THE mower to the shed in the back. It was too dark to mow now. Her mind was filled with thoughts of her conversation with Carson. Even as farfetched as her story sounded, she got the feeling he believed her.

And, to her dismay, she understood his reluctance to talk to his father.

For years she'd dreamed of revenge, but after a few hours in Willow Creek she was surprised to find her desire for it wasn't as strong as before. She needed only peace now. Asa Corbett was already in hell—stoking the fire would accomplish nothing. She just wanted information about her child. Carson would get that.

Jared had often said his older brother was the heroic type, the kind who would rescue a kitten from a burning building without any thought to his own safety. He was honest and straightforward. Jena had already sensed those qualities in him. Even though it would hurt his family, he would do the right thing. He'd confront his father.

Jena had to put her trust in Carson, and she found the thought oddly disturbing and uplifting at the same time.

Hilary swerved into the driveway, headlights blinding Jena. Jumping out, Hil said, "Hey, sis, I brought chicken-fried steaks for supper."

"It's been a long time since I've had Mabel's chicken-fried steak."

"Then you're in for a treat. I brought chocolate pie with mile-high meringue, too."

They walked toward the steps, and Hil suddenly stopped. "Didn't get the yard mowed, huh?"

"Why didn't you buy a self-propelled mower?"

Hil shrugged. "They cost more, and the guys usually mow, but they've been busy. I thought I'd get it done by the time you arrived."

"I did the back, and, believe me, my muscles will be protesting tomorrow. As I was pushing that blasted thing to the front, the constable drove up."

"What did Carson want?"

"To ask questions about that night."

"Is he going to do anything?"

"Yes. I believe he is."

"Hmm. You sound different than you did this morning. Are you developing a soft spot for the constable?"

"Of course not. Don't be silly."

"If you say so. But he's s-o-o good-looking if you like tall, strong and masculine."

"Shut up." She held the door open and Hil laughed, walking inside.

"Hey, Mama, time for supper," Hil shouted.

Norma clicked off the television. "I wondered where you girls were."

"She seems fine," Hil whispered in the kitchen.

"She's been that way all afternoon."

"Told you. It comes and goes."

Hil ran around the kitchen in her cute cowgirl boots like a bunny on steroids, putting the meal on the table and fixing tea.

"How much coffee have you had today?"

"Enough." Hil made a face.

They sat around the old Formica-and-chrome table and ate. It was reminiscent of better times. Before her dad started drinking heavily. Before Jared. *Before...*

"It's nice to have my oldest home," Norma said. "I was going to bake a cake, but I couldn't get the stove to work."

"It's just temperamental," Hil replied. "I can make it work, but I brought food and pie. We're good."

"Okay." Norma continued to eat, but Jena noticed a change in her. She became quiet and stared at the refrigerator. Wrapping her arms around her waist, Norma mumbled, "It's getting chilly. We'll probably have ice in the morning. I saw on the TV it was snowing some-where."

Hil choked on her pie, coughed and took a quick gulp of tea. "What the hell was she watching?" Hil mouthed.

"Wheel of Fortune," Jena mouthed back.

Hil shrugged. "It's not that chilly, Mama."

"I wonder where my flannel gown is." Their mother stood and meandered to her room.

They cleaned the table and put the containers in plas-tic bags. "I'll take the trash to the café in the morning." Hil tied the top of the bag into a knot.

"What do we do about Mama?" Jena asked.

"I don't know. I just agree with whatever she says. That seems to work best."

They went to their mother's bedroom and found her standing near the bed in a flannel nightgown, looking confused. "Where's my electric blanket, Hilary?"

"It's on the bed." Hil winked at Jena.

"Good. I wanted to take a bath, but it's just too cold."

"That's okay, Mama." Hil helped her into bed.

"Is the blanket on?"

Hil knelt and pretended to fiddle with something. "How's that?"

"Much better."

Her sister got to her feet and kissed their mother. "Night."

"Now, don't you girls talk all night. You have school tomorrow."

"We won't."

Her mother was in another time and another place. Maybe after all she'd been through it was a better place for her. And she had the resilient strength of Hilary to help her. Once again Jena was amazed at her sister's patience and compassion.

She kissed her mother's forehead. "Night, Mama."

"I'm so happy to have my beautiful daughter home."

"Hey. What am I? The ugly duckling?" Hil teased.

"You're my sweet, good daughter."

Hil flicked off the light. "Yeah, like that's gonna get me a date with Ryan Reynolds?"

"The actor?" Jena asked as they walked out.

"Yeah."

"Isn't he married?"

"So? I'm not picky."

"You're a nut."

Before Hil could respond, Jena's cell buzzed, and she ran into the bedroom to get it. "It's Blake," she said.

"I'll take a bath and give you some privacy." Grabbing a T-shirt out of a drawer, Hil disappeared into the bathroom.

"Hi, Blake." She sat on the bed.

"I was getting worried. You didn't call."

"I didn't realize you wanted me to."

"Of course. I worry about you going back to that place."

"I'm fine."

"Did you talk to the constable?"

"Yes, and he's being very cooperative."

"I don't know why you don't let me handle it. Then you wouldn't have to go back there."

She drew a deep breath. Blake was a master manipulator. "My mother and my sister are here, and I wanted to see them. If I need help, you'll be the first person I call."

There was a long pause. "The office is not the same without you."

"I've been gone one day."

"It feels like a month."

She gripped her phone. Blake was ten years her se-
nior and good to her, but he tended to push too hard
and that immediately sent alarms sounding through
her. When she'd started working for Blake's firm, she
was hired as a receptionist, and she was happy to get
the job. It paid well. Then one evening Blake and his
team were working a major high-profile case and one
of the assistants called in sick. Blake's secretary asked
if she could stay late and help out.

The next day Blake complimented her on her hard
work and that made her feel good about herself. The
personal assistant who'd been ill soon quit because she
was having a difficult pregnancy. Blake offered Jena
the job, and she'd gladly accepted. Her job was basically being at Blake's beck and call. Between his secretary and Jena, they kept him on track and on time.
Jena usually joined the entourage who went with him
to court, and she loved that part of her work.

Jena looked on Blake as a father figure. He looked
on her as something more. They'd gone out a few times,
and she made it clear she wasn't ready for the kind of
commitment he wanted. She didn't know if she would
ever be.

Of course, he'd wanted to know why. She had to
be honest, so she told him about her ordeal in Willow
Creek. As a lawyer, he was outraged and determined to
get justice for her. He offered to do it pro bono.

But she refused to let him fight her battles. If she
did, it would move their relationship to another level,
and she didn't want that. She listened when he told
her that her rights had been grossly violated and Asa
Corbett should be in jail. Nine years was long enough,
she'd decided. She had to face her past. She had to know
about her child.

"Jena?"

"Oh…sorry." She'd drifted away from the conver-sation. "I'll probably stay longer than I'd planned. My mom is not well, and I need to help my sister with her."

"Take as long as you need, but don't let that country constable take advantage of you."

"I won't." She couldn't imagine Carson doing that, but then, she hardly knew him.

"I could take care of everything, and you wouldn't even have to see the Corbetts."

She gritted her teeth. Blake did not get the mean-ing of the word *no*. "I've got to go. I'll call tomorrow. 'Bye." She clicked off and slipped the phone back into her purse.

"Through?" Hil asked from the doorway in a T-shirt that had Kiss My Grits on it.

"Yeah." She got her nightclothes out of her suitcase and went into the bathroom to calm down. Blake could be so sweet. Other times he was controlling. She would only ask for his help as a last resort. She could handle this on her own.

When she came out, Hilary was sitting on the floor, her back against the bed, her head resting on the mat-tress as she stared at the ceiling.

Jena followed her gaze and slid down beside her, looking up. "You painted that?" A mural of a baby-blue sky, fluffy white clouds with a rainbow shooting across, graced the ceiling.

"Yeah. It's relaxing, isn't it?"

"Mmm."

"I sit here or lie in bed and dream about what's at the end of the rainbow. A place where the phrase 'poor white trash' doesn't exist. Where rumors and gossip are unheard of. Where there are beautiful homes with manicured lawns and gorgeous flowers. And I live in one of them with a man who loves and respects me." Hil turned her head to look at Jena. "What do you dream about?"

She swallowed hard. "I dream one day this big empty hole in my heart will be filled. I'll wake up one morning and be free from the past. But most of all I dream of holding my child in my a-arms." Even though she tried to stop it, her voice cracked.

"Oh, Jen-Jen."

Hilary hugged her, and then they both burst into tears—two girls from the wrong side of town dreaming of a better way of life. For Hilary, her dream would probably never come true. She was stuck in Willow Creek. That broke Jena's heart.

For herself, her dream was just within her grasp.

CHAPTER THREE

ASA DIDN'T FEEL well and went to bed early. Aunt Fran gave him something to help him rest, so Carson didn't get a chance to talk to him. The next morning Asa was still asleep when Carson had to take the kids to school, but he told his aunt to call when Asa was up. He wasn't sure how to confront his father, considering the man's mental state, which was precarious, but he had to do it.

He had a sick ache in the pit of his stomach at what had been done to Jena Brooks. For he knew beyond a shadow of a doubt that her baby had been taken by his father. He just couldn't figure out why, especially since Asa didn't believe the baby was Jared's.

A life for a life, his dad had told her. Could that mean…? He couldn't even finish the thought in his head. What kind of a monster would kill an innocent newborn? Not one he wanted to be related to.

There had to be an answer somewhere. There were other people involved in this, and the only way to find out who, was to look through Bernard Milliner's files, as he had been the constable at the time. Since Jared's case was a murder, the sheriff's office would have handled the investigation, but it happened in Bernie's precinct, and he would have been there on the scene of both murders.

When Carson reached his office, he started looking through the files. His office was filled with regular office equipment and filing cabinets. He also had a small storage room that housed old files. Nothing much happened in Willow Creek, but all cases were documented, and the records went back over fifty years.

He found the paper work and sat down to read. Jared's body had been found by Roland at 8:12 p.m. on a Thursday. Bernie had a note jotted on the side: *Asa sent Roland to look for Jared when he didn't come home.* Carson already knew this. He had been able to fly home three days after the murder, and Asa was still ranting and raving about revenge. Carson had asked the doctor to give him something to calm him. But Asa had still been frighteningly angry. To him, it seemed Lamar's death wasn't enough. He wanted more. Did he get what he wanted?

It had been a horrific time, and Carson didn't look forward to the thought of reliving it. To find answers, though, he had to go back.

Lamar Brooks was found at his house at 6:05 a.m. the next morning. Just like Jared, he'd been killed with a shotgun blast to the chest as he got out of his truck. Asa was the logical suspect, but ballistics could not match the gun with Asa's. The murder weapon had never been found and neither had the murderer. What a mess.

The door opened and his friend Levi Coyote strolled in with two cups of coffee. "Hey, I haven't seen you in a week, so I thought I'd stop by for a minute. I even brought coffee." He and Levi had been friends since they were kids. Along with Ethan James, another friend, they'd been as inseparable as brothers growing up. Ethan was a detective in Austin and Levi was now a private investigator, but their roots ran deep in Willow Creek.

"Thanks. I could use it." He took a sip from the disposable cup.

Levi pulled up a chair. He was a tall, muscled guy. Carson and Ethan decided a long time ago that in case of a fight it was always good to have Levi on their side.

"What's the hangdog expression about?"

"Jena Brooks is back in town."

"Shit." Levi almost spit coffee all over the room. "Is her child with her?"

"No, and that's the problem." He told his friend what Jena had told him.

"Man, that's quite a story."

"Yeah, but she's not lying. I found the bloodstain in the basement."

Levi shook his head. "Asa's always been a little off-kilter, but since losing Jared he's been way off."

"He hasn't been able to cope with Jared's murder, and I'm so afraid…that baby is dead."

"If he did something so heinous, you'll never find the body on the Bar C. It's too big. Where would you start digging?"

"Oh, man." He ran his hands over his face. "This is hell. I might have to arrest Asa. I can't do that, Levi. I can't do that to my own father."

"Just take it slow. You'll need more than that stain in the basement to prove Asa was involved. Start searching for info. You know people around here love to talk, and I'll help. I'll be away on a case today and tomorrow, but I'll check with you when I get back."

"Thanks." Carson placed his hand on the papers on his desk. "I've been going through the murder files, and I can't understand why Lamar would kill Jared. You were around at the time. Did he hate Jared?"

"Just the opposite. He bragged about his daughter marrying a Corbett. She'd never want for anything."

"Did Jared ask Jena to marry him?"

"Not to my knowledge, but I remember he was crazy about her."

"Maybe it was more about the sex than something long-term. Maybe Lamar confronted Jared and demanded he marry his daughter and one thing led to another."

Levi shrugged. "Could be. But it was real stupid of Lamar to leave his shotgun at the scene."

"Mmm." Carson flipped through the files. "After my dad was ruled out as the murderer, no one else was ever questioned."

"Nope. They closed the case and no one objected."

"Why? That's not normal police procedure."

"I was clocking a lot of hours as a cop in Austin at the time, but Pop said the sheriff investigated and a Texas Ranger got involved. Then suddenly the case was closed. Like I said, no one was too concerned who killed Lamar Brooks. He'd murdered an innocent boy, and everyone felt he got what he deserved."

"That's not justice." Carson had a bitter taste in his mouth that so much about what had happened back then seemed to be overlooked and easily forgotten.

Levi shrugged.

Carson shifted through the papers. "Bernie doesn't have too much, but I'll read through all of it, and then I'll go to San Marcos to see what the sheriff has on the murders."

"Don't expect too much." Levi crushed the cup in his hand. "The case was wrapped up quickly. My advice is to talk to Minnie again. She's your weak link. And, of course, Asa."

"He had a bad night. When he wakes up, I plan to confront him."

Levi stood and aimed the cup toward the trash can.

It landed perfectly. "Bam. Three points. Coffee's on you next time."

"You got it." He picked up the lawyer's card from his desk. "Ms. Brooks works for a criminal attorney now. She's giving me a chance to find her child, and then she's turning it over to the attorney."

"Damn. That's the last thing you need."

"Yeah. Because of Pa's involvement I can't let her do that. I'll have to call Ms. Brooks and ask for more time."

"Do you think she'll agree to that?"

"I don't know. She seems...nice."

"Nice?" Levi lifted an eyebrow.

"She was determined at first, but when I talked to her last night she seemed more amenable. She just wants to know what happened to her child, and I understand that. I feel for what she's been through."

"Oh, crap."

"What?"

"You're getting...hmm?" Levi's eyes narrowed in thought. "What is that word women keep telling us we don't have?" He snapped his fingers. "*Emotions.* Yeah, that's it. You're letting your emotions rule your head."

"I am not!"

"This is how it starts, you know. The dance. The romance."

Carson leaned back in his chair. "I can honestly say there will never be any romance between Ms. Brooks and me. There are a million reasons why. The number one reason is her father murdered my brother, and there's no love strong enough to overcome that. Besides, I have no romantic interest in Ms. Brooks. My goal is to find her child and try to keep my father from being arrested."

"What does she look like now?"

"What?" He was thrown for a second.

"She was a pretty teenager. I bet she turned into a beautiful woman."

"I didn't look that closely." He frowned at his friend. "Besides, the first time I saw her, she was hurling accusations right and left, and I just wanted to get her out of my office and out of my life."

"Good." Levi glanced at his watch. "I've got to run. Talk to you when I get back."

As Levi walked out, Carson linked his hands behind his head. He had lied to his friend. He knew exactly what Jena Brooks looked like: she had sad, soulful dark eyes, dark flowing hair and a smooth curvy body that was titillating when bathed in sweat. He'd never admit that to anyone but himself. Since Beth, he hadn't even looked at another woman, and it bothered him that he'd noticed Jena.

No, there could never be anything between him and Jena except a past they both wanted to forget.

JENA WAS ON her way back from Dripping Springs. Last night she and Hilary had talked until after midnight. Jena wanted to do something for Hilary in appreciation of everything she'd done for their mother. That led to a long discussion. Hilary didn't want anything. She was her mother, too, she'd said. In the end, they agreed to fix up the house. It was long overdue.

Hilary wanted a buttercup-yellow house with white shutters, so Jena bought all the supplies and Hilary's friends would do the work. In a fit of indulgence, she went ahead and bought shingles to finish the roof.

Her cell buzzed and she reached for it in the console. "Hey, Hil."

"Did you get everything?"

"Yes. A soft yellow, just like you wanted. It's going to look so nice with the white shutters. Are you sure the guys will do this?"

"Yes. I told them this morning, and Billy Jack said he'd bring the paint sprayer over tomorrow."

"I went ahead and bought shingles. And we have to get new screens, but I have to measure them first."

"Wow. You are being generous."

"I left everything at the store for Billy Jack to pick up."

"Good deal. I can't wait to see the new look. I'm tired of that drab house."

"That's why you paint murals all over it?"

"Yes, I… Hold on. I've got another call."

In a minute Hil was back. "Sis, it was Carson. He wants to see you. You didn't give him your cell number."

"Oh, crap. I forgot. I'll check on Mama and then head over to his office."

"I'll check on Mama. You go to his office. He might have some news."

"Okay. I'll see you later." She clicked off and felt a rush of excitement run through her. Maybe he'd talked to his father. Maybe he knew… Oh, God. Her hands grew clammy on the steering wheel.

She turned into the parking area of the constable's office and took several deep breaths to calm herself. Grabbing her purse, she got out and stared at the building. Was it only yesterday she'd come here with every word rehearsed in her head? With every dream intact in her heart?

Opening the door, she went inside. Carson sat at his desk, reading through a big file.

"Come in," he said. "Have a seat." His eyes looked

worried and his hair was tousled as if he'd been running his fingers through it.

She sat in a chair, placed her purse on the floor and pushed her sunglasses to the top of her head. Yesterday she'd been dressed in her best clothes. Today she was casual in white capris, sandals and an olive-green sleeveless top. She was thinking inane things when the most important subject was almost too painful to broach.

"Did you find the bloodstain on the basement floor?" she asked, her heart beating a steady tattoo against her ribs.

"Yes."

"And you talked to Asa?"

"No. Sorry." He looked up, his green eyes tortured.

She ignored that look. "You saw the stain, but for some reason you haven't talked to your father?"

"No."

She got up, grabbed her purse, intending to leave and call Blake right away. This was unacceptable.

But he was faster than her, blocking her path to the door. "Please, Ms. Brooks. I'm asking for more time."

"I've been without my child for nine years. That's enough time."

"Please."

Something in that one little word said in earnest got to her and she weakened. Or maybe it was the broad chest and wide shoulders that held her attention. A light citrus scent teased her nostrils. Swirls of brown chest hair peeped out from the V of his white shirt. Jared had had boyish good looks, but Carson had a raw masculinity that made her aware he was a man and she was a woman.

"I was going to talk to him last night, but he wasn't

feeling well and my aunt gave him a sleeping pill so he could rest. When he wakes up, I'll try again, but you have to understand he's not the strong domineering man you remember. He's never gotten over Jared's murder, and he's very fragile in his body and in his mind."

"I understand that." She hitched the strap of her purse higher. "My mom is not doing well, either. She's in her own little world. The tragedy has affected so many people, and it still lingers. My father's murder was never solved. Either the authorities covered up for Asa or they didn't care."

"Could we talk about that?"

"The murders?"

"Yes. I have a lot of questions."

She sighed. "What good will that do except to dredge up old heartaches and pain?"

"The cases were closed very quickly, and I feel there is still evidence out there to help corroborate your story."

What was it about this man that made her see his point of view? "Okay. Okay. I'll answer questions. Again, I might add."

"I appreciate that."

She turned toward the chair and noticed he was still standing by the door. "Are you afraid I'm going to sneak out?"

"Just making sure," he replied with a half grin. The tired expression was gone from his face, and she knew he could be quite persuasive if he applied himself.

She resumed her seat, as did he. As she placed her purse back on the floor, she noticed the photo on his desk. Her nerves had been so helter-skelter when she was in the office before she hadn't even seen it.

"Your children?" She pointed to the photo.

"Um…yeah. Trey and Claire."

The boy had brown hair and favored Carson. The little girl was her mother all the way. She remembered Beth Corbett—a beautiful blonde. Hilary had told her about Beth's death. That had to have been hard to lose his brother and wife within a few years.

"I'm sorry about your wife." She felt she had to say something.

"Thank you," he replied in a neutral tone, signaling the subject was off-limits.

He shuffled through the file. "Why did your dad shoot Jared? Was there an ongoing feud between them?"

She lifted an eyebrow. "You mean because of me?"

"Yes." He looked up, his green eyes intense.

"It may surprise you to know that my father had no interest in my or my sister's lives. When he learned I was pregnant, he said at least I had enough sense to sleep with someone who had money." She clenched her hands in her lap. Her childhood had been riddled with strife. Her father had been a decent person until he started drinking. Then he became abusive. They used to dread the sound of his truck in the driveway. Their mother would get them out of their beds and hurry them outside in the dark to hide. She would then take the brunt of his drunken rage.

"Your father killing Jared makes no sense." Carson's voice penetrated her disturbing thoughts. "He had no motive."

"The sheriff and his deputies made up a motive by talking to people around town. They said my dad was trying to force Jared to marry me and nothing could be further from the truth."

"What was the truth?"

"We graduated in May and worked all summer. The

baby was due the first week in October, and we wanted to save enough money to rent an apartment in Austin. Before the baby was born, we planned to run away and get married."

"Who knew about the plan?"

"No one. I didn't even tell Hilary. We didn't want Asa to find out."

"Can you prove any of this?"

"Why do I need to prove anything?"

His eyes held hers. "Because it would mean your father didn't have a motive."

"My father didn't know we were getting married," she said rather tartly.

He pulled a pad and pen forward. "Did you get a marriage license?"

"Yes. In San Marcos."

"Did you rent an apartment?"

"Yes. In Austin." She gripped her hands again to keep the memories at bay. "Jared was killed the day before we were to leave."

Complete silence followed her words, and she took a moment to gather her shattered composure. Memories of that day were still very real and painful. But it was only a prelude of the misery to come.

"Mr. Corbett…"

"Could you please call me Carson?" His green eyes held hers, waiting.

"I'd rather keep this formal." She didn't know why she was hesitating. She just didn't want to be on friendly terms with him.

"Willow Creek is as informal as you can get."

"But you and I are not friends. You and I will never be friends."

"I see," he said in a flat tone, and for a moment she

felt a twinge of guilt. But it passed quickly. He made her feel weak and she hated that. She would never be weak again.

She reached for her purse and stood. "Dredging up the murders is not the reason I'm here. My child is the only reason I came back, and your father is the only one who has the answer. You're stalling because you know I'm right."

He stood, too, his green eyes turning dark. "I've asked before, and your answer wasn't satisfactory. Why are you coming back now? Why not eight years ago? Five years? You've left it rather late to play the mother card."

"How dare you! I don't have to explain anything to you, and I'm not answering any more questions. You have until eight o'clock tonight to speak to your father. If I don't hear from you, I'm calling my attorney." She turned on her heel and walked out.

In the car she was trembling so badly she had to take several deep breaths. She'd known this wasn't going to be easy, but she'd never counted on her emotions betraying her. There was an attraction between them, very subtle, but it was there. No way was she letting her heart get involved with the enemy. And that was who Carson Corbett was—her worst enemy.

CARSON RAN BOTH hands through his hair. Son of a bitch! What had just happened? They were having a normal conversation and the next minute she was tearing into him like a cornered bobcat.

He closed the folder and jammed it back into the storage box. She was right. Dredging up the past was pointless. He had to deal with the present.

His cell buzzed and he reached for it on his belt. It was his aunt.

"Carson, your father's awake. He's had a late breakfast and now he's watching TV."

"I'll be right there."

He locked up the office and headed for home. Driving down the winding road to the house, he glanced at his cows feeding on new coastal hay. It had taken him years, but he'd slowly built a good-size herd again. Yet the ranch was far from what it used to be. He couldn't afford help, so when he wasn't doing his constable job, he worked the ranch. His life ran at a grueling pace, but it kept him from thinking.

Parking at the garages, he took a moment and then went in through the sunroom. Aunt Fran was in the kitchen, loading the dishwasher.

She looked up, her face worried. "What's this about, Carson?"

"It's not good." He told her about Jena Brooks's allegations.

"That can't be true." She wiped her hands on a dish towel. "Asa wouldn't do something like that."

"I'm not so sure. He was out of his mind with grief."

"I wish I could have gotten here sooner after Jared died, but I was in Australia and…"

"You know Pa. You couldn't have changed a thing. Where is he?"

"In the den. Carson," she called as he turned away. "Be patient."

He nodded and walked into the large Western-style room with dark walnut paneling, leather sofas, horse sculptures and a brightly colored area rug. His father sat in his chair, watching TV, a remote in his unsteady hand.

Carson was reminded of the years he and Asa went head-to-head on just about everything. His father was a hard man, and his sons knew that better than anyone. Work was always on Asa's mind, and he'd made sure his boys started working at an early age. Carson could remember pushing hay off the back of a truck to feed cows at six. After school, it was ranch work. Weekends were the same. Vacations were nonexistent. The only fun they'd had was hanging out with friends and playing sports. His father was the reason he'd joined the Marines. He'd had to get away to be his own man apart from his father's insane views of life.

His father was also an unforgiving man. He could remember the time Asa beat Jared to within an inch of his life for leaving a gate open. Cows got out and Asa was furious. Carson jumped in and pulled Asa off his little brother. They'd slept in the barn that night, and the next day Asa acted as if nothing had happened. There were so many days like that. Yet through it all they'd loved their father.

But Jared's murder had broken Asa. So much so that he'd allowed a worthless ranch hand to squander away everything he'd built. Carson shook the memories away.

"Hi, Pa."

The chair buzzed as Asa turned it to face him.

"I need to talk to you."

"About…what?" His robust voice was now a gravelly whisper.

There wasn't any way to do this but to say the words. "Jena Brooks is back in town."

"Bit-ch," he spat, his leathery, lined face suffused with rage. "Killed…my…son. Bitch!"

"Lamar Brooks killed Jared."

Asa heaved several deep breaths and drool ran out the corner of his mouth.

"Stay calm." Carson handed him the washcloth on the arm of the chair.

Asa dabbed at his mouth.

"Pa, there's more." He hated to keep on, but if he didn't an investigator from the sheriff's office would. "You okay?"

Asa nodded.

Carson measured his next words. "Ms. Brooks says Minnie Voltree gave her something to induce labor in the basement of this house. That you then took her baby from her and told her to get out of town or you would kill her."

There was no reaction on his father's face, and Carson wondered if he'd heard what he'd said.

"Pa, she's come back for her child."

An evil grin spread across Asa's face. "She…will… never…find it."

CHAPTER FOUR

CARSON SANK ONTO the arm of the sofa. Stunned. Speechless.

No denials. No indignation. No shock. Nothing but a glee in his dad's eyes that was hard to explain. It was as if he'd been expecting this. Had been waiting for it. Waiting for the day he could have this moment. Of what? The ultimate revenge.

He marshaled his chaotic thoughts. "You kidnapped Jena Brooks and took her baby?"

Asa nodded once.

"Why?

"An eye…for an eye. A life…for a life. She…took… my boy. I took…her baby."

"That's insane, Pa. And illegal."

His father stared at him with triumph in his dull eyes.

Carson stood and raked both hands through his hair. "Where's the baby?"

Asa shook his head.

"You don't know? Or are you refusing to say?"

Asa just stared at him.

"Damn it, Pa. Jena Brooks works for a lawyer, and he will speak to the sheriff about her claims. The sheriff in turn will have questions for you. As the constable, I'm supposed to work closely with the sheriff. Do you understand that?"

"So? Arrest…me." Asa tried to hold out his shaky hands, but the left one barely left his lap.

Carson drew in deeply, trying to figure out how to handle the situation. "Pa, talk to me. Tell me what happened. After Jared's death, you were under a lot of stress and everyone knows that. Just talk to me, please."

Asa shook his head.

Carson watched the mulish expression on his father's face. He'd seen it many times, and he was especially reminded of the day he'd beaten Jared. He'd been bent on teaching his son a lesson. And now he was determined to teach Jena a lesson. Nothing would stand in his way. Not even jail. Nothing.

But maybe there was something that would grab his attention. Something other than revenge. "Pa, that baby is Jared's, so whatever…"

"No!" he shouted, his whole body vibrating with rage. "Bitch…lied. Had Ro-land follow…her and…"

"Roland lied to you just like he lied about everything else."

"No!" This time the denial wasn't so forceful.

"Whatever you did to that child you did to Jared."

"You…believe…that bitch?"

Carson heaved a long sigh. "It's not a question of belief. You freely admitted to taking the child. I'm just trying to figure things out. If you tell me the truth, I'm sure the D.A. will go easy on you. It was a difficult time. Please work with me. Think about your grandkids. What will you tell them when the sheriff arrests you for two kidnappings? Think about that."

Asa looked toward the TV and pushed a button on the remote to turn it off. Carson hadn't even been aware of the sound. He'd been so focused on his father.

Asa was silent, so Carson hoped that was a good thing. Maybe he'd gotten through to him.

"Talk to me, Pa," he said again. "I'll do everything I can to protect you. Just talk to me."

Asa looked at him, his eyes cold and hard. A chill ran through Carson. "Never. She will…suffer…like me. Forever."

Carson threw up his hands in despair. "If that's the way you want it. Forever for you will probably be in a sanitarium, and Aunt Fran won't be there to wait on you hand and foot."

"Don't…care."

"Fine." Carson walked out.

Aunt Fran was outside the door, and she followed him into the kitchen.

"You heard?"

"Yes. Asa's not in his right mind."

"I'll agree with you on that." He opened the refrigerator and grabbed a bottle of water. Twisting off the cap, he took a big gulp. "He kidnapped Jena Brooks, had Minnie induce labor and then took Jena's child. That's against the law. Once Jena's attorney gets here, speaks to the sheriff and an investigator starts digging, it will be just a matter of time before Pa is arrested."

"He's a crippled old man out of his mind with grief. What can they do?"

"Once they verify Ms. Brooks's baby was stolen by Pa, and there's no doubt they will since Pa freely admits it, they'll book him and probably put him under house arrest until the trial. If he's convicted, they'll put him in an institution for the rest of his life."

"Oh, Carson." Aunt Fran touched his arm in distress. "You can't let that happen."

"I don't have any choice, Aunt Fran." He set the bottle on the kitchen island. "I just have this bad feeling."

"About what?"

"Pa's been waiting for this."

"What do you mean?"

"He's been waiting for Jena to come back. I could see it in his eyes. He keeps saying 'a life for a life,' and I'm so afraid he's been waiting to tell Jena that her baby is dead— just like Jared is dead."

"Oh, no, Carson." Aunt Fran covered her mouth in horror. "My brother would not kill an innocent baby."

Carson reached for the water and took a swig, wishing it was hundred-proof alcohol. He wanted to agree with her or say something to get rid of the hollow feeling in his gut. Instead, he spun toward the door. "I have some thinking to do. If Pa wants to talk, call me."

At his car he heaved a sigh and glanced toward the barns and corrals—a peaceful ranch scene with live oaks, scrub oaks, yaupons and a hilly prairie that stretched to the beautiful Texas Hill Country. Cows munched on grass, and a windmill whirled in the distance, pumping water into a trough. Peaceful—though there was nothing peaceful about the Corbett family.

With long strides he made his way to the barn. The horse stalls were empty compared to the heyday of the Bar C, when they'd been filled with thoroughbreds. He walked through the large barn to the other end and pushed open the double doors that were an entrance to a corral and then the horse pasture.

He whistled. A black horse with three white stocking feet cantered to the fence. Carson undid the gate, and the horse pranced through and into the barn to a feed trough. Within minutes, Carson had a saddle on his quarter horse, Jet, and they galloped away into a bright sunny day. He had no idea where he was going. He had to clear his head, to get his thoughts straight.

He rode through his herd, but he barely noticed them. All his thoughts were on what he had to do in the next few hours. He dismounted at Willow Creek and sat in the grass.

Two years ago the creek had dried up from a severe drought. Due to heavy rains it was flowing again. Large willows hugged the creek, and the tips of their slender branches played with the water. He picked up a pebble and skimmed it across the surface. After three skips, it landed on the other side. He and Jared had done this so many times, each trying to outdo the other.

Back then, they were kids and happy in their own way. They had Aunt Fran, their friends and each other. Their father was someone who yelled at them and, when they displeased him, gave them a sharp lash from his belt.

Asa had a softer side, too, but he rarely showed it. He'd brought a puppy home one time for Jared and let him keep it in his room. Asa had fed it on occasion. Then there were times he'd take them to horse and cattle auctions, and he'd proudly tell people, "These are my boys." He gave them money, trucks, anything they wanted. But he never gave them his love. At least, Carson never felt it. He was pretty sure Jared hadn't, either.

There was something about DNA, though. It bound people together, overlooked faults, accepted imperfections, and even if those three words were never spoken, instinctively they were understood.

Carson skimmed another pebble across the creek. How did the Corbett family get so messed up? There wasn't an answer.

Glancing at his watch, he rose to his feet. He had to

get his kids from school. They were the bright spot in his life. He would never let them down, and he made sure they felt his love every day.

With one foot in the stirrup, he swung into the saddle and turned Jet toward home. The last thing he wanted to do was talk to Jena. He'd rather take another lash from Pa's belt than tell her she would never know what had happened to her baby.

JENA WAS RESTLESS and had to do something to let off some steam. She pulled the mower out of the shed and finished mowing the yard. After that, she used the Weedwacker to trim around the edges. There wasn't a single blade of grass peeping up its head. The yard looked better. But it would look even better with flower beds.

In the shed she found a hoe and started digging. She didn't stop until she had a bed on each side of the porch. Her back and shoulders ached, so she thought she'd stop for the day. After the house was painted, she'd buy mulch and finish the beds.

All day she'd forced herself not to think of Carson and their talk, but she'd looked at her watch about a hundred times. She'd given him until eight o'clock, and she intended to keep her word on that. Wiping sweat from her brow, she decided to take a break and sat on the porch. A light breeze fanned her heated skin.

Carson had wanted to know why it had taken her so long to come back. Her reason was personal and private, and she would not share her life with him. Hilary and cousin Nan knew, but other than them she hadn't told a soul, not even Blake.

Realizing it was six o'clock, she went inside to fix supper for her mother. At least Hilary didn't have to rush home for that. She made ham-and-cheese sandwiches, and her mother ate very little. She had a far-away look in her eyes as she picked the cheese off her sandwich.

"Is Hilary still at school?" Norma asked.

Jena was taken aback. Her mother had been fine all day. Now she seemed to be in another place.

"Um…yes." She followed Hil's example and agreed with her.

"I don't like her walking home in the dark."

"Hilary's fine, Mama. I'll check on her later."

Her mother touched her arm. "You're a good sister. Have you finished your homework?"

"Um…yes."

Norma suddenly sat up straight, her head cocked to one side. "Did you hear that? Is that the sound of your dad's truck?"

"No, Mama. It's just a noise on the highway."

"I don't know." Norma jumped up and went into the living room, peering out the window. "I don't see anything."

Jena followed her. "It's nothing."

"I'll sit in my chair and wait." Norma sank into her recliner. "If I holler, you get out of the house. I don't want him beating on you again."

How many times had she heard those words? More than she wanted to remember. In that moment she realized her mother had spent most of her life listening for the sound of her husband's truck. No wonder she was losing her mind. Without any happiness, the mind had found its own kind of peace.

After putting ham and cheese back into the refrigerator, she slammed the door just a little too hard. Why did life have to be like this? As a kid she used to dream of a happy family with loving parents. She'd tell her dad about her day and he'd smile and encourage her. Reality was far removed from the fantasy. But when their grandmother had been alive, their life had been almost normal. Their dad had supper with them every night and he didn't drink. At least not in Grandmother's presence.

After her death, life became a nightmare. Her father lost his job, and he was angry all the time. The drinking, arguing and fighting started. Life was never the same again.

She cleaned the kitchen counter with a deep sigh. There had to be happy families somewhere. Maybe they only existed beyond the clouds in Hilary's mural.

To stop the depressing thoughts she went to take a bath. Afterward, she slipped on clean shorts and a tank top. She hadn't brought many clothes, and it was a good thing Hilary had the washing machine. After putting a load on to wash, she checked on her mother. She was sound asleep in her chair. At peace.

She went outside and sat on the porch, swinging her legs off the side the way she had as a child. It was after seven and Carson hadn't come by or called. She'd wait until after eight and take it from there. She hadn't called Blake today, and she'd wait on that, too. Right now her thoughts were on her child. Carson would come, she kept telling herself. He'd have news. But they'd parted on an angry note, so she shouldn't expect much. Still, she kept hoping.

The white constable car turned into the driveway and her heart raced. He was here. She ran her sweaty palms down her bare thighs and waited.

He strolled toward her, and there was something in the way he moved. Was it dejection? Despair? She couldn't decide. Either way, it wasn't good.

"Good evening, Ms. Brooks," he said, his voice cordial yet hesitant.

"Good evening," she replied. "Have you talked to your father?" The words rushed out before she could stop them.

"Yes."

"And?"

"He admits to taking your baby."

Her heart skyrocketed. She hadn't expected Asa to admit that so easily. "Oh" slipped from her throat.

"Don't get your hopes up," he warned.

"Why?"

"He's never going to tell you where that baby is."

"What?" She was confused.

"Revenge, Ms. Brooks. The ultimate revenge. In his mind you took Jared from him, and in return he took your child. And since he can't get Jared back, you're not getting your child back, either. I'm sorry, but that's just the way Asa is."

Her hands curled into fists. "How can he be that evil?"

"Like I said, I'm sorry for what you've been through, but I've done what you asked. It's out of my hands now. Call your lawyer and let him do what he can, but nothing on this earth will make Asa tell his secret. I know him well enough to know that."

"It's illegal to steal someone's baby," she said with barely controlled anger.

"Yes, and Asa will be arrested because he freely admits to everything, but in his condition very little will be done. He'll probably be put into a home."

She fought the tears forming in her eyes. "I don't understand any of this. Asa was so mean to Jared, and

all he wanted to do was get away from his father. Now
he's acting like Jared was a son he loved dearly."

"In his heart I guess he did."

"He doesn't have a heart," she spat. "How can he
keep a child from its mother? Jared's child!"

Carson shrugged. "I don't profess to understand my
father. He's all the things you say he is, but that's not
going to change a thing. He will never tell you what
happened. That secret will die with him. I'm sorry for
what he put you through, but for me this is over. There's
nothing else I can do."

She stood on unsteady legs. "It will never be over
for me, Mr. Corbett."

"I understand that."

"Do you? Do you know what it's like to have your
baby forcefully taken from you? Do you know what it's
like to be in fear of your very life? Do you…?" Tears
clogged her throat, and she had to stop.

He stepped forward as if to console her.

She flung out her arms. "Do not touch me. Ever."

"Ms. Bro…"

Not able to take any more, she turned and ran into
the house. Tears ran from her eyes, and her body shook
violently. They would not break her. She would not give
in to the pain. She sank onto the floor in the bedroom
and stared at Hilary's clouds and drifted away to a better place.

WHEN CARSON WAS in Afghanistan, he'd often wondered
what it would feel like to be hit by a sniper's bullet. Now
he knew. It had to be similar to the paralyzing fear that
controlled his body and his mind. And touched his soul.

After Jared's and Beth's deaths, he'd felt a deep sadness and didn't know how he was going to go on without

them. They were a big part of his world and adjusting to a new life wasn't easy, but he had his kids. Jena had nothing.

Somehow he felt responsible for her pain because he'd delivered the bad news. That hopeless look on her face got to him, and he just wanted to comfort her in some way, but there was no comfort in the knowledge she would never see her child.

He got into his car, cursing his father's stubbornness and life's cruelty. Maybe she could move on now and find happiness. That was, after Asa was arrested. Maybe that would bring her some peace. For him it would be another nightmare to get through.

He and Beth had vowed to have a happy, loving family, and they had for a while. They were ecstatic when they found out she was pregnant with Trey. In her sixth month, they'd decided it would be better if she came home to Willow Creek to have the baby.

Beth had called her mother, who'd said it wasn't a good time to come home. After many years of marriage, Connie and Don Kirby were getting a divorce. Beth had packed and gone home anyway, trying to save her parents' marriage. It hadn't worked. Her father had already moved out, and her mother was planning to relocate to Maine to be with a truck driver she'd met at Mabel's Café.

Beth was devastated and Carson was so far away he couldn't help her. That was when Asa had stepped in and invited Beth to live at the Bar C. Beth was one of the few people Asa liked, so Carson hadn't worried about how his father would treat her. He doted on her, hiring a housekeeper and making sure Beth had everything she needed.

Beth's parents' marriage was another statistic in the

marriage game. Don moved to Oregon and started another family. Beth rarely heard from her father. He was in the hospital having knee surgery when Beth died. After that, he'd called several times, but Carson hadn't heard from the man in years. Connie married the truck driver and lived in Maine. She'd returned to Willow Creek for the funeral but soon left. Carson hadn't heard from her since.

Even though both of their parents' marriages had failed, he and Beth were determined to make theirs work. That was when he first thought about leaving the Marines. He and Beth needed to be together, especially since they were starting a family. Maybe Asa had mellowed and Carson could run the ranch now. So many maybes had filled his head, especially since Beth had told him that Asa continued to push Jared hard, and she feared he would leave and never come back. But then the unthinkable had happened. Jared was killed and life became a daily nightmare.

He backed out of the Brookses' driveway and turned toward home. Tonight after he put his kids to bed, he'd think about Jena and the pain she would endure for the rest of her life.

Happiness was just an illusion, he decided. All one could do was hope for the best, and he wished that for Jena. He prayed she found peace, in whatever way she could.

"Jena."

Jena blinked at the light on her phone. She was still sitting on the floor in the bedroom, but now it was completely dark.

Hilary flipped on the light. "What's going on? The house was in complete darkness when I drove up. Mama's in bed and I thought you were, too. Why are you sitting on the floor?"

Jena gripped her phone. "What time is it?"

"After ten." Hil slid down beside her. "What's wrong?"

She told her sister what Carson had said.

"That sorry old bastard. Someone needs to slap him."

"I got the feeling it doesn't matter. You can slap him, jail him, kill him and Asa's still not telling his secret. You see, it's his last revenge on me. He doesn't have his son because of me, or so he feels, and so I will never have my child."

"That's insane."

"Yeah, but how do you reason with someone who's insane?"

"I don't know, Jen-Jen. I'm so sorry."

She lifted the phone in her hand. "I've been sitting here trying to call Blake. I've punched his number about ten times, but I click off before it goes through."

"Why?"

"Blake is a cutthroat lawyer, and if he comes here he can cause all kinds of trouble."

"That's good. Maybe he can scare the truth out of Asa."

"And he can make the whole town hate us. You have a good relationship with everyone here, and I don't want that to change. And I certainly don't want anyone to upset Mama."

"So you're going to give up?"

"I will never give up. I just haven't figured out what I'm going to do, but I've come to the conclusion I don't need Blake. I can handle this on my own."

Hil's mouth fell open. "You're going to confront Asa?"

"I'm not sure yet, but by morning I'll have a plan. If Carson thinks I'm going to quietly leave town like before, then he's in for a shock. One way or another I'm going to find my child."

CHAPTER FIVE

THE NEXT MORNING Carson drove into the parking spot for his office, which was part of the paved area for the convenience store and gas station next door. He didn't need a lot of space. People rarely came to see him—when he got a call, he went to whoever was calling in a disturbance or a complaint.

For years Willow Creek hadn't had a constable's office, but Asa had built the current building for Bernie about thirty years ago. Back then Asa was the law in Willow Creek, Texas. Bernie did exactly what Asa wanted him to.

He spotted Ms. Brooks's car parked to the side. What was she doing here? Reaching for his office keys from the center console, he opened the door and got out. When she saw him, she got out, as well.

He tipped his hat. "Mornin', Ms. Brooks."

"Morning."

Her eyes were sad and had that cried-out look. Once again, he felt sympathy for her situation. In jeans and a white knit top that barely came to her waistband, she managed to look incredibly sexy. And that was the last thing he should be noticing.

"I'm not sure why you're here," he said to shift his mind in the right direction. "I told you last night there was nothing else I could do. I'll fax my report to the sheriff, and he will take it from there." He looked around. "Is your lawyer meeting you here?"

"I want to talk to you."

"Oh…okay." He walked toward the front door, wondering why she needed to talk. There wasn't much left to discuss. But he didn't mind talking if that was what she wanted. He just didn't see the point.

He unlocked his office door, flipped on the light and turned on the air conditioning. The room was stuffy from being closed up. Hooking his hat on a peg, he took a moment and then sat down. She'd already taken a seat in the chair across from his desk.

When she didn't say anything, he asked again, "Is your lawyer meeting you here?"

"I've changed my mind about that."

"Why?" That surprised him. She'd been so adamant.

"Blake would come into town with guns blazing, so to speak. His investigators would be relentless in getting answers."

"Isn't that what you want?"

"Yes, but my sister, Hilary, has a very good relationship with everyone here, and I don't want to do anything to change that or to hurt her. And I really don't want anyone to upset my mother."

"I'm not quite following you."

"I thought about this all night, and I'm not slinking out of town like I did before. But on the other hand I can't cause any more stress for my family."

"So that leaves what?"

She brushed at something on her jeans with a nervous hand. "Yesterday you said the cases had been closed quickly and there was still a lot of evidence out there."

"When I said that, you became very offended."

"I know, but now I'm thinking about it a little differently."

"How differently?"

"I'd like to find what other evidence is out there. There has to be someone other than Asa who knows what happened that night."

He picked up a pencil and twirled it in his fingers, wondering how to phrase his next question. "I don't want to upset you, but have you thought of the obvious?"

She moved restlessly in her chair, and he knew she'd thought of every scenario concerning her baby...even though it was painful. "I don't want to believe Asa could be that cruel. That evil." Her voice was barely a whisper.

He didn't, either, but they had to look at the possibility, as he had for the past twenty-four hours. It was burned into his brain. Asa had wanted revenge, and Carson was so afraid he'd found the ultimate way to get it.

"What do you expect from me, Ms. Brooks?"

Her dark sad eyes found his, and he felt a catch in his throat at all the pain he saw there.

"I'd like for us to look for new evidence like you mentioned."

"Us?" He motioned from her to him with the pencil.

"Yes. I'm Blake's personal assistant, and I'm very familiar with these sorts of files and court documents. I can help you go through all the files, and maybe we can catch something that no one else has."

"Don't you think you're grasping at straws?" He had to point that out.

"You didn't think so yesterday."

"Yesterday I hadn't talked to my father. You have to remember that Asa is my father."

"I realize that, but he committed a crime. And you are the law here in Willow Creek."

His stomach churned with uneasiness. The line between family and loyalty and his job was clearly blurred. Yesterday digging through the files was a good idea because he'd been looking for answers. Then he got the answers he didn't want to hear. Now he was torn in two ways. Suddenly, she did something unexpected.

"Carson, please, help me."

The entreaty in her voice and the way his name sounded on her lips, soft and seductive, hijacked his senses and sent his thoughts spinning. He hadn't expected that. And for a moment he was at a loss for words.

"It's Jared's child, too," she added forlornly. "Doesn't that mean something to you?"

"Yes." Jared had created a baby with her, and they'd planned a life together. For that reason he was still talking to her. "But it's also about my family, my father. I know he's guilty, and there's no way around that, but my kids adore their grandfather, and I don't know how I'll explain all this to them. I really think it's best if I don't get involved."

She stared down at her hands, and he felt that twist in his heart again. But what else could he do?

She raised her eyes to his, and, for a moment, he was lost in those dark depths. "I have this need to see my child's face. Each year it grows stronger and stronger. I want to know if he or she is happy and with a loving family. I have to know or I'll never have any peace."

"I—"

"I'll make a deal with you." She stopped him. "If you help me find my child, I will not file charges against your father. Years ago I would have loved nothing better than to hurt him severely, but now, as I said, I just want some peace."

"Jena… May I call you that now?"

"Yes. I'm sorry I was testy about that yesterday."

"Well, this is an emotional situation." He ran his hands over his face, telling himself it was best to stay out of this mess. But his heart wasn't listening. "Okay," he found himself saying. "I'll give it my best shot, but we have to set some ground rules. First, I'm in charge, and you will follow my instructions to the letter."

"Why?"

"Because I'll be responsible for everything we do."

"Okay, I get that."

"Good. And we will be civil to each other and respect each other's feelings."

"Okay."

"And when I say it's a dead end, we quit."

She lifted her chin with renewed determination. "I don't know if I can agree to that."

He stared at the stubborn glint in her eyes, knowing how hard this was for her, and it surprised him that he sensed her feelings so well. "You have to accept we may not find anything."

"I'm sorry, but I'll never be able to do that."

He admired her honesty. "As they say, we'll cross that bridge when we get there."

Scooting forward in her chair, she asked, "Can we start now?"

The file box was still on the floor. He reached down and pulled out the file on the case. As he slid it across the desk, she moved her chair forward. For the next thirty minutes they read through the papers several times and nothing jumped out at them.

At the oddest times he found himself watching the way her hair gently fell forward across her face. Almost unconsciously she'd tuck it behind her ears. It was a graceful motion that seemed to hypnotize him. Or maybe he just hadn't been around a woman in a very long time.

She sat back in the chair. "That doesn't tell us anything, other than facts we're very familiar with."

"Yeah."

"What do we do now?"

He closed the file and put it back in the box. "Let's pay Minnie a visit. I didn't press her yesterday, but I have a feeling she knows a lot more than she's saying." He got to his feet. "Are you up for that?"

"Sure. I have to call my sister to tell her I won't be at the house. We try to keep a close eye on our mom."

He reached for his hat and settled it on his head. Had he made the right decision? Whether he had or not didn't seem to matter. It just seemed important to help her. He had a feeling there were very few people in this world who had ever helped her. Except Jared. And maybe the lawyer. He wondered about their relationship...but that was none of his business.

His main objective was to keep his father from being arrested. Yet he could feel Jena pulling him into her life, her problems, and he didn't seem to mind. He liked her. Whatever the next few days held, he hoped he still liked her at the end.

JENA WAS ALMOST giddy with excitement. Carson had agreed to help her. Last night she was so hurt, so alone, and everything seemed lost. So many times she tried to call Blake, but in her heart she knew that wasn't what she wanted to do. Too many people had been hurt already, and she couldn't run the risk of putting Hilary in a bad situation. Sometime during the night Carson's words had come back to her, and it seemed feasible they could work this out in a non-confrontational manner.

As they walked out of the office she felt much better. She had hope. And she was putting a lot of trust in Carson Corbett.

"We might as well go in my vehicle," Carson said. "There's no need to take two cars."

She got in on the passenger side of his car and caught a delicious scent. Chocolate. He had chocolate in his car. She found that whimsical for a man.

Attached to the dashboard was a police radio. A coffee cup rested in the console along with bows, ribbons, hair clips and ponytail bands—little-girl stuff.

Carson slid into the driver's seat, and suddenly the car was way too small, too intimate in a way she couldn't explain. Or maybe she could. She just didn't want to.

"You like chocolate?" she asked to get her mind on something else.

"Why?" He turned onto the highway that ran through Willow Creek.

"I can smell it."

A smile touched the firm line of his lips, and her stomach flip-flopped for no reason. "I keep it for my kids. It's a treat for them after school. I'm more of a peanut-salty-taste type guy."

She could have guessed that one. He was a man's man all the way. She fiddled with a ponytail band from the console.

"That's my daughter's. We have this fight every morning about her hair. She's four years old and has all these ideas about how she should look. Her friend Chloe has a mother who does her hair into a French braid and does fancy curls with a curling iron. I told Claire her daddy doesn't do curling irons and my fingers just will not do a French braid. When she gets older, she can do her hair any way she wants, but as long as Daddy's in charge, it's a ponytail. I've got the ponytail mastered."

She could hear the love in his voice, and she knew he was a good father. "I saw a gadget advertised on TV that makes French-braiding hair easy. You might look it up."

"Oh, please, we spend entirely too much time on Claire's hair the way it is. Now, Trey, he's easy. Sometimes I have to remind him to comb his hair."

"I remember when Beth was pregnant with Trey," she said before she could stop herself. He didn't seem to mind the reference to his late wife, though.

"I was here for the birth and in the delivery room. I was the first person to hold him. It's a moment a parent never forgets."

Her throat clogged with tears, and he must've sensed her distress. "I'm sorry. That was callous."

"It's okay. It hurts, though, that I will never get that moment back. It hurts that it was stolen from me for no reason other than revenge."

Silence ensued and she was fine with that. She'd rather not talk anymore. He crossed the railroad tracks and turned down a dirt road that led back into the hills where the Voltree family lived.

As they crossed the cattle guard, he asked, "Are you sure you're ready for this?"

"I'm more than ready." But she braced herself for the encounter with Minnie.

Chickens scurried to get out of the way, and an old hound dog barked at them. The mobile home was old and showed its age with rusted spots and rotted wood, similar to the Brookses' property—unkempt.

They got out and she followed him up the steps to the front door. He knocked but no one answered.

"Let's check around back," Carson suggested.

They walked around the trailer, and the hound dog sniffed at their feet. Minnie and her husband, Bilford, were on a makeshift patio, sorting through fresh vegetables from the large garden that took up the rest of their property. They had a vegetable-and-fruit stand on the outskirts of town. For as long as she could remember, that was how they made a living.

Minnie carried a crate of tomatoes to the bed of a truck that was backed up to the patio. When she turned, she saw them. Nervously, she wiped her hands on her apron.

"Constable," she acknowledged.

At the sound of her voice, Bilford swung around and hurried over to shake Carson's hand. "Whatcha doing out this way?"

"We've come to talk to Minnie."

Bilford squinted at Jena. "Do I know you?"

"I'm Jena Brooks."

"You don't say. My, you've turned into a pretty little thing."

She didn't know how to respond to that, so she didn't. He didn't mean anything offensive. It was just the way he talked.

Carson stepped forward. "Minnie, I have more questions."

Minnie walked beneath the roof of the patio, which was basically sheets of tin nailed onto two-by-fours. "I told you I don't know nothing."

"Before you tell me a pack of lies, I talked to my father and he admitted to everything."

Her eyes grew big and wild. "Now, Constable."

"What's this about?" Bilford wanted to know.

Carson turned to him. "Minnie delivered Jena's baby."

"What?" The man looked from Minnie to Carson. "She left town to have the baby. Everybody knows that."

"No, I did not leave town to have the baby." Jena couldn't stay quiet any longer. "Roland and Curly kidnapped me and took me to the Bar C ranch, where Minnie was waiting. She gave me something to induce labor, and then she took my child from me."

"I did not!"

"This is crazy," Bilford said.

"It's not crazy," Carson told him. "It happened. We just want to know what Minnie did with the child." He looked directly at Minnie. "I'd advise you to cooperate."

"Okay. I delivered it." Minnie sank into a folding lawn chair. "That's all I did."

"Why would you do that?" Carson asked.

"Asa holds the note on this property, and he said if I helped him, he would deed it over to us. We barely make ends meet, and he was only asking for me to deliver a baby. I've done that all my life. I didn't see the harm until it was too late."

Carson shook his head. "Did Asa deed you the land?"

"Yes," Minnie replied.

Carson motioned to the older man. "Sit down, Bilford. If Pa deeded you this land, you knew exactly what your wife was doing. Don't give me any more I-didn't-know-what's-happening crap."

Bilford sank into the other folding chair. "I told ya this was going to bite us in the ass someday."

Carson placed his hands on his hips. "I want the whole story, Minnie."

She smoothed her apron with a shaky hand. "Roland

and Curly brought her to the basement, and I gave her something to induce labor. Everything should've gone smoothly, but the baby was breech and things got difficult. I eventually turned the baby and..."

"What was it?" Jena could barely get the words out.

Minnie shook her head. "I don't know."

"Don't lie, Minnie," Carson said. "What was the baby? Girl or boy?"

"I told you I don't know. There was so much blood. It was everywhere, on the baby, the bed, everywhere. As soon as the baby came out, Asa pushed me away and wrapped the baby in a big towel. He barely gave me time to cut the cord. With the baby in the towel I didn't get to look at it really good."

"You don't expect us to believe that, do you?" Carson asked.

"It's the truth," Minnie cried. "Asa took that baby covered in mucus, blood and fluids before I could do anything."

It seemed as if they were talking about another person, not her. But suddenly that night hit her full force. She could see the blood drip, dripping onto the floor, feel the excruciating pain, hear her cries going unheard and sense the loneliness of that room where there were no friends—just enemies.

"If you're lying," Carson was saying, "I'll make sure you do some jail time."

"Tell them everything you know," Bilford urged.

"I have."

"What happened after the baby was born?" Carson asked.

"I took care of Jena."

"Took care of me?" Jena's patience snapped with a vengeance. "There was blood because you botched the delivery. You botched it so bad I bled for days. I eventually had to have surgery to stop the bleeding, but I still had problems years later. Six months ago I had to have a partial hysterectomy. Do you know what that means, Minnie?"

Minnie looked down at her hands, unresponsive.

"I will never be able to have children. You took the only child I will ever have and gave it to a madman. And your ineptitude scarred me for life. I don't understand how you could do something like that to another woman—to a teenage girl."

"I'm sorry." Minnie hung her head.

"*Sorry* doesn't change anything. I'm begging you to tell us everything you know."

"I did."

Jena curled her hands into fists, wanting to hurt the woman, wanting her to feel some of the pain that Jena had endured. But that would accomplish nothing.

"What did Asa say to you when he took the baby?" Carson continued with the questions.

"He was talking crazy. Saying she would never pass the kid off as a Corbett. She'd taken his son, but she would not take his name. It made no sense to me."

"What happened next?"

"Asa went upstairs, and Roland and Curly followed him. I cleaned up and tried to make Jena comfortable."

"After that?"

"I just wanted to get out of there. Roland and Curly came for Jena and I left."

"You left me with those two goons!" Jena shouted. "You had no idea what they were going to do to me. How could you just leave?"

"Honey, I had to get out of there."

Jena's vision blurred with anger. "You let two of the

meanest men in Willow Creek manhandle me. That angers me so much I could pull your long gray hair out by the roots and strangle you with it."

"That's uncalled for." Bilford got to his feet.

"Sit down and shut up," Carson told him, and then he turned to her. "Are you okay?"

She nodded but realized her body was shaking with years of pent-up rage. She took a long breath to calm her nerves.

"As you left the house, did you hear anything? A baby crying?" Carson asked.

"No."

"Did you see anyone?"

"Just Roland and Curly."

"My wife was in the house with a new baby and you didn't see or hear them?"

"Asa said Beth had a rough night with the baby and for us to be quiet."

"Now, see, you didn't mention that. What else are you not telling us?" Carson kept firing questions.

"I just forgot."

"What else are you forgetting?"

"Nothing. Leave me alone."

"You put yourself in the middle of this mess, Minnie. Now you have to face the consequences."

"Don't you think I've worried about it all these years? It wasn't right. I knew that, but Asa has a lot of power. I was just trying to save our home. I'm sorry for the pain I've caused you, Jena. If I knew anything else about your baby, I would tell you."

Jena turned and walked back to the car. She couldn't handle any more. So much heartache, and there was no end in sight. Had she made the right decision coming back here? In her mind she knew she had, but her heart was struggling to stay in one piece.

Carson joined her, and they drove away from the Voltree property. They didn't speak. Emotions were very raw. Without her knowing it, tears slipped from her eyes. She quickly wiped them away, but more followed.

Carson pulled over to the side of the road. "Are you okay?"

She flipped back her hair. "Yes. I just keep wondering when the pain will stop."

"I'm sorry she wasn't much help, but I believe she was telling the truth."

"That's what's so sad. Your father is holding all the cards. He made sure no one knew what he did with my child but him. He's won."

"There was another condition I forgot to mention. Don't give up on the first day."

She looked at him through her tears. "It's hard not to."

"We're just starting."

She wiped away the last of the tears. "I'll have to grow a thicker skin."

There was silence for a moment, and then he asked, "The reason you came back now is because of the partial hysterectomy?"

She looked down at her locked hands. "That child is the only one I will ever have. As the years passed, my need to see its face grew stronger. I thought if I could look upon my child, know that he or she is in a good place, I could move on. But now I have to brace myself to face the fact my baby probably died within minutes of its birth." She drew a sharp breath to stem the pain the words caused.

He reached out and touched her arm, a soothing sensation that gave her strength. "There's something you should know about me. I never give up."

She stared into his confident green eyes. "What do you have in mind?"

He glanced at his watch. "It's early yet. Brett Evans, a Texas Ranger, helped with the investigation. I spoke to him several times after I returned home. He's very thorough, and his memory is uncanny. If you're up to it, we could drive to Buda to visit with him. He interviewed Roland and Curly, and I'm curious as to what they said."

Something in his tone irritated her. "Do I appear weak to you?"

"Excuse me?"

"You've asked several times if I'm okay and if I'm up to it. I assure you I am not fragile, and I will not fall apart. I'm a little shaken at times reliving the bad stuff, but you don't have to treat me like I'm about to have a nervous breakdown."

"Okeydokey." He ran his hand across the steering wheel. "You know, you have a tendency to pounce without warning."

A twinge of guilt pierced her chest. She wasn't apologizing, though. "Well, then, stop making me mad."

"Okay, Ms. Brooks. What would you like to do now?"

"Now you're being condescending."

He turned toward her, his green eyes dark. "I'm not going to apologize for being concerned about your well-being. You've been through a traumatic ordeal and it's not over. It could get worse. If my being considerate bothers you, then maybe it's time for us to stop and you can call your lawyer."

They stared at each other, two adversaries, angry

and determined. She was the first to look away from the fire in his eyes.

"Okay. I'm being touchy."

"Again," he mumbled under his breath.

She gritted her teeth. "Yes. I'd like to talk to the ranger."

He reached for his phone. "I think I have his number on my cell." He talked for a few minutes and clicked off. "He's home and will see us if we can get there within the hour." Without another word, he pulled back onto the road.

After a few minutes, he asked, "Do you think you could stop taking everything I say the wrong way?"

"I'll try."

She didn't know why she was being so testy. Maybe she was building a solid defense around her heart out of barbed-wire quips to keep her emotions in check. Carson was handsome and charming, and even though she'd been away from Willow Creek for nine years, she was still very naïve when it came to men. She had to stay muleheaded and stubborn and not fall for another Corbett.

CHAPTER SIX

THE RIDE TO Buda was quiet and that was fine with Carson. Talking to Jena was like talking to a porcupine. She wasn't letting anyone get too close, and if someone did, she was immediately on the defensive, inflicting pain. He supposed she had good reason. She was protecting herself. He understood that.

But it was aggravating to have her pounce every time he said something she didn't like. He wasn't sure why he was involved with her in the first place. But then, saying no to Jena didn't seem to be an option for him. If he could keep his kids from seeing their grandfather arrested and put in a home, he would stick this out. And he was doing it for Jared, too. Somehow he knew his brother would want him to help Jena. And that might prove to be his biggest challenge—helping her while protecting his father.

The ride was scenic with a rolling lush landscape of farms and ranches. Brett lived on a small ranch outside the city limits. Once they turned off U.S. 290 onto a rural route the landscape was more rustic with thick woods and houses set miles apart.

"I've met Ranger Evans," she said.

Her low sincere voice startled him, but he asked, "When?"

"The day after Jared was killed."

"He interviewed you?"

"Yes. He wanted to know when was the last time I saw Jared."

"When was that?"

"I saw him about 4:00 p.m. He said he had to get home before his dad sent Roland out for him. We didn't want Asa to get suspicious of what we had planned, so he was trying to follow orders."

"Where did you see him?"

"At my house."

They were talking again, sharing information. He hated that he'd offended her, so he carefully chose his next words. "Was your father home?"

"My father was rarely home and he wasn't that day."

"Jared's body was found a little after eight on an old country road. What made him go there?"

She glanced at him. "That's a question no one could answer."

"Did Ranger Evans talk to your mother?"

"Yes. He asked all kinds of questions about my father, but we were as mystified and devastated by the shootings as everyone. Like you, Ranger Evans was looking for a motive, and the only one he and the sheriff could come up with was me. My father killed Jared because of me."

He heard the hurt in her voice and he almost didn't say anything else. But they were looking for answers. "Was he satisfied with that motive?"

"I don't think so because he couldn't find anyone who could say that my father threatened to kill Jared."

"You never spoke to the ranger again?"

"No."

"After your baby was taken, did you ever think of calling him?"

Looking down at the hands clasped in her lap, she

admitted, "Honestly, no. I was scared, grieving and almost afraid to breathe. And I knew no one would believe me, not even the ranger."

He wouldn't have believed her, either, because he'd wanted to believe the worst of her. His brother was dead. And, like his father, he'd wanted her to pay. But now that he knew her, he found her to be an honest and open person. No one had been hurt more than her.

He turned off the rural route road and crossed a cattle guard. They passed cattle feasting on grass as they sped toward a farm-style ranch house with a long veranda. He parked by a worn board fence and they got out. The wind blew her hair across her face, and he watched as she tucked it behind her ears.

"Do you think we could stop butting heads for today?"

"Maybe." A slight smile touched her lips, and he was lost in a kaleidoscope of new emotions, ones he hadn't felt in a long time. And he shouldn't be feeling them now.

"Come on in," Brett shouted from the veranda.

Two blue heelers charged out to greet them. After sniffing their feet, the dogs charged back to Brett. Carson opened the gate and they walked to the veranda. Large baskets of blooming flowers hung from the rafters.

Brett shook their hands. He was a tall, lean man in worn jeans and boots. A thatch of gray hair crowned his head.

"Ms. Brooks, it's nice to see you again."

"Thank you."

Carson didn't like the way Brett was looking at Jena—as though she was an attractive woman he couldn't take his eyes off. But then, Carson proba-

bly looked at her the same way, which was a sober-
ing thought.

"Come, let's go to my study."

They followed him into the house. It was open, warm
and inviting with old hardwood floors and antiques. A
woman appeared from the kitchen area.

"This is my wife, Charlene." Brett made the introductions.

"Would y'all like some coffee?" Charlene asked.

He looked at Jena and she shook her head. "No,
thanks," she replied.

They followed Brett into a large study off the den.
The room was the same as the rest of the house, except
there was a wall of framed newspaper clippings and
awards Brett had received as a Texas Ranger. Several
antique guns were in glass cases.

"Sit, please," Brett said, easing into a leather chair
behind his huge oak desk.

A small sofa was the only place to sit, and he and
Jena barely fitted on it. This was the closest he'd been
to her. She wore a tempting fragrance. He'd had a hint
of it in the car, but now it intrigued him. What was
it? It wasn't strawberry or lavender or lilac or vanilla.
What was it?

"You wanted to talk about the Willow Creek murders?" the ranger asked.

Carson quickly shifted his wandering thoughts.
"Yes."

"I hope you don't mind me saying, but I find it a little
odd that you two are here together."

Carson didn't blink under the ranger's sharp eye.
"Jena has some questions about her father's death, and
I have some about my brother's. I thought you would
be the best person to talk to, other than the sheriff."

"What would you like to know?"

"My father's murder case was closed very quickly." Jena joined the conversation. "Why?"

Brett didn't balk under the question, but Carson sensed he was nervous or uncomfortable.

"Lack of evidence," Brett replied. "To be quite honest no one else had a motive to kill Lamar Brooks but Asa Corbett. And there was no way Asa could have done it. Once Jared's body was taken to the morgue, Asa never left it. No one was touching his son's body without his permission. Roland and Curly were with him the whole time. At six that morning Asa was at the funeral home. Later, Asa gave us access to his gun cabinet, and we ran ballistics on his shotguns. Nothing matched."

This was the first time Carson had heard his dad was at the funeral home all night. In grief, he'd missed so many things. He hated to admit to himself, though, that Asa could have sent Roland or Curly to kill Lamar.

Brett pushed his chair back to a large filing cabinet and pulled out a file. "I keep notes and papers from every case I investigate. The evidence and records from both cases are stored at the sheriff's office." He opened the file on his desk. "There were so many things about the two cases that didn't add up."

"Then why were the cases closed?" Carson asked. "If Pa didn't kill Lamar, that means someone else did."

"Mmm. I always hated the thought that someone got away with murder."

"Why didn't you or the sheriff continue to investigate?"

Brett leaned back in his chair. "After your brother was buried, Asa was in a full-blown rage. He wanted the sheriff and the Texas Rangers out of Willow Creek. Two weeks later we were told that if we didn't have a viable suspect for Lamar Brooks's murder, we were to close the case."

"By who?" Jena wanted to know.

"An aide to the governor."

Carson blew out a breath. His father had that much power because Asa poured money into campaigns for politicians who were quick to do his bidding.

"You said some things didn't add up." He focused on the ranger's words. "What things?"

Brett flipped through some papers in the file. "We had a timeline on Jared. He left Ms. Brooks's house about 4:00 p.m. He then went to the convenience store and bought an ice-cream sandwich, a Coke and an orange-and-white baby T-shirt with Hook 'em Horns on it."

"Oh," Jena gasped. "I didn't know he'd done that. What happened to the T-shirt?"

"I suppose it's in the evidence box stored at the sheriff's office."

She looked down at her hands, her hair falling across her face to hide her expression. Jared had bought the baby a gift and she was struggling to control all the emotions the gesture implied.

Carson had to bite his tongue to keep from asking if she was okay. He wouldn't make that mistake again.

"Ma'am, are you okay?" Brett asked, and Carson wondered how she would respond to the question from someone else.

Jena's head jerked up. "Yes. Thank you."

She glanced at him, and he lifted an eyebrow. He got the distinct impression she wanted to smack him but resisted.

There was silence for a moment. Carson kept waiting for Brett to ask about the baby, and he wondered again what Jena would say. Would she keep her word and not incriminate his father?

To keep Brett from dwelling on the baby, he asked, "Where did Jared go from the store?"

Brett looked down at his notes. "Ella, who runs the convenience store, said Asa called Jared while he was checking out and Jared told his father he was on his way home. She saw the red Dodge head toward the Bar C."

"So something or someone distracted him."

"That was our theory at the time. Lamar called Jared to talk about his relationship with his daughter. Things got heated and Lamar pulled out his shotgun."

"My father didn't have a phone, cell or otherwise," Jena pointed out. "We couldn't afford one."

"Yeah." Brett tapped his fingers on the desk. "There was that, but we concluded Lamar could have called from anywhere."

"My father did not know Jared's cell number."

"I told you nothing about the cases made sense. Then there's Willie Bass."

Carson glanced up. "What's ol' Willie got to do with this?"

"The next morning he came into town and said Lamar couldn't have shot the Corbett boy because Lamar was drinking with him down at Willie's shack on Willow Creek."

Carson frowned. "What happened with that?"

"Later, Willie recanted everything. Said he was drunk and didn't know what he was saying. And that was it."

"My dad drank with Willie all the time because Willie sold his homemade moonshine for a dollar a gallon. He stayed more at Willie's than he did at home."

Carson leaned forward. "That's a hell of a lot of evidence left on the table uninvestigated."

"Yeah." Brett agreed with him. "That's always bothered me."

"Wait a minute." Something clicked in Carson's mind. "What about Jared's phone? If Lamar called him, it would be on there."

"The phone was never found. We searched the truck and a mile radius around it. We even searched Lamar's truck. Nothing. Jared had the cell at the convenience store, and it was always my feeling that whoever pulled the trigger on the shotgun took the cell."

"But the phone company would have a record of the calls," Carson said.

"Yep. They sure did. It took a while, but we finally got a list of calls Jared made and a list of people who called him. Besides friends at school, Asa was the only one who called Jared that day. The only explanation left was that Jared met someone on the way home and agreed to meet them on the country road. And that someone was Lamar Brooks."

"Did the sheriff agree?"

"Yes, but then the investigation stopped." Brett leaned back in his chair. "I don't like to tell tales out of school, but everyone knew the old sheriff was pretty much in Asa's pocket. When Asa wanted us out of Willow Creek, we left. I investigated some on my own but soon got caught up in another case and had to move on. The Willow Creek murders kept me awake many a night. I guess they always will."

When Carson had thought there was evidence still out there concerning the murders, he never dreamed there was this much. His father was right in the middle of it. Why did he stop the investigation?

"For what it's worth—" Brett placed his forearms on the desk "—I felt that Lamar Brooks did not murder Jared Corbett. How Lamar's shotgun got there I can't tell you, but it was very damaging evidence that was hard to ignore. It was all Asa needed to see. And the shotgun that killed Lamar was never found."

"I knew that," Carson said, getting to his feet. "My wife said Asa freely opened his gun cabinet to the sheriff." But Carson knew his father could have easily gotten rid of the gun.

"That was the only thing that Asa cooperated on." Brett stood. "We wanted to search Jared's room, but Asa adamantly refused."

Jena rose to stand by Carson. "What did you expect to find?"

"Anything to give us a clue as to what had happened that night. I was really hoping Jared had made it home and gotten a call there. But Asa repeatedly said Jared never arrived at the house and the phone was not in his room. We had to take him at his word."

Carson held out his hand and Brett shook it. "Thanks for sharing your information, even though it creates a lot more questions."

As Jena shook the ranger's hand, he said, "I hope you're doing well, Ms. Brooks."

"I live in Dallas now and work at a law firm."

"That's good." Brett nodded his head. "Glad you put it behind you."

Carson could almost read the man's mind. He wanted to ask about the baby, but being a ranger he wouldn't cross that line.

They drove away in silence. Jena twisted in her seat to face him. "That was an eye-opener."

"My father's hand is in everything."

"I didn't find that surprising."

He drove over the cattle guard and turned onto the road. "I don't understand why Pa wouldn't let them continue the investigation."

"Because, obviously, there's some sort of cover-up."

He glanced at her. "That makes no sense."

"It does to me. Asa would do anything to get his way. I wouldn't be surprised if he planted my father's gun at the scene."

"Whoa. That's a stretch. Next you'll be saying my dad killed Jared."

"Now there's a thought."

That was a blow to Carson's heart. Somewhere in the back of his mind the thought lurked like a traitor about to pounce. There was no doubt in Carson's mind that Asa loved his boys, but something had gone very wrong the night Jared had died. Secrets, lies and confusion mingled inside him like a virus, making him feel weak and unsure of what to believe and what to expect next.

"This is all hard to grasp," she said. "Take the next turn to the right."

"Why?"

"The dirt road meanders around to Willow Creek where Willie Bass lives. Maybe he can tell us more about that night."

"When Willie sees the constable's car, he'll hide or run."

"Are you afraid of what he might say?"

He glanced at her and saw the gleam in her eyes. "Okay." He made the turn. "You're taking this very well."

"I've had years to prepare myself. I came home to find my child, but I have so many unresolved feelings about that night, and it's time to get it all out into the open. To find answers. To know the truth. And maybe if we're lucky, it will lead us to what I need to know."

Carson didn't respond, just drove on down the road, dust boiling around his freshly washed white car. But he wondered if he wanted to know the truth. The fact that his father took Jena's baby without any qualms was still reeling in his mind. How much more did he want to know? Asa was his father and he was still holding on to his last hope that there was some goodness in him. There had to be or the world just wouldn't make sense anymore. But even facing pain or disillusionment, he was seeing this through to the end. He had to for his own peace of mind.

CARSON TURNED DOWN a dirt track that led to Willie's place. Jena and Hilary had come here with their dad when they were little. The place still looked the same—a run-down, weather-worn shack with a trail in the grass that led to the front door. Gallon jugs and jars were stacked high in the grass. A rusted barrel overflowed with trash.

But beyond the shack was a beautiful scene. Large live oaks and willows shaded the flowing creek. Serene, quiet, private—the way Willie liked it, away from the prying eyes of the community.

"His truck's not here, so that means Willie isn't, either," Carson said. "What do you want to do?"

She undid her seat belt, got out and strolled to the water's edge.

"Where are you going?" Carson called, following her.

She sat in the grass and watched the easy rhythm of the water. It calmed her with its serenity. It boosted her courage with its power. And gave her a sense of reality in this unreal day.

He sank down by her. "Nice, huh?"

"It's good to see it flowing. Hilary said it had almost dried up due to the drought."

"Everyone was happy to see the rain again." Carson looked over his shoulder. "Willie may not be back for a while."

"It's a beautiful day. Can we wait?"

Carson glanced at his watch. "Sure."

"In Dallas I don't get to see things like this."

"Do you like living there?"

"I didn't have much of a choice." She raised her knees and wrapped her arms around her legs. "But I got used to city life."

Carson plucked at the grass. "You and Jared met in school?"

"Of course. We were in the same class."

"I was in Afghanistan during Jared's high school years. When did you start dating?"

She looked at his face but didn't see any derision, only curiosity. "I had classes with Jared, but we didn't move in the same circles. Then one day there was a bad thunderstorm with heavy rain, and Hilary and I were walking home. He stopped and gave us a ride."

"He was nice like that."

"Yeah." She rested her chin on her knees. "After that, he would look for me to offer a ride home. I would refuse. Then one day it was raining again and I accepted the ride. But I told him that was it."

"Why?"

She watched a leaf float by. "Because the boys usually only wanted one thing from me and I wasn't willing to do that."

"But Jared was different?"

"Yes. He was having trouble in English, and he said if I would help him, he would give me a ride home without any strings. Just friendship."

"But it turned into something more?"

She kept her eyes on the water, hardly believing she was sharing her thoughts about Jared. With his brother. But it seemed natural and comfortable.

"Not for a long time. After a football game, we kissed for the first time. It was nice, and I thought maybe we could be a couple." The water lapped against the bank and she was mesmerized by it. "Then one day in school I heard Jared's friends teasing him about me being easy and I refused to see him anymore."

"But that wasn't the end of it?"

"No. He was very upset I had overheard and said his friends were idiots. I still wouldn't give in. Then he started following me home in his truck, day after day, until I finally caved. We studied together but didn't date. We were friends, very good friends."

"But things changed?"

She lifted her head and gazed into his eyes. "Why do you need to know about Jared and me?"

Carson leaned back on his elbows and stretched out his long legs. His white shirt stretched taut across his broad shoulders. She forced herself not to look away. She wasn't a naïve girl seeing a handsome man for the first time. But, oh, it felt like it.

"I'm curious about my brother's relationship with you—how it started and how it ended."

Her eyes held his. "You know how it ended."

"I'm not judging you, Jena."

At the warmth in his voice she felt a weakening in the defenses she'd built around her heart.

"You said you were friends, so something had to have changed," he persisted.

She thought for a moment and saw no harm in telling him. And for some reason she had a need to hear the words said out loud. Or maybe she needed to see his reaction.

"Everyone knew my dad beat my mother, but no one ever tried to stop it. One night he was in a rage. I hid Hilary under the bed and tried to help my mom. But he was much stronger than the both of us. It was a terrible scene. My face was badly bruised, and I didn't go to school the next day. Later, Jared came looking for me and he was shocked at my face. We drove to the bridge over Willow Creek and sat there for a long time. He said no one was ever going to hurt me again. He wanted us to run away, but I told him that was crazy. I couldn't leave my mom and my sister. He started kissing me and one thing led to another. We had sex for the first time—and the only time."

"What?"

She saw the disbelief on his face. "It's true. I was upset and he was upset that he'd done something I didn't want to do. I could have stopped, but I didn't. I needed to feel close to someone. I told him it was okay. We huddled together like two lost souls, and it was just our bad luck that I got pregnant. Eventually, we accepted it and made plans. It wasn't what we wanted, but we figured it was a way out for us. We would start a new life together for our child."

Carson sat up. "That's different from what I'd imagined."

"It's different than everyone imagined, especially your father. Just because I was poor and the daughter of a drunk, it didn't make me a slut."

Nothing was said for some time. "I get the feeling that Jared was deeply in love with you, but you considered him just a friend."

She moved her legs and sat cross-legged. "I didn't know what love was then and neither did Jared. As I said, we just needed each other." She ran her hand along the denim of her thigh, admitting a deep-seated truth. "If I had remained strong, and refused to see Jared, none of the bad stuff would have happened. So you see, your father is right. I really am to blame for Jared's death."

"Jena…" He scooted closer and put his arm around her. The world stopped turning as warm, real emotions engulfed her. A heady masculine scent excited her and she wanted to lean into him, feel his strength, his comfort. But she immediately rejected the urge.

Pulling away, she said, "Please don't do that."

"Jena…"

"No. Don't try to console me. Don't try to make things better. The time for that has long passed. Let's just do what we started out to do—sort through the evidence. Anything other than that is out of the question."

He looked at her with eyes that said she wasn't fooling him. That almost tangible attraction between them was growing. He knew it. She knew it. She just didn't know how to stop it. And the sad part was she didn't know if she wanted to.

CHAPTER SEVEN

THE PUT-PUT OF a truck echoed through the trees. "Willie's here," Carson said and got to his feet.

Jena stood and brushed grass from her jeans. Carson wanted to say so many things, but the right words were lost in the stunning information she'd just shared. Two young kids brought together by the cruel actions of their fathers. He had misjudged Jena on so many levels, and he had to make that right in some way. That would come later. Now they had to face Willie.

Willie's truck rattled into the yard. Surprisingly, he got out, doing exactly the opposite of what Carson thought he would do. In worn overalls and a dirty Dallas Cowboys baseball cap, Willie squinted at them. He was short and thin with leathery wrinkles that marked his advanced years.

They strolled to meet him.

"I gave up making moonshine, Constable, so there ain't no need for you to come out here."

Carson knew that was a lie, but he wasn't interested in Willie's illegal activities. Putting Willie in jail served no purpose other than to clutter the courts with frivolous arrests. People who bought the illegal moonshine usually drank at home and didn't hurt anyone other than themselves.

Willie stared at Jena. "You're Lamar's girl."

"Yes," she replied. "I'm Jena."

"You've grown up."

"Yes."

"What y'all doing out here?"

Jena stepped forward. "I'd like to talk to you about the night Jared Corbett was killed."

Willie's tired brown eyes narrowed. "I don't know nuthin' 'bout that."

"But you said you were drinking with my father that night."

"Ah." Willie waved his hand. "That was drunk talk."

"Are you sure? Or did someone change your mind?"

Willie frowned. "Like who?"

"Asa Corbett."

Willie removed his dirty hat and scratched his head. "Why would you think that?"

"Because my dad's shotgun was at the scene and Asa wanted him to pay."

"Now, girl, let's just let that old hound dog sleep. There ain't no need to mess with the past."

"But, Willie—" Jena moved closer to him, and Willie didn't take his eyes off of her "—if my father was with you, he couldn't have shot Jared. That means someone else did. Just tell me the truth. That's all I'm asking."

Willie shoved his hands into the pockets of his overalls, giving it some thought.

"My father can't hurt you now." Carson wanted him to know that just in case it might help him to make up his mind.

"Ol' Asa's in a hell of his own," Willie mused. "But I'm not afraid of Mr. Asa."

"Who, then?" Jena asked.

"Lamar was a friend of mine. We spent many a night drinking down at the creek. He was real happy his daughter was going to have a better life than he'd ever given her. He'd drink himself into a stupor talking about it."

"Did he that night?" Jena pressed, her voice anxious, but Carson could see she was keeping her emotions in check.

"Yeah," Willie finally admitted. "Woke up about five-thirty that morning and went home. It was the last I saw him."

"Why did you alter your story?" Jena kept on. "If my dad was with you, he was innocent."

"That's why I went into town as soon as I heard. I told Bernie everything."

"Who made you change your mind?" Carson asked.

"I got a visit from Roland, and he said if I didn't want to be the next one in the ground, I better come up with another story quick."

"Did he mention my father's name?"

Willie shook his head. "I didn't ask no questions. Roland's mean and I didn't want no part of him. Besides, Lamar was dead and I couldn't help him."

"How did my father's shotgun get to the scene?" Jena wanted to know.

"I don't know nuthin' about the shotgun," Willie replied. "But Lamar was with me from about three that afternoon."

"Could you have fallen asleep and Lamar left for a little while?" Carson asked.

"Nah. I was making moonshine and I was as wide-awake as a hoot owl. Lamar never left. He sat drinking, watching me."

Carson held out his hand. "Thank you, Willie. I appreciate your honesty."

"Don't know how it can help now."

"More than you think."

Jena also shook his hand. "Please accept my thanks, too. It's good to know my father was not a killer."

"Not ol' Lamar. He just liked to drink."

"A little too much."

"Yeah. That's the nature of the devil."

They walked to the car and got in. Driving away, he said, "With just a little more investigating, the sheriff could have found all this out years ago."

"But no one would go against your father."

"Mmm. Now I'm wondering what else he's hiding."

She didn't reply and she knew as well as he did that none of this was leading them to her child. Just more lies and secrets to add to the mix. Where would it end?

JENA SAT IN a daze. Her father wasn't a cold-blooded killer. A gigantic scar eased from her soul. So many years she thought of her father as a heartless, despicable person who had killed someone she'd loved. And it was all lies. She felt numb inside. Now she really wanted to find out who had killed Jared. Who had made her father into a murderer?

She glanced at Carson. "What's our next move?"

"We really don't have a lot, just hearsay. Willie's admission doesn't change much. We don't have concrete evidence to put Lamar at Willie's—just Willie's word, which at this stage is not reliable since he's changed it more than once."

"I believe him."

"I do, too, but we need more."

She sighed. "How do we do that?"

Carson turned onto the highway from the dirt road. "First, I plan to talk to Pa again. Then I'm finding a way to get into Jared's room."

"Why do you have to find a way? Can't you just open the door?"

"After Jared died, Pa locked it up. He's maniacal about anyone disturbing Jared's things. When I came home for good, the cases were closed, so I humored him and left the room alone.

"Four months later, Bernie retired and I was elected constable. I had no reason to dig into the cases. It was over for me and my family. But there might be something in the room to tie all this together."

"But will it lead us to my child?"

"Hopefully. Roland and Curly are in the middle of everything that was going on. Roland is still in prison, but Curly is out. I might try to track him down. He was there at the house the night the baby was born. I'd like to get his side of the story."

"When you go, I want to go with you. I'd love to kick him where it hurts."

He grinned. "You got it. My kids get out of school tomorrow for the summer, so... Damn."

"What?"

"I didn't realize it was so late. I have to pick up my kids from school."

"Just drop me at your office."

"The school is up ahead and I don't want them to wait."

"But..." She didn't really want to meet his children or be seen with him and give the town more fodder for gossip. Then again, what did she care? She wasn't eighteen anymore. Her nerves were rock solid, her demeanor cool, her attitude kick-ass tough, so she had nothing to fear. Except that one reminder about her crappy childhood from ill-mannered townsfolk could shatter her well-earned confidence. But not unless she let them. And it wasn't going to be today.

The school was up ahead on Willow Creek Drive, about a half a mile from the railroad tracks and her house. A wealth of emotions swamped her as she saw the large buildings with the white stone fronts. Since the town was small, the elementary, junior high and high school were here, just in separate buildings. A gym and a football field were to the right.

After school, she would hurry and find Hilary, and they would walk through the woods to the tracks and home, even on the coldest days. They had one vehicle and her father was usually off somewhere in it. On cold mornings he might take them to school, but they had to make their own way home.

All the debilitating memories of hand-me-down clothes, welfare checks, food stamps seemed to choke her and she had trouble breathing. But she and Hilary had survived and that was good. They were both strong women because of their upbringing.

Buses waited in line for the children and soon they came pouring out the front doors. She and Hilary could have ridden the bus, but it meant getting home an hour later—their house was almost the last stop. They preferred the short walk.

Carson got out and shook hands with several people. He waved to the throng of chattering kids and two of them came running, a little girl and a boy she'd seen in the photo on his desk.

As she watched, Carson hugged both of the kids and they walked toward the car. The girl and the boy crawled into the backseat. Carson buckled the little girl in and took the driver's seat.

"Are you under arrest?" the boy asked, buckling his seat belt.

"No, son, this is Jena Brooks, and I'm taking her to her car at my office." Carson answered before she could.

"Ah, shucks, nothing fun happens around here," the boy complained.

"Jena, the kid who craves fun is my son, Trey, and the blonde cutie is—"

"I'm Claire—" the little girl jumped right in "—and I'm four years old. My best friend is Chloe. We're the same age and everything."

"Dad, Mr. Walt is taking Kelsey fishing this week and she asked me to go. I said yes. I can go, right?"

"Don't you think you should've asked me first?"

"Ah, Dad, it's Kelsey and Mr. Walt. They're like family."

"We'll talk about this at home."

"Ah, shucks."

Jena wasn't given a chance to get a word in edgeways, and she could see the easy rapport Carson had with his kids.

"Chloe and Kelsey are Ethan James's kids." Carson drew her into the conversation.

"You were friends way back when," she said.

"Yes. And now our kids are friends."

How nice that must be to be a part of a long-lasting friendship, like an extended family. She had only her mother and her sister. And a baby she may never see.

As Carson pulled up to his office, his phone jangled. He reached for it on his belt. "Okay, Harry, I'll be right there."

"The Baxter brothers are fighting at the Rusty Spur," he said to her. "Do you mind watching my kids just for a minute? It won't take long. Here's the key to the office."

"But…"

Carson didn't hear the *but*. He quickly got his children out of the car. "You can take them to the convenience store. They can have a drink and a cookie or candy. Tell Ella to put it on my bill. I've got to go. Thanks."

"But…"

He backed out and roared off down the highway while she was still stammering. She stared at the two kids who were staring up at her. Now this was a fine mess. She was going to walk into the Willow Creek convenience store, the busiest place in town, with Carson Corbett's kids. That should set a few tongues wagging. But she was up to the task.

"Who are you?" Trey asked.

How did she explain this? She spied the café across the highway. "Do you know Hilary?"

"Yeah. She makes good sundaes and she always puts two cherries on mine. She's cool."

"I'm her sister. I'm visiting."

"Oh."

"I'm thirsty," Claire said. "I want an ICEE."

"Dad said you can't have any more of those," Trey told her. "It makes your head hurt and then you cry. You like pink lemonade and a chocolate chip cookie."

"Yeah."

That settled, Jena took Claire's hand and they walked the twenty or so feet to the store. Trey spoke to several people and they stared at her, but no one said anything. Jena opened the door and they trailed in. That old familiar scent assailed her—freshly popped popcorn. Some things in life just never changed.

Trey headed for the coolers at the back. "I'm getting a Big Red."

Jena looked down at Claire. "You still want a lemonade?"

Claire twisted in her sandals and stared at her with big green eyes. "Yes, please."

Ella was waiting on a customer and then she turned and saw Jena. Her mouth fell open in shock. "Jena, my girl."

Back then Ella had always been nice, always trying to help her.

"Hi, Ella."

"Girl, it's so good to see you." Ella ran around the counter and hugged her—one of her big motherly squeezes. She had to be in her fifties now but still looked the same as she did the day Jena had left. A little overweight, sometimes cranky, but blessed with a loving personality that benefited everyone in Willow Creek. She had one flaw, though; she loved to gossip. "Are you home for a visit?"

"Yes."

"Hon, you're a sight for sore eyes. I thought I'd never see you again."

"I live in Dallas now. I work for an attorney."

"Good for you." Ella leaned in and whispered, "Did you bring your kid?"

Jena froze, not expecting that question so abruptly. She licked her suddenly dry lips. "No." It wasn't a lie, but it wasn't exactly the truth. It was all she had at the moment, though. As much as she liked Ella, she knew whatever she said would spread through the town quicker than Jena could bat her eyelashes. There would be a lot of questions about her pregnancy, but she wasn't willing to answer them. Not to protect Asa, but to guard the privacy of her child.

"Oh, hon, I don't know why you had to leave town

so quickly. Nobody blamed you for what happened to Jared."

"I want a lemonade, please," Claire said, and Ella hurried to serve her customers.

"Coming up," Ella said. She reached for a disposable cup, filled it with ice and lemonade from the pink machine, as all the kids called it. After placing a plastic lid on top, she inserted a straw. "I thought of you so often and it breaks my heart to know what you've been through."

Jena saw Trey coming from the back. "Could you bring me a diet Dr Pepper, please?"

"Okay." He swung back to the coolers.

Jena didn't want him to hear Ella's gossip.

Ella handed Jena the lemonade and she gave it to Claire, who immediately sucked thirstily on the straw.

"Slowly," Jena advised. "Or you'll get a brain freeze."

"Hon," Ella whispered, "what are you doing with Carson's kids?"

Jena tensed, but she didn't let it show. "I had some things to discuss with him and he got a call so…"

"Get all you can out of 'em, hon. We all believed it was Jared's baby. No one listened to that idiot Roland. Though the Corbetts have fallen on hard times like the rest of us."

No one had ever said to her they knew her baby was Jared's and it was cruel of Ella to mention it now. She bit her tongue to keep from saying anything. It would only create gossip. And it would do no good to tell her it wasn't about money. It was about something much more important and Ella would be the last person she'd tell.

A woman walked up to the counter with a Coke and chips. Ella immediately turned to her. "Hey, Stacey, look, Jena's back."

Jena looked at the girl she'd gone to high school with.
Her brown hair was pulled back into a ponytail, her
face devoid of makeup, and she'd put on at least twenty
pounds. Stacey had been one of the popular girls and
she never had much to say to Jena and Jena didn't have
much to say to her now.

Stacey shouted over her shoulder. "Charla, come
here. Jena's back."

A very pregnant strawberry blonde waddled forward.
Charla was also one of the popular girls, but she'd always been nice to Jena.

"My goodness," Charla said, eyeing Jena from head
to toe. "You look gorgeous."

"Thank you" was all Jena could say.

Charla placed a hand on her stomach. "My third one.
I feel like a blimp."

"You look great."

Trey came back with the drinks. "Chocolate chip
cookies for everyone?" she asked, trying to get out of
the store before they started asking questions.

Trey nodded and Jena made the order. She reached
in her purse for her wallet and paid for everything. No
way was she putting it on Carson's account. She wasn't
sure why that bothered her, but it did. It was important
to pay her own way.

"It was nice seeing everyone." She put her wallet in
her purse and hurried to the door.

Holding it open for the kids, she heard Stacey whisper, "What's Carson thinking leaving his kids with her?
Her father killed his brother."

"Stacey!" That was Charla.

"Where's her kid?" Stacey asked Ella.

"I don't know," Ella whispered back. "She wouldn't
say."

"Wonder who it looks like."

"Stacey, she can hear you," Charla said under her breath.

Jena didn't wait to hear any more. The gossip didn't destroy her composure like it used to, but it made her aware that Willow Creek had changed very little. And it made her more eager to continue investigating with Carson. Lamar Brooks wasn't a killer. She firmly believed that now. Soon everyone would know.

In seconds they were walking to Carson's office with their snacks.

Ella poked her head out the door. "If you need a job, just call me, Jena."

"Thanks." *Like when hell has an early frost.*

"Do you need a job?" Trey asked.

"No, but I worked there as a teenager."

"That must have been cool. You could eat anything you wanted."

"I had to pay for it." And she'd had to budget wisely.

She unlocked the door and they went inside. Trey sat in his father's chair, and Jena pulled a chair to the desk for Claire. She sat across from them sipping on her drink. Glancing at her watch, she realized Carson had been gone more than thirty minutes. What was taking so long?

The kids finished their cookies in record time. "What do we do now?" Trey asked.

Evidently she was supposed to entertain them. Claire sucked on the straw of her drink, and, as Jena watched, Claire's ponytail came undone and her hair fell all around her.

"Oh, no," Claire wailed. "Daddy never does it right."

So much for Carson's claim he had the ponytail mastered.

"Well, Claire, at least it didn't happen until we were out of school this time." Trey laughed.

Claire brushed the hair from her eyes. "Ponytail bands are in Daddy's car."

Jena picked up her purse. "Let's see what I have." She dug around and found her brush. "I can brush it, and I bet your dad has some rubber bands here somewhere."

"Can you do hair?" Claire asked excitedly.

"I can try."

"Oh, boy." She stood on her knees in the chair.

Jena walked around the desk and started brushing Claire's hair. It was long, thick and had a slight curl to it. The girlish highlights were to die for, and she'd seen women in Dallas pay a fortune in an attempt to duplicate them.

"Trey, see if you can find a rubber band in your dad's desk."

Claire twisted her head to look at Jena. "Can you make a French braid?"

Trey laid his head on the desk and groaned. "Not again." He lifted his head. "Dad said you had to stop fussing about your hair. You're driving us crazy."

Claire stuck out her tongue at him.

"I'm going to tell Dad," Trey warned.

"You're a tattletale," Claire shot back.

"No arguing," Jena said. "Did you find a rubber band, Trey?"

"Yes," he replied.

"Please make a French braid," Claire begged.

"Okay. Let's see if I can remember how." She brushed the long blond hair into her right hand and then gathered the hair from the top into three sections, letting the rest hang loose. As she crisscrossed the strands, she took hair from the right and then from the left and added it into the braid. She gripped it tightly so it wouldn't be loose and continued all the way down. Trey handed her a rubber band and she tied the end. She looked at her handiwork and smiled. She remembered.

"What does it look like?" Claire asked.

She looked around for a mirror but there wasn't one. "I'll get my compact from my purse so you can see."

Claire touched the braid with her hand. "I got to see. I got to see."

Jena opened the compact and held it so Claire could take a peep. "Oh, wow. Wait till I show Daddy."

"Thank God that's settled." Trey sank back into the chair. "Now what do we do?"

Jena glanced at her watch. What was taking Carson so long? How did she entertain two kids? She had never been around children that much, but surely she could come up with something.

"I left my stuff in my backpack," Trey said. "I can't play with my Nintendo DS."

"Let's play a game the old-fashioned way," she suggested.

"Like what?"

Since Claire was walking around looking at herself in the compact, Jena took her seat and grabbed a couple of pieces of paper from the desk. "Ticktacktoe. Have you ever played it?"

"Sure. It's with *x*'s and *o*'s?"

"Yes." She drew the grid of four lines and nine spaces. "Wanna play?"

Trey scrunched up his face. "That's for little kids."

"Okay, smarty-pants, let's see if you can beat me."

"You're on."

They played for a few minutes, and Jena could see

Trey was very smart. He focused, paid attention and beat her more than once.

Out of the blue, he said, "Our grandpa is sick."

Jena's breath caught in her throat and she didn't respond.

"He's had a stroke, and Claire and I help him with his exercises," Trey went on.

"Yeah." Claire put down the compact. "His hands shake and I kiss them to make them better. I love Grandpa."

Those were words Jared had never said about his father, but it was clear his grandchildren adored him. Maybe Asa had changed in the past nine years. Believing that, though, might take an act of God because when it came to Asa there was no forgiveness in her soul.

Claire grew bored and crawled into her lap, wanting to play, too. The little girl felt comfortable in her arms, and she wondered, not for the first time, what her child would have looked like. She often envisioned a brown-eyed girl with Jared's blondish hair, but she could never make out the features. She just always had a sense her child was a girl.

"Claire, you don't know how to play," Trey complained. "Look at your hair again. Jena and I were playing."

"Let's be nice," Jena said, even though Claire was scribbling on the grid.

"She's making a mess." Trey laughed in spite of himself.

Jena laughed, too.

The door opened and Carson stood there staring at them with a strange expression on his face, as if he

was seeing her for the first time. The childish giggles
faded away and all she was aware of was the warmth
in Carson's eyes.

CHAPTER EIGHT

"DADDY. DADDY!" Claire jumped out of Jena's lap and ran to Carson. "Look at me. Jena did my hair. Am I pretty?"

Carson picked up his daughter, hardly able to tear his eyes away from Jena. She looked so comfortable with his kids—as if she belonged there, which was the craziest thought he'd ever had.

"Absolutely. You're my pretty girl." He kissed her soft cheek.

"The ponytail bombed again, Dad," Trey quipped.

Claire turned her palms upward. "Again, Daddy."

Carson saw the teasing light in Jena's eyes and felt a kick to his heart. He set Claire on her feet. "Trey, take your sister and get in the car. Aunt Fran has already called."

Trey bounced out of his seat. "I bet Grandpa's worried about us."

"Yeah."

The kids trailed out the door but suddenly stopped. "Thanks, Jena." Trey waved.

"Thanks for doing my hair," Claire called.

Carson looked at Jena. "I'm sorry I was so late, but I couldn't call because I don't have your number. And Hilary didn't answer her cell." He pulled out his phone. "What is it?"

They exchanged numbers quickly, and Jena asked, "Did you have a problem with the Baxter boys?"

"They were drunk and fighting over that piece of land their parents left them."

"I wasn't aware the Baxters had passed away."

"Mrs. Baxter passed away about five years ago, and Mr. Baxter followed about six months later. They left the house and ten acres to Carl. Roy has a mobile home on the site, and they left him fifteen acres. Since Carl got the house, Roy feels he received more, and when they're drinking it's always brought up. This makes the third time this month I've had to deal with this. Today they were drunker than usual and started cursing at me. I called the sheriff's office and waited for a deputy to pick them up. I only had one pair of handcuffs, so I had to sit it out until the deputy arrived."

She got up and slipped the strap of her purse over her shoulder. "It's okay."

He thought how graceful her movements were—she kind of had the appeal of a young Jackie O, especially the stoic no-one-will-break-me expression.

"Though it was a little awkward walking into the convenience store with your kids. The community will be alive with gossip by tomorrow morning."

"Sorry. I hadn't thought of that."

Her eyes met his. "I would say don't do that to me again, but I stopped caring a long time ago about what people think of me."

He could see that she had. Nothing and no one was ever going to shake her confidence in herself again.

"What do you want to do with the leftover drinks?"

He was completely lost in thoughts of her, and her question went over his head for a brief second. "Oh… I'll pour the remains down the sink in the bathroom."

He picked up half of a Big Red and half of a lemonade and marched into the bathroom off his office. After emptying the contents, he threw the bottle and cup in the trash. Turning, he stopped short.

Jena stood in the doorway, a breath away. Her dark eyes were warm, inviting, pulling his senses into an almost forgotten dance. A delicate fragrance that had tempted him earlier clouded his judgment, and the urge to touch her gnawed at his willpower.

"Here's another." She handed him a Dr Pepper can.

"Oh." He was careful not to touch her fingers. Pouring the dark liquid down the drain, he watched it swirl around and disappear, similar to his control. He hadn't been this attracted to a woman since Beth and he didn't understand it. After Beth's death, the sensual part of him seemed to die, too. He didn't want anyone else. What was Jena Brooks doing to him?

He took a long breath and walked back into the office.

"Where do we go from here?" she asked.

Good. He relaxed. They were back to business.

"I plan to talk to my dad again, and I'm going to find a way to get into Jared's room without upsetting Pa. And I'd like to talk to the sheriff to see whose fingerprints were on the shotgun. If Lamar wasn't at the scene, then how did his gun get there?"

"It must have been stolen."

"Did your dad ever mention that?"

She shook her head. "Not to my knowledge."

"My kids get out of school tomorrow, so I'll have a conflict once they're on vacation, timewise, but we'll continue if that's what you want."

She tucked hair behind her ear. "I don't have much

choice, and now I want my dad's name cleared, too, so I don't plan on stopping."

They moved toward the door. "After I drop the kids at school in the morning, I'll call you."

"Okay."

Locking the door, he said, "Thanks for watching my kids."

"Don't make a habit of it," she replied with that teasing light in her eyes before she sashayed to her car.

Unable to stop himself, he watched until she drove away. Two days with Jena and he was feeling seventeen again, which on a scale of one to ten had to be the worst thing that could happen.

He didn't need another problem. Another headache. Another way to complicate his life.

But then…

JENA CROSSED THE tracks and took the first right turn, slowing as she saw trucks parked around their home. Hilary's friends had arrived. Two men were nailing shingles to the roof. Two others were on a scaffold scraping the house while two more were also scraping lower down. They worked fast.

She parked alongside a truck in the driveway and got out. Hilary ran to her. "Hey, sis."

Jena looked at the men. "I'm impressed."

"They'll get the roof on and finish scraping today. Tomorrow they'll paint the house. I'm so excited." Hil did a jig in her boots. Today the tops were yellow. Her sister must spend a fortune on boots.

"Me, too. I just never dreamed they'd do it this fast." The pound of staple guns echoed through the trees along with manly chatter.

"They have jobs and wanted to do this as fast as possible."

Jena glanced at her sister. "For you?"

"Yeah." Hil shoved her hands into the pockets of her short skirt. "I have some neat friends. Come on. I'll introduce you."

They walked closer to the house. "Hey, guys," Hilary yelled above the noise. All the pounding, hammering, scraping and talking stopped. "This is my sister, Jena. You remember her?"

"Hey," they chorused.

"Nice to have you back in Willow Creek," one of the guys on the scaffold called.

"Thank you for doing this," she shouted to them.

"No problem," the man on the roof said. "We get a free meal and pie out of this. And Boots will babysit when we ask. Can't beat that."

"Not every time," Hil told him. "I have a job, you know."

They laughed.

"That's Billy Jack," Hilary whispered to Jena. "He's always busting my chops, but I love him to death—as a friend. Only."

"We hear you, Boots," one of the guys who was scraping said. "Otherwise our wives wouldn't let us come here."

"Appropriate nickname."

"Yeah."

Jena could feel the easy rapport her sister had with her friends. Evidently the wives were included. Jena was glad about that. She wanted her sister to be happy and she seemed to be.

"How is Mama taking all this noise?"

"She's fine," Hilary replied. "She's watching television and doesn't seem to notice it."

"I'll check on her." Jena went into the house, side-stepping a couple of ladders, and Hilary followed her. The noise inside sounded as if Santa and his reindeer were stomping on the roof.

Norma sat in her chair, oblivious to what was going on around her.

"Hi, Mama," Jena said.

Norma's cloudy eyes stared at her. "I was hoping you'd all make it home from school before it started raining. The thunder's getting louder and louder."

Hilary sank down by their mother's chair and stroked her arm lovingly. "Mama, remember, I told you we're putting a new roof on the house. That's what the noise is about."

"Oh. I forget sometimes."

Hilary continued to stroke her arm. "It's okay, Mama. I understand."

Tears stung the back of Jena's eyes and she knelt on the other side of her mother. "It's okay, Mama."

Norma reached out and touched Jena's hair. "My baby, you can't stay long. It's too dangerous."

"I know." Taking her cue from Hilary she knew there was no need to tell her mother otherwise. She wouldn't remember. It broke Jena's heart to witness this, but it lifted her heart to see her sister being so strong and mature. Hilary had grown up in the years that Jena had been away, and the bubblehead was now a very compassionate woman. Jena admired her.

Later, the guys went home, and she and Hilary fixed supper. Norma was stuck on it raining and couldn't seem to get it out of her mind.

"Is it still raining?" Norma asked for the fifth time.

"No." Hilary removed the plates from the table.

"Still—" Norma wrapped her arms around her waist " it's a chilly winter day and I think I'll just go to bed."

"I'll help you," Jena offered, and before long she had her mother tucked in bed under a blanket. How she stood a blanket in May was mind-boggling, but then, it was all in her mind.

After baths, she and Hilary sat on the floor in the bedroom looking at the mural. She told her sister what they'd found out about their father.

Hil stood on her knees. "You're freakin' kidding me."

"No. Willie said Dad was with him, but I'm not sure anyone's going to believe him now."

"How did y'all go from looking for your child to investigating the murders?"

Jena drew up her knees. "I didn't have much choice. Asa's the only one who knows where my baby is and he's not talking. Carson mentioned something about the cases being closed quickly and that there was still a lot of information out there. I was hoping some of the information would lead me to the baby."

"But why didn't you call Blake?"

Jena tightened her arms around her legs. "It's complicated, Hil."

"Do a little uncomplicating, then."

She looked into brown eyes similar to her own. "Because too many people have been hurt and I don't want that to happen again."

"I'm not following. I say call Blake, have Asa arrested and let the whole ugly truth come out."

"Hilary." She sighed. "For that to happen Blake's team of investigators would come here and interview just about everyone. And the community would not like the intrusion. They'd hate me. They'd hate you, and I just can't have that. I don't want you hurt in any way. Mama, either."

Hil sank back against the bed. "I love that people like me and don't look down on me anymore, but they're not my friends if they turn on me because of an investigation."

Jena wrapped an arm around her sister. "Have I told you how grown-up you are?"

"Come on, Jen-Jen. I want you to find that peace you're looking for. You deserve it."

"But not at the expense of your happiness."

Nothing was said for a few minutes. They rested their heads on the bed and stared at the mural. A happy place. A dream life. Were they always going to be dreaming?

"So you and Carson are going to continue investigating the murders?" Hilary asked.

"For now, yes. We're trying to figure out how the shotgun got to the scene of Jared's murder."

"Dad always kept it in his truck."

"Do you remember him talking about someone stealing the gun or losing the gun?"

Hilary shook her head. "No, but he could have sold it for liquor money."

"I don't think so. His dad gave him that gun. I can't see him selling it even for booze."

"That's a real mystery right here in Willow Creek."

"Please don't tell anyone," Jena said. "We don't want this to get out just yet."

"My lips are sealed."

Jena stretched out her legs. "All these years I believed our dad was a cold-blooded killer, and it's such a relief to know that he wasn't."

"Yeah, but it doesn't make us forget all the other bad things he did."

"But we loved him in spite of them," Jena wanted to make that clear.

"Love is funny like that," Hil mused. "I guess that's why women stay in abusive relationships."

"Like our mother."

Hil sprang to her feet. "Not going there."

Jena's phone buzzed and she reached for her purse. "It's Blake. I'll take it in the living room."

"Night, sis." Hilary pulled back the comforter. "I'm going to bed."

"Night." Jena clicked on. "Hi, Blake."

"You haven't called. Are you okay?"

"Yes." She eased onto the sofa and sat cross-legged in the dark. "I'm taking things slowly."

"How's it going with the constable?"

Jena tensed. "We've been talking."

"I'm surprised you're talking to him."

Her nerves stretched tighter at the tone in his voice. "Why?"

"He's the son of Asa Corbett, the man you said stole your child."

She gasped. "Are you checking out my story?"

"Honey, I always check my facts."

"I resent you checking into my personal history without my permission."

"It's only because I care about you."

She gritted her teeth. "This is my problem and I will handle it my way."

"I don't understand why you won't let me help you."

"I've told you but you're not listening to me. My sister and my mother live here, and I do not want to disrupt their lives."

"What about *your* life?"

"Blake, I admit I'm going through a lot of emotions

right now and I don't know if I'm making the right decisions or not, but if I'm not, they're still my decisions. Please try to understand that."

"Okay. The longer you're away the more I fear I'm losing touch with you."

"I have to deal with my past before I can even think about a future. That's important to me."

"You're one stubborn lady. I guess that's why I'm so attracted to you."

She blew out a breath, knowing that his attraction was driving a wedge between them. She wasn't ready for it. And that told her so many things she'd just as soon not face right now.

"How is your mother?" he asked when she didn't say anything else.

"Not good. She's out of it most days and I want to help my sister as much as I can while I'm here."

"You have lots of vacation coming, so take all the time you need. Besides, you know your job is secure."

She took a moment before responding. What she said next could cost her her job, but she had to say it. "Blake, when I come back, we really have to talk. I've told you many times I'm not ready for a relationship and I don't want special favors from my employer."

There was a long pause. "I'm aware I push too hard, but you're unlike any woman I've ever met. I know you're not ready and I appreciate your honesty."

Was that her allure? She wasn't like his other women? But what he'd meant to say, she was sure, was that she wasn't easy.

"Like I said, we'll talk later." She couldn't handle Blake's pressure on top of everything else, but she wanted him to know, to her, they were employer and employee.

"Sure, and you'll call if you need me?"

"Yes, and thank you for being so understanding."

She clicked off and stared into the darkness. She'd made a deal with Carson and she wouldn't go back on her word, yet it was very tempting to let Blake take care of her problems. But she was stronger than that.

Today when she and Carson had been standing in the doorway of the bathroom, she sensed a change in the relationship. It wasn't anything she could put her finger on. It was just something she could feel. The way he looked at her. The way he purposely tried not to touch her. The way she wanted him to. That was what frightened her the most. She couldn't be falling for Carson. That was out of the question. Out of the realm of possibility and could make a complicated situation explosive. She didn't do explosive anymore.

For heaven's sakes she just wanted peace and quiet. Where did she find that? Maybe in the darkness of this room, where there was no one but her and her thoughts. Did she walk away and leave the past where it was—in the past? Or did she keep searching for that elusive dream?

God help her, all she could feel were his green eyes looking at her, trusting her, and she knew she would see it through. She could do no less.

TREY AND CLAIRE were outside playing and Aunt Fran was watching them through the kitchen window. Carson thought it was the perfect time to talk to his father.

He walked through to the den. Asa sat watching TV—or staring at it was more accurate. Carson didn't think he was seeing or hearing it. His shoulders were slumped and he had a defeated expression on his face. That struck a chord with Carson and he felt sympathy for his father. He understood the pain Asa had endured after losing his youngest son. It didn't erase the bad stuff he'd done, though. It just made Carson aware of his love for his father.

"Pa."

No response. Carson could see what held his dad's attention. The large TV was built into a walnut bookcase. Family photos and books surrounded it. Asa's eyes were on a picture of Carson and Jared when they were about ten and fifteen astride paint horses Asa had bought for them.

Carson sat in a chair close to his father. "Pa, I'd like to talk."

"Nothing...to say."

Carson let that pass. "I spoke with the Texas Ranger who worked Jared's murder case, and he said you called off the investigation. Why would you do that?"

His father looked at him with a weary expression. "I didn't."

That threw Carson. The ranger wouldn't lie. "Are you sure? You were very angry at the time."

"Ranger wanted...to see my boy's room. Said no. That's it."

"Did you talk to the sheriff?"

"No need to. They had...the killer."

Something wasn't adding up again. "Why wouldn't you let the ranger see Jared's room?"

"Nobody touching...his things!" he said with a burst of anger.

Carson rubbed his hands together, staring at the pattern on the area rug. "What if Lamar didn't kill Jared?"

"Bitch...turning your head."

Once again Carson let that pass. "Pa, I'm trying to

work things out. You took Ms. Brooks's baby and now is the time to make it right."

"Never. She will…suffer."

"Do you know how insane that sounds?"

His dad only stared at him and Carson knew he wasn't going to budge an inch. He took a deep breath. "Where is the key to Jared's room?"

"Leave it…alone."

God, he wished he could do that, but there was no turning back now. He had to keep his father from being arrested one way or the other.

Before he could respond, the kids came running in. "Grandpa, the last day of school is tomorrow," Trey told him, sitting on the rug, his eyes bright with love for his grandfather.

Claire stroked Asa's shaky hand. "Do you feel okay, Grandpa?"

Asa nodded. "My babies…are home."

Claire twirled around. "Look at my hair. A lady did it, but I don't 'member her name."

"Trey, do you have homework?" Carson asked to divert their attention. He was sure Trey remembered and could blurt out the name at any minute.

"No, Dad," Trey replied. "It's the last day of school and we're just going to have fun. We get out at noon, so don't forget."

"I won't." Carson walked into the kitchen.

Aunt Fran was stirring something in a pot. "I'm making spaghetti," she said. "I hope you're hungry."

"Yeah." His mind churned with so many doubts and confusion he wasn't really hungry, but he wouldn't disappoint Aunt Fran. Leaning against the cabinet, he asked, "Do you know where the key to Jared's room is?"

She glanced at him briefly. "Asa has it, I guess."

"Have you noticed it in Pa's room?"

"No." She placed a lid on the pot. "Why are you asking?"

"Pa wouldn't let the officials into the room when Jared was murdered, and I want to see what's in there."

"Carson, please leave this alone."

"I wish I could, but after looking into both murder cases a lot of things aren't making sense. I need answers. I need to know what happened to my brother."

"He was murdered. Please don't dredge it all up again."

He shook his head. "Aunt Fran, you don't seem to understand that Pa committed a crime. I don't want to see him spend his last days in a mental institution. Jena Brooks wants to know where her child is and she deserves to know. Please help me get into Jared's room."

She wiped her hands on a dish towel. "There are some keys in Asa's top dresser drawer. One might be to Jared's room. I don't know. I've never tried them." She gave him a disapproving look. "Please don't upset your father."

"I'll try, but he upsets himself with this crazy idea that he has to hurt Jena."

"He's just grieving."

"It's been nine years, Aunt Fran—it's time to face the facts."

She brushed that off with a wave of her hand. "I just hate all this tension."

"Me, too, and it affects my kids. But this won't be over until Pa agrees to cooperate."

Aunt Fran turned away, so he went down a short hallway to a large master bedroom. Another master bedroom was upstairs along with four more bedrooms. When Pa had the house renovated for their mother, he'd updated and modernized it. As Carson got older he often wondered what had happened between his mother and his father for his mom to leave so suddenly. And for her to leave her children.

All the years he was growing up nothing was ever said about her. They learned early if her name was mentioned, Asa became enraged, so they never brought her up. For Asa to redo the family home, he had to have loved her dearly. Maybe it was more of a prison for her—he knew his father was a very jealous, controlling man. Whatever it was, it had nothing to do with the situation now.

He stopped at the door to the master bedroom and slowly strolled in. The big bed had been removed and in its place was a hospital bed. That sight was always a little jarring when Carson entered the room. A reminder of how the times had changed. And a reminder of his father's poor health.

Opening the dresser drawer, he saw the keys on a ring. They didn't look familiar, but he took them, hurried upstairs and tried every last one on Jared's door. None of them worked.

"Damn!"

What was behind the door that Pa wanted no one to see?

CHAPTER NINE

"No. No. No!" Claire screeched and darted under the bed before Carson could stop her.

"Claire, come out of there." Carson was about to lose his patience. Last night she'd cried and cried when he'd wanted to undo the braid, so he'd let her sleep in it. But now she wouldn't let him undo it and comb her hair for school. She was a restless sleeper and her hair was mussed and straggly. He wasn't sure when he'd lost control of the situation. "It's time for school."

"Okay, but you can't touch my hair. I want it to be pretty for school."

"Claire…"

Trey entered the room. "What's going on?"

"We're having a problem with Claire's hair," Carson told him.

"Not again. Every morning it's the same thing. Dad, we just need to shave her head."

"No!" Claire wailed from under the bed.

"Why don't you call that lady," Trey suggested. "I bet she'd fix Claire's hair."

That was the last thing Carson wanted to do, but he didn't have much time or the kids would be late.

Claire poked her head out from the bed. "Call her, Daddy."

Carson groaned, knowing when he was beat. "Let's go." He grabbed Claire's brush and comb just in case.

Within minutes they were in the car and on the way to school. Aunt Fran shook her head as they went out the door. She was as inept as he was at doing hair. That was why she had hers cut short.

"Call her, Daddy," Claire insisted.

"You look like you stuck your head in a fan." Trey made his thoughts known. "Somebody better fix your hair or you're going to scare everybody."

"Daddy."

"Trey, stop teasing your sister."

"Call her, Daddy."

"Claire, she might be busy or asleep. It's early." He knew his daughter was going to keep on until he put his foot down, and that time was now.

"She'll do it, Daddy. Call her, please."

He stared in the rearview mirror at his beautiful daughter. How could he say no to her? He would see Jena later anyway, so what was the big deal? But... something was holding him back.

They had known each other only a few days and their lives were getting entwined too quickly. There was no way they could be friends. No way they could be anything else, either. It was strictly... Hell, he didn't know what it was. He didn't want his kids involved, though.

So what did he do?

A NOISE WOKE Jena at 5:00 a.m. She raised herself up and noticed a light in the kitchen. Was her mother awake? She usually slept late. Crawling out of bed, she intended to find out.

Norma was mixing flour and buttermilk in a bowl, making biscuits.

"Mama."

Her mother glanced at her. "Oh, I'm making breakfast, but I can't get the oven started. Is Hilary awake?"

"Uh...not yet." Her mother seemed fine this morning; like her old self.

"She knows how to start the oven."

"I'll get her."

Hilary was sprawled across her half of the bed; her head was buried in a pillow and her hair covered her face.

Jena shook her. "Hil, wake up."

Hilary moaned. "What time is it?"

"A little after five."

Hil curled into a ball. "Go away."

"Mama's cooking breakfast. How do I turn on the stove?"

"What?" Hil flopped onto her back.

"Mama seems fine. I'll watch her. How do I turn on the stove?"

"The wrench is in my nightstand. The valve is at the back of the stove. You just turn it and be sure to turn it off again."

"Got it." She found the wrench and went back to the kitchen. Her mother was busy rolling out biscuits. Jena looked at the back of the stove and saw the valve. There were scratches on it from being turned so much. While her mother's attention was elsewhere, she bent down and gave the valve a twist with the wrench. She quickly returned the wrench to the drawer. Hil was still out.

In the kitchen, she reached for matches in the cabinet and tested a burner. It came on. Kneeling on the linoleum, she opened the oven door and lit another match. Finding the hole, she inserted the match and turned the knob. The oven fired up.

Sitting on her heels, she remembered doing this so

many times as a child. They had no heat in the kitchen, and it was a must in the wintertime to light the oven first thing to warm the house. Life was so different then, but in other ways it wasn't. Back then she wasn't happy and she still wasn't. Was there even such a thing?

The shrill of Hilary's alarm brought her out of her thoughts. She stood and helped their mother fix breakfast. Bacon was through frying when her sister breezed in.

Hil snatched a slice. "Are those buttermilk biscuits I smell?"

"Yes," Norma replied. "Sit down. They'll be ready in about five minutes."

"Sorry, Mama, gotta run. I have to open the café. I'll bring you a muffin about midmorning." She kissed their mother's cheek and mouthed at Jena, "Don't forget to turn off the stove."

Jena gave her a thumbs-up sign.

After Hil left, Jena had a nice visit with her mother. She ate two buttermilk biscuits slathered with butter and strawberry jam. Nothing tasted as good as her mother's biscuits and she hadn't had them in nine years. She enjoyed every bite.

"Do you like your job?" Norma asked.

"Yes. I've met a lot of nice people." Jena licked the jam from her fingers.

"I'm happy for you."

"Thank you, Mama."

"Sweetie, you can't stay here too long. It's too painful for you, I know."

It was a surreal moment, as if her mother knew her thoughts just as she had when she was a child.

"Sometimes it is, but I'm stronger now, Mama. No one will hurt me like that again."

Norma got up and hugged her. "Don't think about the bad stuff. It's over."

Tears welled in Jena's eyes. Her mother was talking about the baby and Norma couldn't bring herself to actually say the words. Her mother's delicate state of mind prevented Jena from forcing the subject. But it would never be over until she knew the truth.

Norma kissed Jena's cheek. "I'm a little tired. I think I'll go rest in my chair for a while."

"Go ahead. I'll do the dishes."

As her mother left, Jena sighed. There was no going back and there didn't seem to be a way to go forward, either. Maybe her mother had the right idea—retreat to a happier place in your mind.

Before doing the dishes, she turned off the gas to the stove. With her hands in soapsuds, she heard her cell buzz. She grabbed a dish towel and sprinted to the bedroom for her phone. Glancing at the caller ID, she felt a flutter in her stomach.

Carson.

He'd said he was going to talk to Asa. Maybe the old man had changed his mind. She quickly clicked on.

"Jena, I have a big favor to ask this morning." His voice was so strong and masculine it seemed as if he was in the room with her. She suddenly knew what *having the vapors* meant. She fanned her face with her hand.

"Jena…"

She quickly collected herself. Heavens, what was she thinking? "Yes. What kind of favor?"

"I have to have the kids at school in fifteen minutes, and Claire won't let me touch her hair and it's a mess. She wants you to fix it again so she'll look pretty for the last day of school. If you're busy, I'll put it in a ponytail."

"Noo!" Claire screeched in the background. Jena was screeching the same word inside her head. She couldn't get involved with his kids. It was too personal and she didn't want any emotional attachments to the Corbetts.

"Please!" Claire cried loudly.

Her resolve weakened. Claire was four years old and would be hurt if she said no. She couldn't do that to a child. She planned to talk to Carson later, so what was her problem? Fear. Good old-fashioned fear. She'd just told her mother she was stronger, but when she looked into Carson's green eyes she felt weak.

"Jena?"

"Okay." She wasn't meeting them at the Bar C. That was out of the question. "I can be at your office in a few minutes."

"Thank you."

She clicked off knowing she was getting too involved, but as long as she was aware of that she could control the situation. At that moment she realized she was still in her nightclothes. She quickly grabbed khaki shorts and a red sleeveless knit top. Slipping her feet into sandals, she reached for her purse.

In the living room her mother was watching a morning news show. "Mama, I have to go out for a few minutes. I won't be long."

"I'll be fine. I don't feel like doing much today."

Jena ran to her car and was at Carson's office in five minutes. He was already there with the kids. She went inside, and Claire was sitting in a chair with her hair all around her.

"I undid the braid and brushed her hair," Carson said. He stepped one way; she stepped the other. After fifteen seconds of this, he caught her upper arms and turned her. An unexpected giggle erupted from her throat and she felt silly, lighthearted and alive.

Ignoring the new sensation, Jena quickly separated Claire's hair and began to braid as fast as she could.

"We're gonna be late, Dad," Trey grumbled.

"Hang on, son. We still have time," Carson told him.

Jena whipped a rubber band around the end of the braid and raised her hands, feeling as if she'd won a contest. "Done!" she shouted, and against every sane thought in her head, she laughed.

They all laughed and a warm inexplicable feeling settled in Jena's heart.

"Thank you," Claire called as they scrambled toward the door.

Carson glanced at her. "Wait for me." There was a wealth of meaning in those three words, and she took them to mean exactly what they implied. Sinking into a chair, she couldn't understand what was pulling her to Carson. Maybe it had something to do with the unattainable. But she wasn't going to think it to death. She had one goal and it was still the same. Somewhere in this maze of confusion, doubts and attraction, she hoped to find a link to her child.

CARSON COULDN'T WAIT to get back to his office. Excitement chugged through his veins as potent as Willie Bass's moonshine. It was crazy, but he couldn't deny this exhilarating feeling. Jena was different and she stirred feelings in him he hadn't felt in a long time.

When he opened the door, she was on her cell. She immediately clicked off. "I was talking to my sister. I wanted her to know where I was."

He sat at his desk and couldn't take his eyes off her.

The red blouse made her skin glow and her eyes bright. She was lovely. And he was getting in a little too deep. He reined in his emotions.

"Thanks for fixing Claire's hair. By the time she reaches her teen years I'll be completely gray."

She smiled. "I'm sure you'll survive."

"Yeah." He leaned back in his chair, mesmerized by the change in her expression. "Beth would have been so much better at this." At the sound of his wife's name a sense of sadness came over him, and he felt guilty for his attraction to Jena.

"When did Beth die?"

He never talked about what had happened that day and no one ever asked. Until now. The urge to change the subject was strong, but instead he started to talk. "Beth had a lot of problems with the pregnancy, as she did when she was pregnant with Trey. The last two months she was confined to bed because of bleeding." He took a deep breath and allowed himself to feel the pain. "We were scheduled to go in for an appointment, but that morning something happened. I got up and dressed and let her sleep. When she didn't get up, I went to wake her. That's when I noticed the blood on the floor. I pulled the comforter back and the bed was soaked. I called 911. An ambulance took her to the hospital. They saved the baby but not my wife."

"I'm so sorry."

"I was in shock for a long time, but I had two kids to raise, so I had to stay strong for them."

"Claire never knew her mother, then?"

"No, and she really misses having a mom."

"She seems well adjusted, though."

"And a little spoiled," he admitted. "I'm not very

good with discipline. It hurts me more than it hurts them."

He was pouring his heart out as though they were best friends, and that wasn't even close, but she was easy to talk to and she seemed genuinely interested. Still, he had to stay focused.

"Well—" he leaned forward "—we better get back to our situation."

"Yes. Did you talk to your father again?"

"No change there." He picked up one of Claire's hair bands from the desk. "May I ask you a question?"

"I suppose, but I reserve the right not to answer."

"Fair enough." He stretched the band with his thumb and forefinger. "My father's hate for you is maniacal. What happened to cause that? It has to be more than Jared dating you."

"Asa was always nice to me when I'd see him at the convenience store or at the café. He'd tip his hat and say hi."

"What changed that?"

She moved restlessly in the chair. "I told you after I heard Jared's friends gossiping about us, I refused to go out with him. I told him to leave me alone and that upset him. After that, Asa was mean to me. He said I was white trash and not good enough for his son and for me to stay away from Jared."

"So Asa was mad that you rejected his son?"

"I suppose so, because it got worse, especially when Jared and I started seeing each other."

Carson thought about that for a minute. "Then the pregnancy happened and Asa thought you were trying to pass someone else's kid off on Jared."

"The baby was Jared's," she stated firmly. "Asa just wouldn't believe it."

"A hell of a lot of heartache for two families," he remarked.

"I didn't ask for any of it. I just wanted to be left alone."

He didn't have a response for that and thought he should get off the subject. He didn't want to hurt her any more than she'd already been.

Her angry voice broke the silence. "You think I used Jared, just like Asa."

He held up his hands. "Whoa. I don't think any such thing. I'm just trying to find a reason for all the heartache and pain."

Her dark eyes slammed into him like a physical blow. There it was—the wall of her stubborn pride. It was years in the making and it was solid steel, tested by fire and tears. She was safe behind her pride. Untouchable. Especially by human emotions. And gossip.

He carefully laid the band on the desk. "I thought we agreed to stop snapping at each other."

"Then stop making me angry."

He nodded. "Okay. Let's talk about something else. I asked Asa why he stopped the investigation of the murders."

"What did he say?" The heat in her eyes was replaced with a deep curiosity.

"He said he didn't."

"And you believed him?"

"He has no reason to lie. I mean, he admitted to kidnapping you, so why would he lie about something like that?"

"Something else that doesn't make any sense," she mused.

"He did say that he wouldn't allow the ranger into

Jared's room. He didn't want anyone disturbing Jared's things and he felt the murderer had been caught."

"What about my father's murder?"

She was determined to keep them at odds. He could hear it in her voice. Considering the circumstances, they shouldn't be talking at all. But they were in this together, and he hoped they could maintain a measure of civility. He wouldn't let himself think about anything else, especially the softness of her skin or her quiet beauty.

He had to be honest, though. "We'll probably never know what happened that morning when your father was shot or who pulled the trigger."

She brushed back her hair. "This is all so frustrating."

"I know." He reached for the folder for Jared's murder, in the box on the floor. "I'm still curious as to whose prints were on the shotgun that killed Jared." He shuffled through the documents. "Nothing here. Maybe the ranger remembers. I'll give him a call before I speak to the sheriff."

"Did you look in Jared's room?" she asked.

He pulled out his phone. "I tried, but I couldn't find the key. Before I break down the door or climb through a two-story window, I'm going to search one more time."

"Afraid of heights?" She lifted a teasing eyebrow and all his senses shifted into full attention when *dangerous* should have been flashing inside his head.

"I...um... No." He tapped the ranger's number, and Jena came around the desk and sat on the edge. His eyes were on her smooth, smooth legs. The ranger's voice came on and he dragged his focus away. "This is Carson Corbett. Sorry to bother you again, but I was

wondering if you remember whose fingerprints were
on the shotgun that killed my brother?"

Jena leaned in and a delicate fragrance wafted
around him. Obviously, she wanted to hear the conversation. He pressed the speakerphone button and laid
his cell on the desk.

"Let me check my files." The ranger's voice came
through loud and clear.

"Do you mind if Ms. Brooks listens?"

"No, of course not," the ranger replied.

She scooted back on the desk and waited. He looked
everywhere but at her legs, which were just inches from
him. There was an almost palpable vibe in the air that
was hard to explain, but maybe not. It was sexual. And
he hadn't been out of the game so long he couldn't recognize it. She seemed oblivious to it.

"I got it." The ranger's voice had come back on.
"Lamar Brooks's and Roland Stubbs's prints were on
the gun."

"Did Roland have an explanation as to why his prints
were on there?" Carson asked.

"He found your brother and picked up the gun without realizing what he was doing."

"I see." He really didn't see, but he would come back
to that later. "Did my father personally tell you or the
sheriff to close the investigation?"

"Most of our conversations went through Roland.
Your father was grief stricken and unable to deal with
it. I spoke to him once about Jared's room and he became enraged. After that, everything else was handled
through Roland."

"Roland told you to close the cases?"

"He told the sheriff as Asa's spokesperson and then
we got word from the governor's aide."

"So my father was mostly out of the picture?"

"I guess you could say that. Did you find information to the contrary?"

"My father said he never told anyone to close the cases."

"Well, I'll be damned. I always had a bad feeling about this."

"Yeah, there's a lot of evidence that should have been investigated."

"If I can help in any way, just let me know."

"I will, and thanks." Carson turned off the phone and leaned back in his chair. "Roland's hand is all over this."

"I'm sure he was taking orders from your father," Jena said.

"I don't think so. Pa was distraught, wanting vengeance against the Brooks family. That's all he had on his mind."

"So you're saying he killed my father?"

He shook his head. "No. I don't think he did. I believe he sat with Jared's body just like the ranger said."

"So you think your father is innocent in all this and you'd rather I just forgive and forget?"

His eyes met the challenge in her dark depths, and feuding families, murder and deception went right over his head. All he could feel was the heat building between them—sometimes in anger and sometimes in awareness. Whatever it was, the flame was there, begging to be stoked.

"No," he replied, getting to his feet. "I'd rather do this." He cupped her face, his fingers sliding into her silky hair, his palms resting against her smooth cheeks.

She drew back slightly, her eyes black, and then she stilled, licking her lower lip. The action drew his eyes like a flickering flame. The heat continued to build, igniting something deep in him, but he waited for her to object or pull away. She did neither. Unable to resist, he took her lips in an explosive kiss of raw, potent emotions.

CHAPTER TEN

JENA'S FIRST INSTINCT was to pull away as fast as she could, but the feel of his hands on her face stifled her natural response. His lips touched hers; gently and against her will she opened her mouth. His tongue stroked her bottom lip, tempting, inviting, until she moaned under the delicious sensations swirling through her. When he covered her mouth completely, she lost all train of thought as she unashamedly kissed him back. Only his hands and lips touched her, but she felt on fire from the onslaught of her senses—too long dormant for someone her age.

The buzz of a phone punctured the moment. Carson drew back and stared at his phone on the desk. "I—I better get that." His voice was hoarse.

She breathed in the heady masculine scent of him and slid off the desk. What was she thinking? Her hand trembled against her lips as she struggled with her emotions. This wasn't supposed to happen. *Ever.*

Through her maze of confusion, she heard Carson's voice. "Yeah, sure, Abby. Thanks."

He laid his phone on the desk, his eyes on her. "That was Abby, Ethan's wife. She's a teacher at the school. The kids cleaned out their lockers, had a party and now they're officially out of school. She's dropping off Trey and Claire."

She heard his words, but nothing registered except what was on her mind. "Please don't kiss me again."

"Jena…"

"Just don't, okay?"

"You didn't seem to object."

"Kissing between us is off-limits for obvious reasons. Don't even think about it."

His eyes narrowed. "Can you stop thinking about it?"

"Yes." She brushed back her hair with a sweep of her hand. "You just caught me off guard."

"So you kiss everybody with that much emotion?"

She couldn't look him in the eye because they both knew she was lying, but she was never going to admit it. "Let's stick to the plan. My only goal is to find my child. That's it."

"Jena…"

"I have to go." She was running. Again. But she couldn't curb that instinct. To protect herself she had to regroup and gain control. It was important that she was always in control.

Before she could make it to the door, it opened and Trey, Claire and two other kids entered, followed by a pretty blonde.

"Oh," the blonde said, obviously startled to see a woman in the office. "I'm sorry. I didn't realize you had someone in here."

"This is Jena Brooks." Carson made the introductions. "She was born and raised in Willow Creek and is home for a visit. Jena, this is Abby, Ethan James's wife."

"Nice to meet you." Abby held out her hand and Jena shook it. The woman was gorgeous, with blond hair and blue eyes. She felt rather plain beside her and she inched toward the door.

"This is our oldest daughter, Kelsey, and our youngest, Chloe." Abby introduced her daughters and the girls smiled at her.

"Nice to meet all of you. I was just leaving."

Claire pointed at her. "She fixed my hair." Claire and Chloe stood together and they looked like twins: same blond hair, height and build, except Claire had green eyes and Chloe, blue.

"We have to go, too," Abby said. "The girls are spending the weekend with my parents."

"Yeah," Kelsey broke in. "They're taking us shopping for summer clothes. Yes!" She raised a fist in the air.

Trey frowned at her. "I thought we were going fishing."

"We have all summer to fish, Trey, but when Grandma wants to go shopping, I go."

"Sometimes you act like a girl."

"I am a girl."

"Not all the time."

"Yes, all the time, and when I get back I'll kick your butt fishing."

"No, you won't."

"Enough," Abby said. "Are you two going to argue on the last day of school?"

"No," Kelsey mumbled, looking at Trey. "We'll go fishing. I promise."

Trey stared at the floor.

"Trey," Carson prompted.

"Okay," Trey mumbled back.

"That's better." Abby herded her two out the door. "See y'all later."

Jena followed without saying another word. She had to get away and she couldn't look at Carson or his kids. Once again she was in over her head.

JENA SPENT THE rest of the day with her mom, trying to come to grips with what had happened. It was a kiss. That was all. Why was she so upset about it? The kisser was Carson Corbett, otherwise known as the son of her sworn enemy. She was kissing the enemy and liking it.

There. She'd admitted it. She liked Carson and had responded accordingly. But now she was on guard. It wouldn't happen again. It couldn't.

To release restless energy she decided to clean the house and do laundry. She stripped both beds and put a load in to wash. She then dusted, vacuumed and mopped the kitchen. While the sheets were in the dryer, she fixed lunch for her and her mother. Her mom seemed her normal self and the day went very well.

Norma even helped to make the beds. As Jena put the sheets on her mother's bed she noticed the mattress had an indentation where her mother's body lay. The mattress was old and needed replacing.

"Mama, is this mattress comfortable?"

"I suppose. Why?"

"It's rather lumpy."

"Like me." Her mother smiled and Jena hadn't seen that in a very long time.

Jena hugged her. "Would you like a new mattress?"

"Oh, no, we can't afford that. Your dad's not working."

That burst of sunshine that had peeped through in her mother's smile suddenly faded. And Jena felt lost. She wanted to help her mother, but she didn't know how.

"I'm getting tired," Norma said. "I'm going to rest in my chair. You better go get Hilary. I don't want her walking home from school alone."

Jena let out a long sigh. Her mother did so well in the mornings but as the evening drew near her mind seemed to shut off. And she drifted into a world of her own—or a time when her life was simpler.

Once the house was spotless, Jena went to look at the plots she'd dug for flower beds and do some planning. Just then, trucks pulled into the driveway. She waved at the guys and they began to unload equipment to paint the house. She went inside so her mother wouldn't be startled by the activity. But her mom was sound asleep.

That didn't last long. Ladders banged against the house and Norma woke up with a blank expression on her face.

"It's okay, Mama."

"Is it storming again?"

"No. Hilary's friends are painting the house."

"Oh. I know she tells me these things but I can't remember." A look of panic replaced the blank expression.

"It's okay, Mama." Jena sat by her mother's chair and gently rubbed her arm like she'd seen Hilary do to calm her. "I'm here and I'll help you. So don't worry." Jena reached for the remote control. "Do you want to watch some TV?"

"I guess."

The sound of the television blocked out the noise outside and that seemed to calm her mother. "Hilary will be home soon and then we'll have supper. Are you hungry?"

Her mother didn't answer. She just stared at the TV. Jena knew she was somewhere where Jena couldn't reach her. Again, she felt helpless.

Hilary breezed through the door in her boots and short skirt, her flashy jewelry jangling. "Hey, sis, come take a look. The house is getting a makeover."

Norma sat up in her chair. "Hilary Brooks, where

have you been? You were supposed to be home an hour ago. You know I don't like you walking home late."

Hilary glanced at Jena and she nodded, indicating her mom was having a bad afternoon.

"Sorry, Mama," Hilary said. "I wasn't looking at the time."

Norma sank back in her chair. "I better fix your dad's supper or he'll get angry." But she made no move to do so.

Jena got up and joined her sister. "She was so good this morning, but now she doesn't know where she is or what year it is."

"The evenings are always bad," Hilary said. "But she'll get better."

"Hil, we have to talk about this."

"Not now, sis. I'm too excited. Come outside. You have to see." Hilary ran from the room and Jena slowly followed. Hilary stood in the middle of the front yard staring at the house. Joining her, Jena did a double take. The yellow house with the white shutters looked like a small cottage she'd seen in magazines. It was beautiful.

"How did they do that so fast?" Jena asked.

"Billy Jack has a sprayer and he's really fast."

At the sound of his name Billy Jack walked over in his white painting clothes. "What do you think, Boots?"

Hilary threw her arms around his neck and hugged him. "I love you guys. It's just the way I pictured it."

"Great. Now you probably have paint on you."

"Who cares?" Hil brushed at her clothes.

"Not me." Billy Jack grinned.

"I wish I could sit out here and stare at it, but I have to go back to work."

"But you just got home," Jena pointed out.

"I know. The café's real busy right now and Mabel

needs me. I brought supper, though." Hilary ran to her truck to get the food and hurried into the house.

Billy Jack stared at Jena. "This is none of my business, and I'm not saying anything that I haven't already said to Hilary. She's killing herself working at that café. She hasn't had a raise since she started working there, and she does just about everything from the cooking to waitressing. I hate that they use her. Hil tells me to mind my own business. I thought she might listen to you. Between the café and taking care of her mom she has no time for herself."

Jena shook her head. "Hilary has worked there since she was sixteen, and I'm sure she's had a raise since then."

"The only time Hilary gets a raise is when minimum wage goes up, and you know how often that happens."

It took a moment for Jena to digest this. "I can't believe she hasn't asked for a raise in all these years."

"She hasn't. When the guys and I push her, she gets mad at us. But no one should have to work that many hours for so little money."

Jena frowned. "You said she does the cooking?"

"She does everything. Mabel and her daughter sit at the cash register and take the money. Visit one day and you'll see how everything works."

"I will and I'll talk to Hilary."

Billy Jack went back to finish the house and Jena went inside. Hilary was putting food on plates.

"Mabel made meat loaf today and Mama loves Mabel's meat loaf." Hilary placed the plates on the table. "I'll get Mama."

"This is Mabel's meat loaf?" Jena asked.

Hilary turned back. "Yes."

Jena lifted an eyebrow. "Are you sure?"

Her sister's bubbly disposition disappeared in an instant, and her dark eyes flashed an old familiar warning that said "leave me alone." But Jena wasn't in a mood to leave her alone. And the thought that someone was taking advantage of her sister made her fighting mad.

Jena looked down at the meat loaf, mashed potatoes and green beans. "This looks very similar to the meat loaf Mama used to make with green peppers and onions."

"So?"

"So—" she stared directly at her sister "—I believe you made this meat loaf with Mama's recipe."

Hilary didn't respond and the warning in her eyes was flashing like a neon sign.

"Why are you doing the cooking?" Jena asked.

"Because Mabel can't see anymore and she has arthritic knees," Hil replied in a low voice.

"So she pays you more for cooking?"

Hilary's eyes narrowed. "Who have you...? Oh, the guys have been yapping. This is none of their business and it's none of yours, either, so please stay out of it."

"Mabel is taking advantage of you.... Can't you see that?"

"That's my business."

"I'm getting tired of that response, Hil. We've been taken advantage of our whole lives, and I refuse to stand by and let anyone do that to you. You deserve more. You deserve everything that's at the end of that rainbow in your bedroom."

Hil looked down at her hands. "It's not that simple. I've made a life here, and please don't do anything to embarrass me."

All the hurt in Hilary's voice blindsided her. She'd heard that tone so many times when they were kids.

"Why are they so mean to us?" "Why don't they like us?" "Why do they talk about us?"

"I would never do anything to embarrass you. But I hope you have enough strength to stand up for yourself. Show them you're a person who has value and not someone they can order about. Show them you have a backbone and they will respect you."

"Oh, yeah, that's easy for you, Jena. You left and live in the big city with a happy new life, but I'm stuck here, and I'm doing the best I can. I've made friends, and everyone likes me."

Hilary's tone grew sadder and Jena knew she should stop, but life wasn't about everything being easy. "Hil, everybody doesn't have to like you and in the real world they don't. It's okay to stand up for yourself. It's okay to have opinions. Please don't let them take advantage of you. I know it's your life but I worry. You deserve better."

"Like you said, it's my life and I have to live here when you're gone."

That was true. But Jena couldn't let it go. "Maybe on Sunday we can do something together with Mama."

"I have to work on Sunday."

"When is your day off?"

Hilary shifted from one boot to the other. "Um…I don't have a day off."

"Excuse me?"

Hilary turned on her heel and walked out. "I've got to go," she called over her shoulder.

"This isn't over!" Jena shouted after her.

"Yes, it is." The door slammed.

Jena heaved a hot breath and eased into a chair. She had to let Hilary make her own decisions even if they were bad. Hil was right. Jena would go back to Dallas, and Hil had to live with the people of Willow Creek. But it irked her that Mabel was taking advantage of her sister. It irked her more that Hilary was allowing it.

Pulling herself out of her funky mood, she finished putting supper together. Norma was completely out of it, talking to Jena as if she was twelve years old. By eight o'clock her mother was ready for bed. She gave her mother her nighttime medications and sat with her for a while.

When Norma fell asleep, Jena went outside and sat on the porch, her legs dangling over the side. The fresh scent of paint lingered in the air, and she could hear the roar of traffic on the highway across the tracks. The rumble of a train echoed in the distance. Familiar sounds.

So many times as a teenager she'd sat in this same spot and listened to the traffic, hoping headlights would turn down their street and into their driveway. In her mind, it would be friends from school inviting her to hang out at their house. But no one ever came, except sweet Jared. And for that alone she loved him. Of course, neither of them was sure about the emotion because love was absent in their family lives. Jared was kind, compassionate and the only true friend she'd ever had. After the murder, she'd missed him so much. She swallowed hard, wiping the memory away. It still was painful.

Almost on cue, car lights turned onto their street. It had to be Hilary, but the car that rolled into the driveway wasn't Hil's. *Carson.* She knew he'd probably come only to apologize for what had happened in his office. What did she say to him?

CARSON TOOK A moment and then got out. As he walked toward her he rehearsed what he was going to say.

I'm sorry seemed cliché and he really wasn't sorry. He should be, but he could still taste her lips, feel the smoothness of her skin. If kissing was a sport, he'd sure like to try for first place with her. The thoughts were so wrong, but he couldn't get them out of his head.

He stopped in front of her. She didn't say a word and he didn't expect her to. That wall she'd built around herself was so strong tonight, he felt he could reach out and touch it. Because of what he'd done. Damn! The last thing he wanted to do was hurt her.

"May I sit down?"

"What are you doing here?" Her voice was low with an edge of steel in it.

"I'd like to talk."

"There's no need…"

"I disagree." He sat on the porch beside her, and she scooted a couple of inches away. "For heaven's sakes, I'm not going to attack you."

"I didn't think you were. I'd just rather not get too close."

"Are you afraid of me or you?"

She scooted until her back was against a post. Drawing up her knees, she asked, "Why did you kiss me? We're not even friends."

He shrugged, not missing the fact that she didn't answer the question. "You were sitting on my desk, relaxed, and it just seemed ironic that we're caught in this web of family lies, deception and manipulation. When you smiled, I thought how nice it would be if we were just two people without all the baggage of the past. I'm attracted to you and I thought I'd see if one kiss could change the situation."

"Nothing can change our situation," she said. "Even

when we find my child nothing will change between us. We will still be enemies."

"Because of my father?"

"Yes."

"I crossed a line and I'm sorry for that, but I'm not sorry for kissing you. I rather enjoyed it and I think you did, too. So I'll ask you again—who are you afraid of? You or me?"

It was a long time before she answered, and the words were so low he barely caught them. "I'm always afraid."

He turned so he could face her in the darkness. The porch light wasn't on, but the moonlight was ample enough. "Why?"

"Do you have to ask that question?"

"Maybe not, but tell me about it."

Again, it was a long time before she replied, "When Hilary and I were growing up, the kids were mean to us. They called us names because we wore hand-me-down clothes and lived off welfare, not to mention our home was across the tracks where poor white trash lived. So we stuck together and grew a thick skin to protect ourselves. But life was hard and at times we were afraid just to walk out the door."

"I'm sorry for what you had to go through" was all he could say. He could only imagine how traumatic it had been for a young girl.

They sat in silence for a while. "May I ask you a question?"

"What?" she asked.

"What happened after you left Willow Creek?"

She sighed. "Haven't we covered that?"

"A little bit, but I'm curious."

"I lived with my mom's cousin. She was a licensed

vocational nurse, and when I didn't stop bleeding from the birth, she took me to see her doctor. She told him I'd just lost a baby and was staying with her to recuperate. I was hospitalized for three days, but he was able to stop the bleeding."

"It didn't last?"

"No, until…well, you know the rest."

To get her mind on something else, he asked, "When did you go to work for the lawyer?"

"About five years ago. First, I got a job at Walmart, saved my money and took computer and secretarial courses at a junior college. Eventually, I got a job as a receptionist in the law firm, and I was noticed because I was willing to work long hours."

"Did you always live with your cousin?"

"Until she had a heart attack three years ago. She lingered for a week, and I sat with her day and night. She was very good to me. I still miss her. Her son got the house, and I moved into an apartment. I was on my own for the first time in my life."

"Did you like it?"

"Not at first. I was alone and scared, but I made friends and had almost a normal life."

"In all those years did you ever think of coming back to Willow Creek?"

"I lost track of the number of times I got in my car to do just that, but I never made it out of Dallas. Asa had said if I returned, he'd kill my mother and my sister. After what he did to me, I couldn't take that risk."

Carson moved uneasily. She was talking about his father, and it was hard for Carson to believe all the bad things Asa had done. Even though he knew they were true.

"So you see, Carson Corbett, you and I should not

be kissing or doing anything together. That's just the way it has to be."

"Yeah. I just lost my head for a moment."

"That's not good for a lawman."

She was teasing and he wished he could see her dark eyes. But then, it was best if he didn't. He was tempted once and he could easily be tempted again. No matter how much they talked about being wrong for each other, it didn't change the fact that he liked her a lot.

"I better go." He got to his feet. "There's a strong smell of paint and I noticed the house has a new color."

"Hilary's friends painted it today." She swung her legs off the edge of the porch again.

"It looks nice."

"Mmm."

He should walk away and leave on a good note, but he had to know. "So where do we go from here?"

"Back to searching for my child," she replied without hesitation.

"My time will be limited now that the kids are out of school, but over the weekend I'll get into Jarod's room."

"Talking to your father again wouldn't hurt, either."

"For what it's worth, I will try."

"Good. Now we're back to dealing with the past… the way we set out to do."

"Yeah. I'll be in touch." He strolled toward his car.

"Carson."

He turned back.

"Thank you for apologizing. I appreciate that."

"Then you don't think I'm as reprehensible as my father?"

"No," she answered. "I'm not upset with you. I'm more upset with myself."

"Why?"

"For responding."

He stared at her through the darkness, hardly believing she was admitting that.

"But we both know that's a dead end and we won't allow it to happen again."

"Yeah. Night." He continued on to his car. There was nothing left to say, but there was a whole lot he wanted to say. Passion between two people was like lighting a stick of dynamite. Once the fuse was lit there was no turning back until the explosion of senses satisfied both of them. She didn't need to know that. Or maybe she already did. But he and Jena were set on a course that would either destroy them or bring them together. For a Brooks and a Corbett the latter wasn't even an option.

CHAPTER ELEVEN

JENA WAITED UP for Hilary and it wasn't by choice. She couldn't get Carson out of her head. Just the sound of his voice in the dark made her feel safe and she had no idea why. Like Jared, he was kind and trustworthy and maybe she responded to that.

If she was comparing them—and she wasn't—the resemblance ended there. With Jared, it had been two teenagers who'd needed each other. Carson was a mature man who made her very aware she was a woman with needs. And that wasn't good. It could only lead to heartache and pain. She'd had her share of both.

She realized in the next few days she'd have to make a decision—call Blake or continue with the unproductive partnership she had with Carson. She couldn't let her emotions sway her.

The last time she looked at the clock it was 11:00 p.m. and Hil still wasn't home. That bothered Jena. If Jena wasn't here, their mother would be left alone in the house at night. In her mother's mental state, that was unacceptable. A serious talk was coming, and Hil wasn't going to like what she had to say.

When she awoke, Hilary was sprawled across her half of the bed, sound asleep. Jena got up quietly and went to check on their mother. She was also asleep. Jena made coffee and was sipping a cup when her mother came in.

"Morning, Mama."

"Morning, sweetheart. I could use a cup of coffee."

Jena jumped up. "Coming right up." Her mother's eyes were bright and clear this morning, and it was wonderful to see that.

"Has Hilary gone to work?"

"No, Mama, she's still sleeping." Jena placed a cup of coffee in front of her mother.

"She doesn't usually sleep this late."

"She worked late last night." Jena opened the refrigerator to see what they had to eat, and there wasn't much. "Would you like some toast with your coffee?"

"Yes, that would be nice."

Jena was spreading jam on the toast when Hilary strolled in. "I overslept. I have to run."

"Just a minute," Jena said before Hilary could get out the door. She followed her into the living room. "What time did you get home last night?"

Hilary sighed. "Please don't start. We were packed last night."

"I'm just worried about Mama being here all alone."

"I knew you were here or I would have checked on her."

"Hil, there's no food here, either."

"I'll bring something."

"I'll go to the grocery store."

"There's no need. Why are you making this hard?"

Jena folded her arms across her chest. "Have you ever heard of burning the candle at both ends?"

"Of course."

"That's what you're doing, and you can't keep it up. You can't please everybody just because you want them to like you."

"Aren't you here to find your child?" Hil fired back.

"Yes."

"Then why don't you do that and stay out of my life."
Hil slammed out the door.

Jena ran her hands through her hair, trying not to let
that oppressive feeling come over her. Her number one
supporter was deserting her and that left a raw ache
inside. But she was not going to back down from her
stance that Hilary should stand up for herself, no matter how upset it made her sister.

JENA GOT DRESSED to go shopping for groceries and asked
her mom if she'd like to come along. To her surprise
she said yes, so they drove to Dripping Springs to the
H-E-B grocery store. Norma got out with her and that
surprised Jena, too. She seemed to enjoy picking out
things she wanted to eat, especially fruit. The cart was
full when they checked out.

On the way home, they passed a small nursery, and
Jena turned around and went back. She needed flowers for the flower beds to add the finishing touch to
the house. Her mother again got out and helped her to
pick out yellow pansies and white petunias. She added
potting soil, fertilizer and mulch. Her trunk and backseat were full.

After a light lunch, she went to work. She had texted
Hil as a peace offering to tell her there was no need to
rush home. Jena would be home all day. She kept her
phone close just in case Carson called, but he didn't.

By the time she finished preparing the ground with
a hoe she was exhausted, but she planted the flowers
and the white crape myrtles she'd bought for the corners of the house. Her mother sat on the porch watching her, and life seemed as normal as it could be. But

by late afternoon Norma's sunny disposition faded and the darkness of her mind took over.

As Jena prepared supper Norma wrung her hands and paced. "If you hear your father's truck, go hide. I'll call you when it's time to come out."

"Okay, Mama. Why don't you sit down and have a glass of tea."

"I'm not thirsty." She hurried into the living room to watch out the window. Jena's nerves were frayed when her mother finally went to bed.

After a bath, Jena sat on the porch and relaxed. The paint scent mingled with the sweet-smelling crape myrtles. Everything was fresh and new—almost like a new beginning. Was there such a thing? How could anything be new when the same old heartache would always be with her?

Her phone buzzed and she reached for it, hoping it was Carson. It wasn't. Her heart sank and she couldn't believe how disappointed she was.

Hilary left a text. Going to be late. Busy night.

She answered. Don't worry. Everything's fine.

She stood and glanced down the road. She could really get used to seeing Carson every night. And that was the most insane thought she'd ever had.

THE NEXT MORNING was a repeat of the morning before. "Don't nag, sis. I'll be home early. Sunday is a short day at the café," Hil called as she went out the door and before Jena could do much complaining. Her sister must have not seen the flowers or she would have been excited. Their talk was coming soon. Hil couldn't avoid it forever.

Her mother sat at the table eating Corn Flakes and a banana. That seemed so ironic to Jena. Corn Flakes were one of the staples they'd received in abundance from the food bank when they were kids. Jena had thought she'd never want to eat the stuff again. Her mother had picked it out yesterday at the store, saying she hadn't had them in a while. So maybe some things weren't so bad.

Her mother was fine after yesterday's outing, and Jena wanted to keep her moving instead of sitting in her chair all the time. After she washed the dishes, she suggested, "Let's go for a walk."

"Oh, no." Norma shook her head. "I'm tired from yesterday."

Jena dried her hands on a dish towel. "I don't want to walk alone. Please come with me."

"Where are you going to walk?"

"Down our road to the railroad tracks."

Norma pushed back her chair. "I'll put on my shoes."

Jena was elated at her mother's easy acquiescence. Maybe all she needed was a little motivation, but Jena wasn't sure that would help the state of her mind. Within minutes they walked out of their driveway and down the road.

Jena had made this trek many times as a kid. It was her route to school. The road dead-ended at the tracks, and this area was full of houses and mobile homes that were run-down like theirs. As they passed a small white house that was usually neater than the rest, Jena asked, "Does Mrs. Carter still live there?"

The night Jena's baby was born, Norma had borrowed Mrs. Carter's car to make the trip to Dallas. Her father's truck had been seized by the sheriff and that was the only way to get Jena out of town.

"I don't know," Norma replied. "But I think Hilary said she died. Mrs. Brown, too."

Her cell buzzed and Jena pulled it out of her pocket. Hilary left a text. Saw the flowers. Fabulous. Tks.

"Just Hilary," she told her mom. She kept hoping Carson would call and say he'd gotten into Jared's room. So far there was nothing but silence on his end.

They reached the three large half poles cemented in the ground and painted black and yellow, signaling the end of the road before the tracks. As they turned, Jena noticed the trail around the poles that led over the tracks to the school. Kids from this side of town still used it.

Her mother began to tire, so they slowed down. When they reached the house, Norma sank into her chair, exhausted. Jena got a bottle of water they'd bought yesterday for her mother. After a breather on the sofa, she planned to visit Hilary at the café.

"Do you know where Hilary put my knitting?" Norma asked suddenly.

"Uh…no, but I'll check in your room."

"I haven't knitted in a while and today I feel like it."

Her mother made beautiful things and used to sell them at craft shows at the community center, especially during the holidays. Sometimes it made the difference in getting a gift for Christmas or not.

She searched through her mother's closet and spotted the red, white and blue bag her mother had made for her knitting. Pulling it out, she stared at the tiny item on top. She picked up the yellow baby's blanket. Unfolding it, she found a yellow baby's cap, sweater and bootees.

"Oh," she moaned, sinking to the floor. Her mother had made these for Jena's baby. She held them to her chest and tears ran down her cheeks. Her baby would never wear them. Her baby…

She quickly wiped away the tears. She couldn't do this anymore. She'd cried enough.

As she meticulously folded the items, a stray hiccup left her throat, and then she placed the items on the top shelf at the back so her mother wouldn't see them. But Jena would know where they were and her heart would ache every time she thought of them.

Finding the baby things gave her the impetus she needed. She wasn't waiting around anymore for Carson. Pulling her cell out of her pocket, she called him. It went to voice mail. That was strange. He was the constable and should be readily available.

She left her mother knitting and went into town. Carson wasn't at his office. Since he wasn't there she drove to the café. The parking lot was full and she had to ease in next to a big truck on the far side. She would check out Hilary's working situation for herself. She was in a mood to take on the world.

The bell on the door jangled as she went through it. Removing her sunglasses, she glanced around. The noise was deafening as people chatted, laughed and visited. Some were in their Sunday clothes, others in jeans. They milled around a buffet that had been set out. The wood tables and chairs were full, as were the red booths along the side wall. A mural graced the far wall—one of Hilary's murals of a rainbow and clouds with children picking flowers along the lower left corner. Hilary was spreading her cheer everywhere.

Red barstools were along the counter. When a man slid off one and ambled toward the door, she maneuvered through the crowd and eased onto it.

Mabel sat at the cash register near the door with another woman. It had to be her daughter, Beatrice. Jena didn't see Hilary.

"Ma'am—" a girl about twenty wearing an apron spoke to her "—it's a brunch buffet. You serve yourself. You have to buy a ticket from Bea." She pointed to the woman at the cash register.

"Thank you." She had no plans to buy a ticket. As she looked around, she didn't see anyone she knew. None of Hilary's guy friends were here. Willow Creek was now full of strangers, and it was just as well. She had no desire to get reacquainted with anyone.

"Hilary," Bea bellowed above the crowd. "We're running out of scrambled eggs and biscuits. Why aren't you keeping up?"

Hilary rushed out in an apron and a hairnet. She removed a large pan from the buffet and slid in another full of scrambled eggs. In a few minutes she was back with a tray full of biscuits.

"You might have to help Sally bus the tables," Bea told Hil, and it took all of Jena's strength to stay seated. Hil was run off her feet, and she wanted to tell the woman to bus them herself, but she wouldn't embarrass Hilary.

Hil brought out a large container and began to remove plates and glasses from a table. People were waiting. She sprayed disinfectant on the table, wiped it and removed the container. As Hil turned, she saw Jena.

"What are you doing here?"

"I came to talk, but I can see you're busy."

"Yeah." Hil frowned. "We can talk at home."

"Hilary, we're out of bacon," Bea shouted.

Without another word, Hil darted off to do Bea's bidding. Jena made her way to the door.

"Hey." Bea stopped her. "Did you pay?"

Jena faced the stout overweight woman. "No. I didn't eat anything."

"Then what are you doing here?"

Before she could answer, Mabel struggled to her feet,

holding on to a cane. "You're Hilary's sister, Jena. Hilary didn't say you were home."

"Yes, I…uh…" Why hadn't Hilary mentioned that she was home? There had to be a reason for that. She'd told Hil she didn't care whom she told. But Hil probably didn't want to stir up all the old rumors. Or Hil was embarrassed by her sister's presence in Willow Creek. "I just came in to tell Hilary something."

"Jena, is that you? Stacey said you were back."

She swung around to see Tammy Sue Faulkner, another girl from high school. "Yes. Hi, Tammy Sue."

"Damn, you look good after having a kid." Tammy Sue thumbed over her shoulder to a group of kids at a table. "I have five now and I get bigger with each one." Tammy Sue looked around. "Didn't bring your kid? I don't blame you. I leave mine whenever I can."

The restaurant became painfully quiet and all eyes were on her. Hilary stood in the kitchen doorway with a horrified expression on her face. The retort on Jena's lips died. "Good to see you, Tammy Sue." She glanced at the older woman who was hanging on every word. "You, too, Mabel."

Jena made a quick exit, feeling the past weighing on her like a heavy blanket. Maybe she was always going to have that feeling, but she would never embarrass Hilary. They would talk tonight, though. There would be tears, yelling and possibly anger. Through it all she hoped they'd remember they were sisters. It bothered her that Hil hadn't told anyone she was home. Was she ashamed of her sister?

CARSON WAS TAKING Trey fishing, and Claire had decided to come along with her Barbie dolls. As he was putting gas into his truck at the convenience store, he noticed

Jena's car at the café. He'd thought of calling her several times over the past couple of days but figured they needed some breathing space.

Getting in his truck, he said, "Hey, guys, let's go over to the café and see if Hilary made chocolate chip cookies today. We can have them after the fried chicken Aunt Fran fixed for us."

"It'll take too long, Dad," Trey complained.

"I want a chocolate chip cookie," Claire said.

"It won't take long, son, and we have all day."

He drove across the highway. The truck next to Jena's car backed out, and he zoomed into the spot. Trey jumped out and Carson helped Claire. As they rounded the truck, Jena came toward them, head down. She seemed upset.

"Jena…"

"Oh."

He'd startled her. Her dark eyes were big and rounded. And sad. She was upset about something.

"I called you earlier and you didn't answer," she said in a rush.

"Did you leave a message?" He reached for his phone to check.

"No."

"Did you need something?" He slipped his phone back into the case on his belt.

"I wanted to talk."

"We're going fishing," Trey said. "Want to come with us? You can talk to Dad then."

Jena looked down at Trey, as if she hadn't realized he was standing there. "Uh…no, thanks. I have to check on my mom."

"I got a new rod and reel for making all A's. I'm gonna catch that big ol' fish in Willow Creek. You have to come watch."

"Yeah, we want you to come," Claire added for good measure.

Indecision flittered across Jena's beautiful face. He should just tell his kids to stop pestering her but found he couldn't. He wanted her to come, too.

"The kids'll be playing and we can talk." Something was troubling her and to his surprise he wanted to help. And she had called him. He wanted to find out why.

"I have to fix my mom's lunch."

Carson looked at his watch. "We can pick you up in fifteen minutes."

"O-okay."

"Yay!" Claire clapped.

Carson watched her drive away. His invitation blew his resolution to play it cool with Jena. He couldn't be cool when he was hot and bothered around her.

And he had no idea where his feelings were going to take him. He just knew he couldn't stop thinking about her.

TWENTY MINUTES LATER, Jena sat on the passenger side of Carson's truck, wondering what she was doing. She probably wasn't thinking straight after the incident at the café, but if this was the only way to talk to Carson, then so be it.

"No constable's car today?" She buckled her seat belt.

"It's much easier to carry a rod and reel in my truck."

"Wait till you see my new rod and reel, Jena," Trey said from the backseat. "It's so cool. It's a Zebco, and Dad put the line and weights on last night. I helped. I'm gonna catch that big catfish Mr. Walt and Mr. Henry talk about."

"That's Ethan's dad and Levi's grandfather," Carson explained.

"I know," she replied, her voice sounding testy for no reason other than she was upset with herself for being a patsy. "I was raised in Willow Creek. Mr. Walt and Mr. Henry are well-known characters."

Carson glanced at her but didn't say anything.

They passed the entrance to the Bar C, and then Carson pulled into a lane that had a barbed-wire gate. "Okay, buddy, you're up." He looked over his shoulder at Trey.

"I'll be glad when Claire gets old enough to open gates," Trey grumbled as he got out.

"Uh-uh, Daddy. I'm not opening gates."

"Okay, princess," Carson said, "but let's make that decision when you're older."

Soon they were off through a pasture of cows, and then they drove through a thicket into an opening. Willow Creek sparkled like a bright ribbon in the distance. Carson stopped beneath an old live oak growing between the willows.

"We'll have lunch first," Carson told the kids.

"Ah, Dad."

"Don't complain, son. Once you start fishing you're not going to want to stop."

"Okay."

Carson unloaded the truck and spread a large old quilt on the ground. Claire plopped in the middle with her dolls.

Trey showed her his new rod and reel. "Isn't it cool? It's black and red."

"Very cool," she replied.

"This line is tough. It'll hold a big fish, right, Dad?"

"Yes, son. Sit down—it's time for lunch."

Jena munched on a piece of fried chicken and watched Carson interact with his kids. They chatted about nonsensical things and Jena relaxed. There were no staring eyes or judgmental attitudes here, just peace and quiet. Maybe a person could never go home again, especially when they'd left under such horrifying circumstances.

"I'm getting the worms, Dad. I gotta fish." Trey jumped up and went to the truck. Claire was asleep on the quilt. Carson rubbed her back with a serene expression on his face.

"Bring Claire's big pillow," Carson shouted after him.

Trey came back with a huge black-and-white velvety-looking cat pillow in one hand and a coffee can in the other.

Handing his dad the cat pillow, Trey asked Jena, "Are you scared of worms?"

"No."

"Really? Most girls freak out, except Kelsey. Look." He shoved the can in front of her.

She looked down into the dark dirt and saw thick worms poking through.

"Gross, huh?"

She smiled. Trey was trying his best to scare her. He probably did this to all girls, especially Claire. Reaching in the can, she pulled out a fat worm. "Not gross at all."

"I don't think you're going to scare Jena, son," Carson remarked.

"She's cool, huh, Dad?"

"Real cool." Carson grinned at her and her stomach fluttered with unwanted excitement. But she couldn't deny that instant attraction.

"Uh…you have to give it back," Trey said. "They're

expensive. We buy them from Mr. Higginbooth. He has a worm farm. Really."

"I know." She dropped the worm into the can. Mr. Higginbooth was well-known for his fishing worms, even when she'd lived in Willow Creek.

"I'm gonna catch Ol' Big today. Kelsey will be so jealous." He picked up the can of worms, his rod and reel and headed for the creek.

Carson tucked the big pillow under Claire's head. "She doesn't have to go to school and she was up at five this morning. I made her go back to bed, but I could hear her playing in her room. She'll be out for a while. I better check on Trey. He's not used to the new rod and reel and he might wrap it around a tree." He strolled to the creek.

Claire whimpered, and Jena scooted closer and rubbed her back like Carson had done. It seemed the natural thing to do. Claire drifted into deep sleep.

The sun burned brightly, but the thick foliage of the live oak kept them shaded. The June day was getting a little warm, though.

Carson sank down on the quilt. "That boy is stubborn. He says he can do it on his own."

Jena watched as Trey cast the line and reeled it back in, over and over. "Why doesn't he leave the line in the water?"

"He says he's mastering his technique for when he catches Ol' Big. In truth, he's playing. That's what little boys do." Carson looked down at his daughter. "Miss Princess is out?"

"Yeah." Jena put the leftover chicken, bread and fruit in the picnic basket.

"You said you wanted to talk," Carson reminded her. "What about?"

She sank back on her heels, seeing in her mind's eye the yellow baby's outfit hidden in her mother's closet. "I wanted you to know that just because we had a moment of insanity I won't stop searching for my child."

His eyes narrowed. "A moment of insanity?"

"God." She closed her eyes and ran her hands through her hair. "What are we doing, Carson? I shouldn't be here with you and your kids having a picnic."

"Why not?"

She stared into his warm green eyes and saw everything that was good and right in a dark confusing world. The green depths reminded her of spring: growth, renewal, rebirth, a new future. How could that be?

Carson Corbett was only going to hurt her.

CHAPTER TWELVE

"Is this what you were upset about when we met you at the café?" Carson asked. Her sad dark eyes were breaking his heart in ways he never dreamed possible. "You think I'm trying to charm you into forgetting about our deal?"

"What?" She blinked. "I wasn't upset."

"Yes, you were. You looked hurt."

"Oh, that." She dismissed it with a wave of her hand.

"What was it?"

She played with the handle on the basket, and he thought she wasn't going to answer. "I went to the café to talk to Hilary and found out she hadn't told anyone I was back."

"Did anyone say anything to you?"

"Mabel recognized me, and then Tammy Sue Faulkner had to say hello and tell me how childbirth hadn't changed my figure. She looked around for my kid. Everyone did. I wanted to tell them my child was stolen, but the words wouldn't come. I left like a coward. Nine years and nothing has changed. I'm still Jena Brooks from the wrong side of the tracks. I'm angry at myself for not saying anything."

"Why didn't you?"

"Because of Hilary. I didn't want to embarrass her. If she hasn't told anyone I'm home, she must not want them to know."

He touched her hand, which had a death grip on the basket. "I'm sorry."

She stared down at his hand. "Don't touch me."

"Why?" He didn't remove his hand.

"You know why."

"I like touching you."

She stared at him and he wanted to tell her everything would be okay, but most of all he wanted to tell her that she could trust him.

"I like you touching me, too," she said in a low voice. "But it's wrong and we both know it."

"Somehow that doesn't seem to matter."

"Carson—" she blinked back a tear "—today I found some knitting of my mother's. She was making clothes for my baby. Clothes my child will never wear. That brought home to me that I must find my child. I must know what happened to it. I need to know for my own sanity."

His hand squeezed hers. "I promise I will do everything in my power to help you find the truth. Just give me some time."

She looked at him again, her eyes not so troubled. "Why do I trust you so much?"

"Because you can. My family has hurt you enough, and I will do my best not to do that to you. I will talk to my father again. He wasn't feeling well and stayed in bed all day yesterday. I'll get into Jared's room, too."

"Why haven't you gone in there yet? You just have to unlock a door."

"Because the kids are home and I'd rather wait until they're not there. I don't know how I'll feel when I go inside and I don't want them to see me upset. It's just going to take a few days until I get the right opportunity."

"That's just it. I don't have a lot of time. I'll have to go back to work soon."

"Give me a week." He held up their clasped hands. "We can do this. Please be prepared for the outcome, though." He wanted to make everything right for her but deep in his heart he knew that might not happen. "And I have to be prepared to deal with my father no matter what he did."

She slowly removed her hand. "Either way I can only see heartache down the road."

"But we're adults and we can handle it."

She looked off to the creek. "I've wondered so many times if I've done the right thing in coming home. Although, I just couldn't seem to do anything else. I have no life until I know the truth."

He had kids, so that was easy for him to understand.

"Daddy!" Trey shouted. "I caught a fish."

Carson jumped up and ran to the water and looked at the fish Trey had on the ground. "Son, that perch is about six inches long, and I think you have to throw it back."

"I know. Where's Ol' Big?"

Carson patted his son's shoulder. "You'll catch him. You just have to be patient."

Carson's cell buzzed and he talked on it as he walked toward Jena. "Okay. I'll be there as fast as I can." He slipped his phone in its case. "Walt called and said some guys are causing trouble at the Rusty Spur. Usually the young guys hang out at the Hitchin' Post, the other beer joint. Do you mind watching the kids? I'll be gone just a few minutes."

"Carson, not again. Why don't they just call 911?"

"Harry, the owner, doesn't want anyone to get arrested. He just wants them to behave. Please. Trey will be really upset if he has to stop fishing."

Her eyes softened. "Okay."

"Promise I won't be long. Thanks." He strolled to his truck. "Trey, I got a call. I'll be gone a few minutes," he called to his son.

"Okay, Dad."

He waved out the window to Jena. She was smiling and it crossed his mind that he'd like to see her smiling for the rest of his life.

THE SOUND OF the truck woke Claire. She sat up and pushed hair out of her eyes. "Where's Daddy?"

Jena rubbed her back. "He got a call."

Claire touched her hair around her shoulders. "My ponytail came undone again."

"Yeah, we have to tell Daddy that you need bigger bands. Maybe there's something in your bag." Jena opened the bag Carson had gotten out of the truck.

"Can we leave it down? It doesn't hurt my head like this."

"Sure." Jena didn't see any harm in that.

"Let's play Barbie." Claire grabbed her dolls on the quilt. Jena watched her dress and undress them, helping when she needed to. When they were growing up, she and Hilary had received used Barbie dolls from different charities. They were like new to them. She exhaled deeply. She had to stop remembering her crappy childhood and accept it for what it was and move on. Yet...

"Can we have a snack?" Claire asked. "Daddy bought cookies."

Jena found them in the basket. She called, "Trey, do you want a cookie?"

"Can you bring it to me, please? I can't leave my rod and reel. A fish might jerk it in."

Jena carried him a cookie and Big Red in a cup. Setting the cup in the grass, she handed him the cookie.

"Thank you, Jena."

"You're welcome." His fishing cork bobbed on the water. "Are you getting any bites?"

"Just perch. I'm waiting for Ol' Big."

"Good luck." She went back to Claire, who was stuffing chocolate chip cookies in her mouth and had a red ring around her lips from the soda.

"Hey, sweetie." Jena sank down by her and reached for a napkin to wipe her face. "Enjoying the cookie?"

"Uh-huh." Claire curled up on the pillow, and Jena moved the red soda out of the way.

"I tired."

Jena ran her fingers through Claire's long tresses. "Go to sleep. Your daddy said you were up early this morning."

"There's no school and I wanted to play."

Sunshine was making Jena a little sleepy herself. All her problems seemed so far away, but they were lurking in the dark corners of her mind.

"I like you," Claire said.

"I like you, too." Jena smiled. It was so easy to like Carson's kids. It wasn't too hard to like their father, either.

Her cell beeped. She tugged the phone from her shorts' pocket. It was a message from Hil: I'm home. She wondered what her sister was doing home so early, but then, she'd said she got off early on Sunday.

"Jena!" Trey screamed.

Jena turned to see Trey standing in the water desperately trying to reel in a fish.

"Help me!"

Before Jena could move, Trey fell face forward into the creek. "Jena!" he screamed again.

"Oh, my God!" Jena ran toward the water. "Hold on. I'm coming."

A fish flopped in the water. Trey held on tight to his rod and reel, his head poking above the water. Jena stepped in, shoes and all, and grabbed Trey around the waist.

"Help me, Jena. I got Ol' Big and he's pulling me in."

She held on to him with all her might, but the tug of the fish edged them farther into the water. The creek was deep in parts and she was afraid of Trey drowning.

"Reel harder," she suggested.

"I can't. Ol' Big has the line tight."

She drew in much-needed air and realized Claire was screaming on the bank. "Shh, Claire."

"You gonna drown!" the child cried.

"It's okay," Jena called back to her.

"I want Daddy."

Me, too, Jena thought, but Carson wasn't here and Jena had to do something about the situation.

"Okay, tiger, you might have to just let go of the fishing rod."

"No. It's my new one and Ol' Big can't have it."

Well, that didn't work. New plan. Her sandals were stuck in the slimy mud. She slipped her feet out of them, feeling the mud squish between her toes. Ignoring that, she planted her feet firmly in the sludge.

"Okay, tiger, you have to stand. I'll help. You'll have more leverage that way. On the count of three I'm going to yank you up."

"Okay."

"One, two, three…" Feet firmly anchored, she tugged

and Trey helped. She had him upright and he still had a grip on his fishing rod. They both were soaking wet. She reached for the reel to help turn it to bring in the fish, but like Trey had said, the line was tight, and she couldn't budge it. Just then, the fish leaped into the air. The thing was huge.

"It's a whale!" Trey shouted.

"Reel, fast," she urged.

They both tried to turn the reel, but it was wet and stubborn. With both hands she lifted the rod forward. At that moment, the fish leaped again and the line popped. Jena and Trey fell forward into the water. She spit and sputtered but never let go of Trey. The water was about waist-deep, and she dragged the boy until they could sit up.

She gulped a breath. "You okay, tiger?"

"Yeah. I almost had Ol' Big. Dang it!" He still held tight to his fishing pole. "Wait till I tell this story. Did you see how big he was?"

"Sure did, tiger. Maybe you'll get him next time."

"Trey," Claire cried and ran into the water.

"Claire, no," Jena called, but it was too late. Claire was splashing, shoes and all, toward them. She fell into Jena's arms and then hugged Trey.

"I scared."

"It's okay, sweetie," Jena reassured her. "Now we have to get out of the water."

The sound of a truck alerted them.

"Daddy's back," Trey said excitedly. "Wait till I tell him." He stood up too quickly and lost his balance in the mud. Jena caught him with one arm while trying to hold Claire, too. The water was muddy, and Trey splashed sludge on her face and her hair, which didn't matter because she was already wet. She was trying to keep them from drowning. And Trey made it difficult by refusing to let go of his fishing pole.

Suddenly strong, strong arms pulled them from the water to the bank. "What the hell are y'all doing?" Carson asked.

Trey heaved a breath. "You're not gonna believe it, Dad."

Carson held Claire against him. "Everyone okay?"

"Yeah, sure." Trey brushed off his father's concern. "I caught Ol' Big, Dad, and he was so huge I couldn't reel him in. Jena tried to help, but she couldn't, either. He's humongous. He broke the line and we fell in the water. Isn't the line fifteen-pound test, Dad? It wasn't strong enough. We have to buy stronger line."

Trey talked so fast that Carson put his hand over his son's mouth. "Take a breath. And let go of the rod."

Trey looked down at his hands clamped on the rod. "I can't. My fingers won't move."

Carson pried them off. Trey worked his hands and then laughed.

"This isn't funny, son."

But Trey couldn't stop laughing and Claire joined in. Despite herself, Jena laughed, too. It was a much-needed release after the stressful time in the water.

The children's laughter was contagious, and Jena saw the corners of Carson's mouth twitch. He embraced his children and laughed with them. His laughing green eyes stared at her, and everything stopped as she saw something she'd never seen before—hope, trust and a promise of tomorrow. All of a sudden her chest felt light. Almost as if the gigantic boulder that had been sitting on her heart had been moved to allow in something marvelous. Could this euphoric feeling be happiness?

Trey hugged Jena and she lost her train of thought.

"Thank you." A suffocating feeling came over her as she realized she was getting attached to Carson's kids.

She swallowed. "You're welcome, tiger."

"Son, why didn't you just let go of the pole?"

"I wasn't letting him have my fishing rod."

"We'll talk about fishing safety tonight. Your life means a lot more than a fishing rod."

"Ah, Dad."

"I just ruined a good pair of boots." Carson yanked off the wet boots and poured out water.

"Sorry, Dad."

"And your reel is probably ruined."

"We can clean it up."

"We'll see. And there will be consequences for risking Jena's and Claire's lives."

"Ah, shucks. I didn't mean…"

"I know, son. We'll talk about this later. Now we have to go home and get cleaned up."

They stood and looked a bedraggled, sodden group. Jena's and Claire's hair was in rattails.

"I lost my shoes, Daddy," Claire said.

"We all lost our shoes, princess." Carson threw his boots in back of the truck and then they picked up the picnic stuff. Jena retrieved her cell from where she'd dropped it when Trey screamed.

Grabbing the quilt from the ground, Carson used it to dry Claire and Trey. While he put Claire in the truck, Jena wiped the water and mud from her body as best as she could.

Trey was quiet as he buckled himself in. Jena felt sorry for him. He wanted to catch the big fish and now he was going to be punished. Carson held the door open for her. "Don't be too hard on him."

"Are you getting a soft spot for my kid?" His eyes twinkled.

"A little," she had to admit.

"He has to learn safety."

"I know…it's just…"

"When you look at yourself in the mirror, you'll probably change your mind."

She touched her mud-soaked hair. "That bad, huh?"

"Not to me, but…"

Their eyes clung for a few seconds, and Jena had the irresistible urge to kiss him, mud and all, right in front of his kids. Of course, she didn't, but the strong impulse to do so was there.

She wasn't sure how she'd gone from revenge to these new, overwhelming, passionate feelings.

CARSON'S HEART WAS still in his throat. When he'd driven up, he didn't see anyone on the blanket. He'd glanced toward the creek and seen them splashing about. He thought they were swimming and then realized they weren't. That was when he knew he could almost fly as he jumped out of his truck and ran to them. His only goal was to get them out of the water and to safety. He'd ask questions later.

Jena had saved Trey. He knew his son would have hung on to that fishing rod until his last breath. He was that stubborn.

How did he repay her for that? The answer was easy—find her child. He'd told her he would and he knew he had to do it. And all the while he'd have to fight his attraction to her.

He dropped the kids at the house so Aunt Fran could get them into dry clothes and then he took Jena home. After he'd parked, he got out and hurried around to her side to help her. She was already halfway out of the truck.

"I'm not helpless, you know," she said. Mud coated her hair and her face and Carson thought she was beautiful.

"Are you okay?" he asked.

"I just need a bath."

He had one hand on the truck and the other on the door, enclosing them in their own private space. "Thanks for what you did today."

"These babysitting gigs are getting harder and harder," she replied in a teasing tone that sent his heart soaring.

His eyes held hers. "You know what I want to do right now?"

"Yes. The same thing that I want." She shocked him with her honesty. "But we won't."

"Why?"

"I don't know. Maybe because the devil lives in Willow Creek, Texas, and he's your father. Or in the real world the poor girl doesn't get the handsome guy. Or you can't build anything on a world of heartache. Or some such crap. But—" she wiped some mud from her cheek "—you've exorcised my desire for revenge."

"Maybe I could exercise a lot more."

"Carson…"

"Jena."

She took a step forward. He didn't move. "There may be insurmountable obstacles between us, but I'm not going to fight my attraction for you." He reached out to slide damp hair from her face. "I realize we have a road full of rocks and thorns ahead, but I sincerely want to help you."

"Sometimes you're too nice."

"Sometimes you're too proud."

She unexpectedly kissed his cheek, ducked under his arm and ran to the house. "'Bye, Carson," she called over her shoulder.

He got in his truck and drove away. Maybe he was too nice, but he would like to have some happiness in his life. If he had to negotiate rocks and thorns, then he was up for it.

JENA OPENED THE door slowly, hoping to get to the bathroom without anyone seeing her. Norma was asleep in her chair, her knitting in her lap. Hilary lazed on the sofa. Silently, Jena tiptoed to the bathroom, but Hil quickly followed.

"What happened to you?"

"I fell into Willow Creek." She didn't see any reason to lie.

"What?"

"I'll tell you later. I have to get cleaned up."

"Whatever." Hil went back to the sofa and Jena sensed something was wrong. Her sister wasn't her cheerful self, but after working like a slave, who would be? In a few minutes Jena was back in the living room in clean, dry clothes.

Her mother was awake. "Oh, you're home. Look what I knitted today." She held up a white bootee. "The baby's going to need lots of clothes."

Jena felt as if someone had sucker-punched her in the stomach. She fought tears and went into the kitchen. Hil was right behind her.

"Why did you have to give Mama her knitting?"

"She asked for it."

"She asks all the time and I tell her I can't find it."

"Why do you do that?"

"Because she starts all this baby stuff and it's hell."

"I'm sorry. I didn't know."

"Well, you should." Her sister was angry. That was more than obvious, and she was angry at Jena. "You come back here and... Why did you come to the café today?"

That anger echoed in Jena's chest. "Am I not allowed there? Or do you just not want me there? Are you ashamed of me?"

"No," Hil mumbled.

"Then why haven't you told anyone I'm home?"

Hil sank into a kitchen chair. "I told you I didn't tell anyone. I didn't want to deal with all the gossip."

"That never seems to stop, does it?"

"No. After you left today, it really started up. Mabel, Bea, Tammy Sue and several others wondered what you were doing back in Willow Creek without your child. Mrs. Tisdale mentioned that Ella had said you didn't bring the kid. And you were seen with Carson, so you must be after money. But Carson wasn't a fool. He'd want proof the child was Jared's. On and on it went. They whispered but I could still hear them."

"Oh, sis, I'm sorry." She hugged her sister. She'd never wanted something like this to happen.

"I quit."

"What?" Jena drew back, shocked. "Why?"

"I...uh..." Hil fiddled with the saltshaker on the table. "I saw myself through your eyes, and I didn't like seeing that girl who allows herself to be used just to be one of the crowd."

"Oh, Hil."

"When the place was almost empty, Bea told me to be sure and get the tables cleaned off and everything set up for in the morning. She was tired and going home to put her feet up. Her tone got to me, and I took off my apron and said maybe *she* should clean off the tables and get everything ready for the morning."

"And she fired you?"

"No. Her face turned red and her mouth worked but no words came out. I took my key out of my pocket and said I quit. She found her voice then and said how ungrateful I was. We had words after that about wages, long hours and no time off. I walked out feeling good about myself. But now I have no job. What are Mama and I gonna do?"

She hugged her sister again. "Don't worry about it tonight. We'll think of something, and I have a little money to keep us going."

"I'm sorry I was so stupid," Hil murmured.

"Hey, my sister is not stupid. Let's fix dinner, watch a movie and just relax and regroup."

Hil looked at her with watery eyes. "You were with Carson. I saw his truck outside."

"Yeah." Jena brushed back her damp hair. "I was being stupid, too. Guess it's in our DNA."

"But…"

"It's beyond complicated, Hil. I knew it would be difficult to come back for my child, but I never dreamed I could be swayed emotionally by a pair of sincere green eyes."

"Jen…"

"I'm okay. I just have to get my head straight." Sitting on the banks of Willow Creek with Carson and his kids, she'd experienced a brief moment of happiness. It was real, poignant and fleeting. She'd felt it in her heart and she would remember it for a long time, probably at the oddest of times and the oddest of places—a fleeting thing that wasn't meant to be.

CHAPTER THIRTEEN

WHEN CARSON ENTERED the house, he heard his kids screaming and crying. He threw his wet boots into the laundry room and dashed into the den. Asa was having a seizure—his body shook as he lay prone in his chair. Aunt Fran was injecting something into his arm. Trey and Claire were holding on to each other, crying.

"Is Grandpa gonna die?" Trey asked, tears streaming down his face.

He gathered his kids close. "Go to the kitchen and get something to drink. I'll take care of Grandpa."

"I scared." Claire clung to him.

"It's okay, baby. Go with Trey."

As the kids slowly left, he asked Aunt Fran, "What happened?"

She put the syringe into a bag she kept Pa's medications in. A home health nurse had taught her how to give injections and how to care for Asa. "I gave him something, so he should relax now." She motioned for him to step aside and he followed her to the doorway.

"While I was getting Claire dressed, Trey came downstairs and was telling Asa about his fishing trip." Her face molded into a frown. "What were you thinking, Carson, taking that woman with you and the kids? The moment Trey said her name Asa became very agitated and I couldn't calm him down."

"First of all, Asa committed a crime against 'that

woman,' as you call her. She's done nothing wrong and Pa had better get used to hearing her name. This isn't over." Carson didn't want to hurt his aunt's feelings, but Jena was not the bad guy here. He walked back to his father. "I'll take care of this. Pa, are you okay?"

Asa raised his head, his eyes glazed. "You…her…the kids."

"Yeah. She probably saved Trey's life today. He wouldn't let go of the fishing rod. You know how stubborn he is."

"Bit-ch."

Carson knew he wasn't getting anywhere with his father. He took stubborn to a new level. There was only one way to reach him. He squatted by the wheelchair. "You want Jena Brooks gone?"

Asa's glazed eyes brightened in a weird sort of way.

"Tell her what happened to her child and Jena Brooks will go away." That wasn't the exact truth, but Carson was trying to make a point and maybe reach his father's heart.

"Nev-er."

He stood and released the brake on the wheelchair. "I'll put you back in bed and maybe tomorrow we can talk."

Aunt Fran followed them into the bedroom. Between the two of them they were able to get Asa into bed. His eyes closed and Carson knew he was asleep. He stared at his father, who still wielded so much power even in his fragile state. And he wondered if there was any end to this nine-year-old nightmare.

He went to the kitchen to check on his kids. They were huddled together in a chair. Claire saw him first.

"Daddy, I scared."

He picked her up and sat with her in his lap. Trey leaned against him as if needing reassurance, too.

"Is Grandpa gonna die?" Trey asked.

Carson had to be honest. "Grandpa is old and sick and one day he's going to die, but hopefully not today."

He put his arm around Trey. "We'll check on Grandpa in a minute. He loves you guys, you know that?"

"Yeah," Trey replied. "I thought he'd be happy I caught Ol' Big."

"Grandpa is not well, son. We have to be patient with him."

Aunt Fran came in and started supper. He rushed upstairs to change into dry clothes. The meal was a quiet affair. The kids said good-night to Asa, but he was out for the night. It did the kids good to see he was all right, though.

After the kids were in bed, Carson had a talk with Trey about fishing safety.

"I didn't mean to hurt anybody, Dad."

He sat on the edge of his son's bed and stared into green eyes just like his own. "I know, son."

"Jena's cool. She didn't mind getting wet or anything like most girls do."

"Yeah, she's cool."

Trey scooted up in bed. "Are you, like, dating her, Dad?"

Trey's bluntness stunned Carson for a second. "No, son." He wasn't lying. They were nowhere near dating. "I'm just trying to help her find someone."

"Oh."

Before his little mind could conjure up anything else, Carson thought it best to deal with the matter at hand. "I was going to let you go fishing to the stock tank by yourself, but in light of what happened today I've changed my mind."

"Ah, Dad." Trey slid down into the bed.

"You can go fishing with Kelsey and Walt, but I always want an adult along. I don't want you risking your life to catch a fish."

"But it's Ol' Big."

"Are you listening to me, son? Your attitude is not helping. I may not let you go at all if that doesn't change."

Trey sat up quickly. "I won't do anything stupid, I promise. I've been waiting all school year to fish this summer. You might as well lock me in my room if I can't go."

Carson ruffled his son's hair. "I don't think it will come to that. Just remember there are rules."

"I will."

Carson leaned over and kissed Trey's forehead. "Love you, son."

Suddenly, two little arms clutched him around the neck. "Love you, too, Daddy. Is Grandpa okay for now?"

His son may be stubborn, but he had a big heart. "Yeah, and I'll check on him before I go to bed."

"Okay."

Carson turned out the light and walked next door to check on Claire. She was sprawled across her bed, cuddling several stuffed animals and sleeping like a princess. He trudged into his bedroom feeling drained and exhausted. Even though his body was tired his mind seemed to be in overdrive.

Falling onto the bed, he tried to relax but there was just so much unrest in his soul. How could he reach his father? That was his main problem. He had to have something substantial, something to cool his father's hatred. Something to open his mind.

He got up and went down the hall to Jared's room. Staring at the doorknob, he saw something so simple he couldn't believe he hadn't seen it the other day. A tiny hole was in center of the knob. He hurried downstairs to find Aunt Fran. She was watching TV in the den.

"Aunt Fran, do you have a hairpin?"

"What?" She blinked and took off her glasses. "No. Why?"

"Are you sure? Could you please check?"

She got to her feet. "What do you need it for?"

"To get into Jared's room."

"For heaven's sakes, can't you leave this alone?"

He stared into her troubled eyes. "You know I can't."

"Oh, all right." She headed for the stairs. "But don't let your father hear."

She protected Asa like a lioness, but if he couldn't get Asa to cooperate, all the protection in the world wasn't going to help him. She brought him back a handful of hairpins and he went to work on the door. Aunt Fran watched. On the third try he was able to unlock it. He didn't even know he'd been holding his breath until he let it out in a rush.

"I don't want to see what's inside," Aunt Fran said and went downstairs.

Carson had an eerie feeling, but he flipped on the light, not sure if it would even work. It did. Light flooded the room full of cobwebs and dust. He stepped inside and the eerie feeling grew stronger. He felt as if he was desecrating his brother's last minutes on earth. Taking a deep breath, he forced himself to walk far-ther into the room.

The bed was neatly made with a brown-and-tan comforter, and it was literally covered in dust. Cobwebs decorated the headboard. Sneakers and socks lay by the bed. On a dresser were Jared's books, a backpack, wallet and keys. The wall had posters of rodeo stars and fast cars. Jared never got to drive that red Jaguar he'd dreamed about.

On his desk were papers, notebooks, a boom box and stacks of CDs by various artists. A poster board hung on the wall above the desk, and school pictures of football, track and baseball covered it. Since Willow Creek was a small school, kids got to play all kinds of sports. Several empty spots were on the board and Carson assumed those had probably been reminders of Jena, and Asa had removed them.

In the bottom drawer of the desk, he found Jared's journals. He started writing about things that happened when he was ten or eleven. He said it helped him to sort out his feelings, especially about his father. Carson flipped through several of them. It was mostly stuff about his horses, dogs, ATVs, kids in school he liked, girls he really liked and his father. The notations ended a year before he died and there wasn't one word about Jena. That puzzled Carson. Had Jared stopped writing? He stowed the journals back in the drawer.

He needed more. He searched the closet and found nothing unusual. A suitcase lay on the floor. Squatting, Carson brushed the dust and spider webs away and unzipped it. Inside were jeans, shirts, T-shirts, socks and underwear. Jared was packing to leave, just as Jena had said. In the top pocket was a manila envelope. He pulled it out and looked at the contents: a marriage license and a receipt for an apartment in Austin. Again, just as Jena had said.

He pulled out the dresser drawers and found nothing.

Jared's phone wasn't here. Picking up the envelope, he went back to his room and paced. What was he missing? What was Jared doing on that road that day when he was planning to leave with Jena? He was packed and ready.

Carson couldn't find any answers, so he took a shower and went to bed. But he couldn't sleep. It seemed odd that Jared hadn't written anything the last year of his life. He was seeing Jena and having problems with Asa. His brother would be stressed, and when he was, he wrote about his feelings. Where was Jared's last journal? Carson felt sure there was one.

Asa always went into their rooms without permission. If Jared was writing about Jena, he probably hid the journal so Asa wouldn't know his feelings or his plans. And it was most likely hidden in his room. Carson got up and went back down the hall. If he could find the journal, it would tell Carson a lot about the state of his brother's mind at the time.

He hadn't locked the door, but he should in case the kids decided to explore. He flipped the switch and light showcased the depressing room, which for some reason reminded him of a tomb. Shaking the feeling away, he began to search again, pulling out all the drawers and looking under and behind them, as well as behind the dresser and desk. Nothing but dust bunnies.

Next, he went through the closet again. Nothing. Then he checked the nightstand and under the mattress and under the bed. Nothing but more dust bunnies.

Damn it! He paced the room. Where would Jared hide it?

"Carson.'" Aunt Fran stood in the doorway in her robe. "What are you still doing in here? It's almost midnight."

"Remember how Jared used to write in journals?"

"Yes."

"I found them in here." He opened the bottom drawer of the desk to show her. "The last year of his life is missing."

"Maybe he stopped writing."

"I don't think so. It was a habit and a stress release for him, and the last year was more stressful than any he'd ever had."

"If it's not here, I don't know what to tell you."

"That's okay. If Pa found it, he probably destroyed it because I'm sure it was a lot about his relationship with Jena."

"Why do you want to find it, then?"

"I thought it might give me a clue about what happened that day. No one has an explanation of what Jared was doing on that old country road. His suitcase is packed and he and Jena were planning to elope the next day."

"You answered your own question. Lamar found out about it and did something to stop the elopement."

Carson shook his head. "No. Everyone I talked to said Lamar was happy about his daughter's involvement with Jared. Besides, I don't think Lamar killed Jared."

"Drunks do irrational things, Carson. We'll probably never know what really happened that night, and like I've said, I think it's best to leave it alone. You can't undo heartache and pain. And you can't undo the murders." A look of pain crossed his aunt's face.

"You think Pa shot Lamar, don't you?"

"I didn't say that, but Asa has suffered enough."

"And he's caused most of it."

Aunt Fran shoved her hands into the pockets of her robe in an angry movement. "You're his son. How can you say that?"

"Because I'm the man who's trying to keep his ass out of an institution." His voice sounded angry and he didn't mean to talk that way to his aunt. "I'm sorry. Go to bed. We're both tired."

She glanced around the room. "It's depressing in here. And sad."

"Yeah." He hugged her. "Night."

After she left, he looked at the space where his brother had spent a lot of his time. He had hoped to find a clue, something to explain that awful day. But there was nothing but items of a teenage boy whose life had been cut too short.

He walked to the door to flick off the light, but something made him glance back. That was when he saw it—a shadow on the bed. What was it? He walked over and tried to touch the spot, and that was when he realized it was a shadow. Of what? Looking up, he saw an item hidden in the hanging bowl-shaped light fixture. He stood on the bed and reached to retrieve it, but he already knew what it was: the missing journal.

Jared had stored it in the safest place he could, where no one would ever see it. The journal was caked with dust. Carson turned off the light, locked the door and carried the journal to his room. In his bathroom, he used a washcloth to clean it. He sat in bed and opened the book.

It began with thoughts of school and his friends and how Asa was pushing him to take control of the ranch. Each notation was dated.

Sep 10—Pa says I need to be a man. I'm eighteen years old and I just want to have fun. I'd rather get drunk on Willow Creek with the guys. That way I can't hear Pa. Only the drums in my head.

Carson read on and saw the first notation about Jena.

Sep 17—Tried to talk to Jena again today. She gave me the cold shoulder as usual. What's her problem?

Sep 20—Pa's on my ass about my grades. Thinking of sleeping in the barn. The rats are better company.

Sep 30—Today I got lucky. Well, not that lucky. It was pouring rain and I gave Jena and her sister a ride home. She thanked me and smiled. Man, I felt weak.

Oct 4—The guys are razzing me about Jena. Told them to shut up or I'd make 'em shut up. I can take 'em. That's me. Toughass. Oh, yeah! I like my friends, but they're idiots.

The journal chronicled Jena and Jared's relationship just as Jena had told him.

Oct 15—Pa wanted to know what I was so down about. I told him I like Jena Brooks, but she won't go out with me. Big Mistake. What made me think Pa would understand? He told me to stay away from that white trash. She wasn't good enough for his boy. Like I'd listen to him. Wish Carson was here. He'd understand.

"Yeah, li'l brother, wish I'd been here, too."

The next notes were about his bad grades and Jena tutoring him. And how much he liked her and wanted to help her.

Nov 5—Things are better between Jena and me. Can't believe she agreed to tutor me. Being dumb is paying off. Ha! Ha! I think she really likes me. I'm nutso about her. She even let me take her home from a football game, and, man, she let me kiss her. Wow! Now I know what fireworks are like in my head.

There was more about them spending time together and then:

Nov 12—When I got home today, Pa hollered for me to come into the den. His belt was wrapped around his hand and he was so angry the veins in his neck were about to pop through the skin. Before I could run, he hit me across the chest with the belt. It stung like hell. He yelled that he'd told me to stay away from that girl and now he was going to teach me to follow orders. This time I caught the belt and jerked it out of his hand. I don't know what would have happened next 'cause Beth came in and I got the hell out of there.

Carson flipped through the pages as he read more about Jena and Jared's developing relationship. And Jared's tumultuous life with Asa.

Dec 18—Carson's home for two weeks. Pa's chewing on his ass now. I get a break for two whole weeks. Best Christmas gift I ever got.

Jan 1—Spent New Year's Eve with Jena. We went into Austin, saw a movie and had dinner. After that, we went to a fireworks display in a park. At the stroke of midnight we kissed. It blew my mind. She was scared; I could tell. I told her I wouldn't force her to do anything she didn't want to.

Jan 5—Something good and something bad happened today. Trying to wrap my head around it. I went to Jena's to see why she wasn't in school. She wouldn't come out, so I kept banging on the door. That was probably rude but I didn't think about that then. She finally came out. One eye was bruised and her jaw was blue. Her father had beaten her. I was so angry I wanted to kill him.

I talked her into coming with me, and I drove to the Willow Creek bridge crossing. We talked about our lousy fathers and then she cried. I didn't know what to do, so I just held her. We started kissing, and, I still can't believe it, we had sex in my truck. It was her first time and she was quiet on the way home. That was bad. I didn't know how to make things right again.

Jan 18— Jena's avoiding me in school. I ruined the best thing in my life.

Jan 20—Pa's on my case again. Said he told Carson he was giving me the ranch and I should learn the business end from Roland. Yeah, like I want to spend time with that jerk. Like Carson, I'll be gone as soon as I get my diploma. Pa doesn't need to know that, though.

Jan 31—Jena met me in the hall at school and said she needed to talk to me. I took her home and she said she thought she was pregnant. For a split second I felt as if my life was over. Pa was going to kill me. Don't know why I thought of him. Guess I was in shock. Jena quickly told me she didn't expect anything from me. She just wanted me to know. I told her, feeling grown-up, I would take care of her and the baby. She told me to get lost. Man, I screwed up bad.

Feb 5—My head is finally on straight, and Jena and I had a good talk. I like Jena, but I don't know if I love her. Not sure if I even know what love is, but I told Jena we could learn to love together. I asked her to marry me. Took a solid week before she agreed.

Entries from February through July were things Jena had already told him as they planned their life together. This wasn't the type of information Carson was looking for, and he felt guilty reading about their relationship. But he already knew most of it. Two kids facing grown-up problems and doing their best to do the right thing.

The young girl in the journal was so different than the woman he knew. She was now mature, confident and able to handle life. The journal made him see how vulnerable and insecure she was as a teenager. And it made him understand why it took her nine years to come back. She was really afraid Asa would kill the two people she loved if she ever returned to Willow Creek.

The Aug 3 entry caught his eye—*I've been work-ing my ass off trying to make Pa believe I'm going to run the ranch. But something is wrong. A lot of equip-ment is missing. I asked Roland about it and he said the equipment was in the shop. Asa liked everything in top shape. I don't believe that. I thought Pa was run-ning the ranch, but Roland seems to handle everything. Going through the Bar C checkbook, I found out why. Pa pays for an apartment in Austin for Tanya LeBeck. That's where Pa spends all his time. Wonder if I should send her a thank-you card. Ha!*

Aug 10—Two drawers are locked in the office and I asked Pa if he had a key. He did. Roland and Curly were out and I wanted to see what was in there. I couldn't be-lieve it. Roland has two sets of books; one for the Bar C and one for himself. The man is embezzling money from the ranch! I took photos of the books with my camera and locked the drawers. Carson's coming home for the birth of his son and I'll send the shots to him once he's here. Sorry, bro, but I have to go.

Aug 21—Confronted Roland today. Didn't mean to. He just got under my skin. I informed him I knew he was funneling ranch money into his private account. If he didn't put the money back, I was calling the sheriff and telling Pa. He tried to scare me, but I held my ground. I gave him twenty-four hours. That's all the time I have because Jena and I are leaving on the 23rd. We want to be settled before the baby arrives.

The entry ended the page and Carson forced him-self to flip to the next note. *Aug 22* was written in bold letters, or maybe they seemed to stand out for Carson. It was the day Jared was murdered.

I met Roland at the barn and he said he'd transferred the money and wanted to give me the paper work. I

*held out my hand, but I should have known there was
a catch. He said he had to get the papers from the bank
and he wanted to meet later on County Road 246. I
told him I'd meet him back at the barn, but he was
afraid Asa would get suspicious. Since I was leaving
early in the morning, I decided to get it over with. I'll
leave the paper work with Beth to give to Carson. He'll
take care of everything. 'Bye, big brother. I'll call. Just
don't tell Pa.*

Carson touched the page. "'Bye, li'l brother."

He closed the book and felt numb. It had been a trap.
The minute Jared had stepped out of his truck Roland
had shot him—with Lamar's shotgun, which he'd probably stolen when Lamar was drunk.

Son of a bitch! He'd never put the embezzlement
and the murders together. Why hadn't he seen the connection? Roland was slick. He'd covered his tracks and
spread rumors about Jena and Lamar, and no one ever
questioned them. Carson certainly hadn't.

He slipped the book into his nightstand. All these
years he'd wondered what had happened that night. Now
he knew. His heart slammed against his ribs in anger.
Roland was going to pay for what he'd done. Jared had
left a trail of evidence that was hard to dispute. He ran
his hands over his face, plotting his next move.

But first he had to tell Jena.

CHAPTER FOURTEEN

CARSON THOUGHT HE wouldn't sleep, but Claire woke him up at 5:30 a.m. "Daddy, it's time to get up."

"It's too early," he mumbled groggily.

"But I want to play."

"Go back to sleep." She crawled in beside him and Trey crawled in on the other side. "Why is it I can barely get you two up during the school year, but during the summer you're up before the sun?"

"Don't know," Trey said and before long they drifted off, as did Carson.

The next time he looked at the clock it was six-thirty. As soon as he moved, the kids woke up.

"Let's go see if Aunt Fran will make us pancakes." Trey jumped out of bed and Claire followed him out the door.

Carson groaned and sat on the side of the bed. It was morning and he had a clearer picture of what he needed to do. Had to do. He opened the drawer and pulled out the journal.

"Jared, I think you hid this for a reason. You wanted me to find it. I know you had no idea you were going to be killed, but in a psychic sort of way you left clues. I just hate that it took me this long to find them. I also know you'd want me to do the right thing—for Jena. Not sure how to handle Pa. Because of his health I'll have to be careful. But he's clinging to a powerful secret that has to be told."

He dressed and went downstairs to his study, placing the journal on his desk. In the kitchen, the kids were stuffing pancakes into their mouths.

"Would you like a couple of pancakes?" Aunt Fran asked.

"No, thanks. Just a mug of coffee." As he poured it, a knock sounded at the back door and Ethan walked in.

"Mornin', all."

"Is Kelsey back?" Trey asked.

"Yep, they got back last night," Ethan replied and then looked at Carson. "Do you have a minute?"

"Sure." Carson poured another mug and they walked to his study. He, Levi and Ethan had an uncanny connection. Ever since they were boys, they seemed to know when one of them was in trouble. And Carson needed a friend to talk to today.

"What's up?" Carson asked as they took seats, Carson behind his desk and Ethan in a leather wingback chair.

"We're taking Kelsey to see a Texas Rangers' game at the end of the week. I thought Trey might like to go."

"Who's we? You and Walt?"

"The whole family, including Dad."

"You do know I have two kids? If Trey goes and Claire can't, I'll have one sad little girl on my hands."

Ethan took a sip of his coffee. "Since we know Chloe will be miserable, Abby's been trying to talk her into staying with her grandma and grandpa, but that's not going over very well. So taking Claire will solve the problem. The separated-at-birth twins can entertain each other."

"It's uncanny how much they look and act alike."

"Yeah, if I didn't know better I'd say Abby's ex had an affair with Beth."

Carson ran his hands over his face.

"Hey, man, I was joking."

"What?" Carson blinked, lost in his own inner thoughts. "Oh, I know you were."

"What's wrong?"

Carson told his friend what had been happening lately and about Jared's journal and what was in it.

Ethan placed his mug on the desk. "So Roland shot Jared and framed Lamar?"

"It doesn't say that. Jared just says who he was going to meet that day on County Road 246, but it doesn't take much to figure out the rest."

"And my cop instincts tell me Roland waited for Lamar that morning and shot him, too. He got rid of the shotgun, making sure it wasn't Asa's because that was his gravy train."

"That's my guess. I'm going to make an appointment to see the sheriff today. This case has to be reopened. Lamar didn't kill Jared and I have to be pretty persuasive to convince the sheriff and the district attorney of that."

"You shouldn't have a problem. It's just going to take time."

"Yeah." He sighed deeply. "I have to tell Jena first."

Ethan frowned.

"What?"

"The way you said her name."

"So?"

"As if you have feelings for her."

Carson couldn't deny that. "Okay, I like her. She doesn't deserve what happened to her. And she deserves to know what happened to her child."

"Man, this is as complicated as it gets."

"I know. I have to read Jared's journal to Pa, and it's either going to cause him to have another stroke or a major heart attack. But he's the only one who knows what happened to the baby."

"Well, now—" Ethan rubbed his hands together "—Roland might know. He did all your dad's dirty work."

"Mmm. A lot more might be uncovered before this is over."

Ethan got to his feet. "I have to get to work. If you need any help, just let me know."

"Everybody in this town branded Lamar a murderer and never questioned it. They believed all of Roland's lies about Jena. Sad to say, I bought into it, too. I believed the rumors."

"Don't beat yourself up."

"I'm going to make sure justice is done this time."

They walked to the door, and Ethan patted Carson's shoulder. "Take it slow, my friend. Take it slow."

CARSON SPENT THE next thirty minutes scanning pages from the journal. If he had to turn it over to the sheriff and the D.A., he wanted to make sure he had a copy just in case it turned up missing. He dug out his leather briefcase and slipped the journal inside.

Evidently the kids were through with breakfast. He could hear them playing in the den.

"Not too loud, guys," he said on his way to the kitchen. They followed like little puppies. "Aunt Fran, I have some police work to do. Do you think you could watch the kids?"

She turned from putting dishes in the dishwasher. "The therapist is coming, and he'll work with Asa most of the morning. Then Asa will be tired and sleep. The kids and I might go for a walk."

He looked down into two smiling faces he loved. "You know the rules. You have to mind Aunt Fran."

Trey nodded. "We know."

"Son, you might clean up your rod and reel and see if it still works. It might need new line, too. Look in my tackle box."

"I'll help him," Aunt Fran offered.

"You know how to put line on a rod and reel?" Trey was clearly surprised.

"Sure do. Caught many a fish in my day."

"Wow." Trey was impressed.

"Go upstairs and get dressed."

"My hair, Daddy." Claire held out her tangled tresses.

"Go." Aunt Fran pushed him toward the door. "I'll get them dressed and brush Claire's hair this one time, but I'm not doing any braiding."

He kissed her cheek. "Thanks, Aunt Fran." Going out the door, he knew he'd have to tell his aunt about the journal. But right now Jena was his top priority.

"What am I going to do?" Hilary wailed as they finished cleaning the kitchen after breakfast.

"You'll find another job," Jena told her.

"Not one where I can run home and check on Mama."

"Do you want to go back to the café?"

"Hell, no." Hilary flopped into a chair. "I've finally found my pride."

"I'm so proud of you."

"Say that in about a month when we have nothing to eat."

Jena shook her head. "I'll get a pen and paper and we'll go over expenses and figure out a way to survive."

"Oh, great, nothing like knowing how really poor we are."

"Will you stop it. I—" A knock sounded at the door, cutting Jena off. "I'll get it.

"Hi, Billy Jack," she said, opening the door.

"Hilary's not at the café. They said she quit."

"You bet I did." Hil spoke from behind her. "You were right. I should have asserted myself before now."

"Hot damn, Boots. It's about time, and in case you're wondering, it's a mess down there. The coffee isn't fit to drink, and Bea is so slow filling orders everyone is walking out."

Hil slid her hands into the back pockets of her shorts. "They'll hire a cook."

"Not for minimum wage." Billy Jack chuckled. "Talk to you later. Just wanted to check on you."

As Jena closed the door, Hil said, "I feel kind of guilty. Everyone depends on me for breakfast before they go to work."

"Oh, please." Jena's cell buzzed, preventing her from saying anything else. She ran to the bedroom to get her phone. It was Carson. She sat on the bed. Her heart raced, she had a ridiculous urge to smile and for a split second that euphoric feeling she called happiness bubbled inside her.

Even though she'd had misgivings, she had a wonderful time yesterday. She'd gone to sleep with a smile on her face. His kids were adorable. Trey was a tough little guy, and Claire was a cutie. They were easy to… No, she wouldn't think that word. She couldn't ignore all the obstacles between them.

And he was waiting.

"Hi, Carson."

"I'm at the office. Do you have some time this morning?" He sounded stressed.

"Uh…Hilary quit her job and she's having a major meltdown, so I really need to be here."

"I wondered what was going on over at the café. A lot of trucks are burning rubber as they leave. I'll have to go over there if it doesn't stop."

"Billy Jack came by. Seems everyone is upset." There was silence for a moment. "Is the reason you want to see me important?" she finally asked.

"Yes."

"Is it about the baby?"

"It's connected to the baby."

"I'll be right there." Nothing was as important as the search for her child. Her hands shook as she slipped on sandals. Any information was important, which was what she told Hil as she rushed out the door. Hil understood.

She made it in record time. Carson sat at his desk with a somber expression, so unlike yesterday. A tremble ran through her as she took a seat.

"What is it?"

"I got into Jared's room last night."

"Oh."

"Did you know Jared wrote in a journal?"

"Uh…no. He never mentioned that."

"He started when he was about ten or eleven. Aunt Fran started traveling about that time, and Pa was even harder to deal with. Jared wrote about his feelings or sometimes just what happened on a certain day. He didn't do it every day, only when he was stressed. It helped him to cope."

"You found his journal?" she asked, knowing that had to be the reason he'd called.

"I found several of them, along with the marriage

license and paper work and a receipt for an apartment in Austin."

She brushed a speck from her shorts. "It was a one-room efficiency. The sofa made into a bed. I didn't know where we were going to put a crib, but Jared said we'd figure it out. It really didn't matter. I just wanted to be away from the prying eyes of the people of Willow Creek." She bit her lip, refusing to let memories take over. "Did you find anything else?"

"Like I said, I found his journals, but the last year of his life was missing. I thought that was odd since his last year was stressful and I'm sure he would have written something down. I searched everywhere and couldn't find it. As I was leaving the room an odd sensation came over me and I looked back. I saw a shadow on the bed. It was coming from the light fixture, and that's when I saw it. The journal was tucked inside the light fixture."

"Oh…why would Jared do that?"

"He wrote a lot about you and I guess he didn't want Pa to find it." He opened the briefcase on his desk and pulled out an old-looking book. He pushed it toward her. "You might want to read it. It tells what he was doing on that county road the day he died."

Jena stared at the book, not knowing if she could read it.

Carson stood. "I'll give you some privacy. I'll go across the street and try to calm the confusion over there."

As the door closed, Jena kept staring at the book. Did she want to go back and read about that turbulent time? But somehow the temptation was too strong.

CARSON GAVE HER as much time as he could. When he opened the door, she was just sitting there staring off into space. He squatted by her chair.

"Hey, you okay?"

She brushed away a tear, and he just wanted to hold her like he did Trey and Claire when they were hurt. But his feelings for Jena were not childlike.

"I'm not that young girl anymore," she mumbled.

"No," he agreed.

"It's so sad. That shouldn't have happened to us."

"No. And Jared shouldn't have been killed."

She brushed away another tear. "He went to meet Roland."

"Yeah. My guess is Roland stole your dad's shotgun and killed Jared. I have a meeting with the sheriff and the district attorney in an hour to see if I have enough to reopen the case."

"I'm going, too," she said, her eyes bright.

"Are you sure?" He got up and went around his desk. "What about Hilary?"

"I'll call her. She'll be fine."

"It's a nightmare at the café. No one can find anything or cook anything. Bea is trying, but she's just making matters worse."

"That's what Billy Jack said. Mabel and Bea don't realize how much work Hilary does."

"They do now." Carson placed the book in the briefcase. "Ready to go?"

She got to her feet, looking down at her khaki shorts and knit top. "I should probably change."

"You look gorgeous." He'd meant to say *fine,* but another word came out instead. With her slim figure, feminine curves and dark soulful eyes, no one would pay one bit of attention to what she was wearing. He wasn't.

She lifted an eyebrow but didn't say anything for a second. "I...I have to call Hilary."

Carson grabbed his hat. "I'll meet you in the car."

Within minutes they were on the road to San Marcos. They didn't talk much. Jena seemed lost within herself, and he hoped something good came out of this for her.

They were shown into Sheriff Bill Ratcliff's office. Bill was in his fifties, balding and a little flabby around the middle, but Carson knew him to be honest and one hell of a lawman. Carson explained what was going on, and Bill agreed the D.A. needed to see the journal. He'd already talked to the district attorney after Carson's call. They walked over to the D.A.'s office.

Riva Stanton was new to the job, and Carson hoped she was an eager beaver for justice. They waited in her office. Jena was too quiet and that bothered him. He gently touched her arm. She seemed to relax.

Ms. Stanton came in wearing a gray suit, her brown hair in a bob. "What have we got, Bill?" she asked as she took her seat.

The sheriff made the introductions. "As I told you, Mr. Corbett has new evidence concerning his brother's death."

Ms. Stanton looked at a file on her desk, which evidently someone had pulled for her. "From what I understand it was an open-and-shut case."

"Roland Stubbs made us all believe that," Carson replied.

The D.A. tapped her pen on the file. "Okay, Mr. Corbett, tell me what you know."

Carson told her everything he'd found since he started investigating, and then he pulled the journal from his briefcase and opened it to the last entry. "We never understood what Jared was doing on that old county road, but in his journal Jared tells us he went to meet Roland. Something Roland never mentioned."

She glanced at the entry. "Mr. Stubbs was embez-

zling money from the Bar C, which is owned by your father, and Mr. Stubbs is now serving time for that crime."

"Yes."

Ms. Stanton looked at Jena. "Ms. Brooks, your father
is accused of the murder. How do you feel about that?"

"I want his name cleared. That's why I'm here."

"The journal is damning evidence, but I need a lot
more to reopen this case." Her gaze settled on him. "If
I'm going to go out on a limb, I need to know everything. I don't like surprises popping up. Surprises that
will make me look like an ass who's wasting taxpayers'
money. Do you understand me, Mr. Corbett?"

"Yes, ma'am." He wasn't expecting to have to make
this decision today. He glanced into Jena's dark eyes
and saw everything he wanted. He also saw fear there,
and right and wrong.

Yet, his family loyalty weighed heavily upon him. He
was about to incriminate his own father, but he couldn't
get Jena's baby out of his mind and off his conscience.
Jared's baby. That child deserved justice, too.

He rubbed his hands together. "There's more, but
I request that you keep what I tell you in the strictest
confidence."

Ms. Stanton leaned back in her chair. "I'm not making deals, but my office is discreet about every case
we handle."

Slowly, Carson began to tell her about Jena's baby
and his father's involvement. The D.A.'s mouth fell open
a couple of times, as she was clearly stunned.

"Ms. Brooks, your child was forcibly taken from
you?"

"Yes. Minnie Voltree gave me something to induce
labor. Roland, Curly Sanders and Asa Corbett were
there."

"Why didn't you tell someone?"

"Asa threatened to kill my mother and my sister if I ever came back to Willow Creek, and I knew he meant it. I was eighteen when my baby was born and scared, but I'm not anymore. I want to know what happened to my child."

"Mercy, this is small-town Texas justice, isn't it?"

"Ms. Stanton, I don't condone what my father did, but in his defense he was grieving and out of his mind."

"I agree with that, Mr. Corbett."

"My father has had a stroke and is in poor health. Before a detective or an investigator is sent to the house, I'd like the opportunity to tell him first."

"We have a lot to do before that happens." She scribbled something in the folder. "I'm going to put an investigator on this, and if he can get more details from Mr. Sanders and a signed statement from Mr. Bass and Mrs. Voltree, we might have enough to reopen this case and get a conviction." She flipped through the file. "No one was ever arrested for Lamar Brooks's murder?"

"No, ma'am," the sheriff replied.

"I really dislike the good-old-boys' network, and I dislike it even more when teenage girls are taken advantage of." The D.A. glanced at Jena. "Ms. Brooks, we might even get a clue as to what happened to your baby. Stubbs and Sanders were there. They know something."

"Ms. Stanton, I'd like to help the investigator."

The D.A. looked directly at him. "That might be a good idea. It will save some time. What do you think, Bill?"

"It will certainly help. Holden is our best investigator, but he's working the Gomez case."

"I know Holden," Carson said. "He's a colleague of my friend Levi Coyote."

"Mmm. Levi's done work for our department before. We can contact him and see if he's interested. I like his work. He's thorough."

"Good idea, Riva," the sheriff replied. "Levi knows the area and the people involved in the crime. He can hit the ground running."

"Sounds good." Ms. Stanton closed the file. "Mr. Corbett, do you have a problem working with Levi?"

"No, ma'am. I would prefer it."

"Good." She folded her hands across the folder. "We'll be in touch with Levi and let him know what we need. Hopefully, we can find answers that will bring the real murderer or murderers to justice. But I will need something substantial. I hope you understand that."

"Yes, ma'am." Carson walked out of the room with a heavy heart. He'd set the wheels in motion and now he had to see it through. He had to find a good lawyer for his dad so that he could stay under house arrest or something. How was he going to tell his kids? And Aunt Fran?

Suddenly, Jena took his hand and held it as they walked to his car. "Thank you," she said with a smile. And in that moment, looking into her bright eyes, it was all worth it.

CHAPTER FIFTEEN

"I CAN'T BELIEVE you did that," Jena said on the way back to Willow Creek. She was so touched by his openness she didn't know what to say. She'd never expected him to reveal his father's involvement.

"The D.A. is willing to take a look at the case, so I had to be completely honest, even though it hurt."

Unable to resist, she touched his arm. "I'm sorry."

He looked down at the hand on his arm. "It was going to happen sooner or later. I just have to prepare my family."

Removing her hand, she felt guilty for the pain she was causing him. How she wished they had met under different circumstances. They were so compatible. Or maybe she was just dreaming.

"How about lunch?" Carson asked. "There's a country diner up ahead."

"Sounds good to me."

The place was packed with a lunch crowd. Country music played in the background. They were shown to a small table in the back—a cozy spot for two. He ordered chicken-fried steak, and she had salad with grilled chicken.

"I like Riva Stanton." She placed her napkin in her lap.

"I thought I'd have to do a lot of talking to even get her to review the case," he replied. "But the two of us together was hard for her to dismiss. And she wants justice, too."

Their food arrived and nothing was said for a few minutes. She watched his strong hands as he cut up the steak, and she felt she could watch him forever. His movements were sure, confident and masculine. She liked the whole package of Carson Corbett, except for a little, annoying fact: Asa was his father.

"Things will start to happen fast as soon as Levi gets on the case," Carson said. "He's like a bulldog with a bone. He doesn't let go until he gets what he wants."

"You trust him?"

"With my life."

She took a sip of her tea. "How long do you think it will take?"

"I don't know. Hopefully soon, but you never know what kind of roadblocks we might run into. Levi and I will put in a lot of time, though."

"I want to be included."

Their eyes met across the gingham tablecloth. "You don't have to be."

"I need to be."

He nodded and placed his napkin on the table. "The main reason I mentioned my dad today was that Roland might know where the baby is. He was Pa's right hand. It could be a bargaining chip."

"What do you mean?"

"If we can get the information Ms. Stanton needs and it points to Roland killing Jared in cold blood, she could go for the death penalty. A lot of things have to fall into place before that happens, but she could offer a reduced sentence if he will tell us what happened to the baby."

"Oh, Carson, then…"

"Yes, I wouldn't have to continue grilling Pa. Roland may have all the information we need."

She stared into his gorgeous green eyes, which were soothing and comforting and a whole lot more. "I want to hug you."

His eyes twinkled. "I want to do a lot more."

She laughed, stood and leaned across the table and kissed his waiting lips. He held her head and kissed her back, and they were oblivious to the crowded diner.

Until the waitress approached. "Will there be anything else?" she asked.

Jena resumed her seat, feeling giddy and young. And happy.

"No." Carson cleared his throat. "Check, please."

The waitress laid a ticket on the table. "You pay up front."

"Thank you." Carson pulled out his wallet and laid some bills on the table. Hand in hand they made their way to the cash register and then out the door.

On the way home they talked about trivial things, letting the heart-wrenching stuff rest for now. It was nice to feel normal even if it was only for a short time. That wasn't realistic, but she couldn't make her heart believe that. She'd found nirvana and she wanted to savor it, even if it was only for this moment. Every woman deserved that.

WHEN JENA MADE the turn onto their road, she had to slow down. Kids and bicycles were everywhere, but mostly in their yard. Hilary had a card table set up and kids milled around it. What was her sister doing?

She managed to park in the driveway as the kids sped off on their bicycles. An old ice-cream maker sat in the middle of the table, and Hilary was stuffing change into her pocket.

"What are you doing?"

"Making money, sis. I just can't sit around, so I got the old ice-cream maker out of the attic. I went into Dripping Springs and got everything I needed. Kids are out of school and they want ice cream. I'm charging fifty cents a cup and I'm sold out. I'm going into the house to count my money."

"What about the table?"

Hilary made a face, but she folded the table, and Jena helped to carry things into the house. Her mom was knitting in front of the TV. Jena prayed she wouldn't bring up the baby, but her mother seemed fixated on the TV.

Hilary emptied her pockets onto the table and sat down to count. Jena was amazed at the difference in her sister's attitude since the morning. With Hilary's bubbly personality, Jena should have known her sister wouldn't be down for long.

"Thirty dollars and fifty cents. Hot damn. Now we can eat." Hil raised her arms in the air. "And you know what else? Ms. Colley called and asked if I'd make a chocolate pie for her. She has relatives coming, and she always buys them from the café. She was sorry to hear that I had quit. I told her I'd make her a pie, and she's picking it up in the morning. Ten more bucks. Yay!"

"Have you been sniffing the paint fumes?"

"No." Hil stuck out her tongue. "I just decided I don't do depression very well. And I… Hold on. My phone is vibrating." She pulled it out of her pocket, and Jena listened to what her sister was saying.

"Hi, Mrs. Rogers. No. I'm not working at the café anymore. Yes, I can make you a coconut pie. You want it delivered? That's all the way out to Willow Creek flat. Probably around fifteen dollars. Yes, I'll put thick meringue on it. See ya at ten tomorrow." Hil clicked off and made a motion like pulling a lever on a slot machine. "Ca-ching. Another sale."

Before Jena could say anything, Hil's phone went off again.

"Hey, Billy Jack. How many? Okay. About six-fifteen. I'll have it ready."

Jena leaned against the cabinet. "Now what?"

"Billy Jack wanted to know if I'd make coffee and cranberry-walnut muffins for the guys in the morning. It's what they usually have at the café, and he said they're not going back in there."

"Hil, you can't run a restaurant out of our house."

"Why not?"

"You have to have a license, which you don't, and that makes it illegal. And as soon as Mabel and Bea find out, they'll report you to Carson or the sheriff."

Hilary got to her feet. "Well, ignorance is bliss. I'll just say I didn't know. I mean, what can they do?"

Jena shook her head. "Not much, I suppose."

"I have to get supplies for in the morning. I won't be long. Mama's been good most of the day, but who knows what the evening will bring."

"I'll be here, so don't worry."

"How did it go with Carson?"

"I'll tell you later." For now, Jena just wanted to hold everything in her heart. There was now hope where there wasn't before and that was thanks to Carson. He'd put her before his family. No one had ever done anything like that for her before, and she was still trying to process his generous gesture. Not to mention her feelings, which were growing every time she looked into his green eyes. More trouble was ahead but she'd just as soon not think about that now. How could she when Carson was making it possible to find her child.

EVEN THOUGH CARSON had done the right thing, he found it hard to face his family. He'd weighed the odds and there just wasn't another way. Now he had to tell Aunt Fran.

As a constable, he'd sworn to protect the people of Willow Creek. As a father and a son, he had to protect his family. Jena's child was family, too, and he couldn't ignore that. Somehow he had to pull it all together and keep everyone safe, including Asa.

When he entered the kitchen, childish chatter filled the room. Aunt Fran was putting something in the refrigerator, and Trey and Claire were right beside her.

"Wait till Dad sees," Trey said.

"What does Dad need to see?"

"Daddy," they squealed and ran to him.

He picked up Claire. Aunt Fran had called to see if it was okay to go fishing at the stock tank, so he knew it had something to do with fishing.

"I got my rod and reel working really good. We caught two bass and Aunt Fran cleaned them. Wow, Dad, she cleans fish like a man. I helped, too. Now we're gonna have them for supper. I was really good and did everything Aunt Fran told me. Grandpa's sleeping, so I didn't get to tell him yet. He'll be so surprised. Claire cried like a little baby 'cause we killed the fish and she said she wasn't eating it. She doesn't understand fishing. She's a girl. Aunt Fran's making her a peanut butter and jelly sandwich." Trey opened the refrigerator door. "See, there's our fish. What do you think?"

"Son, I think you need to take a breath."

"Ah, Dad. I'm excited."

"I know." He ruffled his son's hair. "I'm glad you had a good time, and I'm happy you minded Aunt Fran."

"They were no problem," his aunt said, reaching for a frying pan.

"I'm going to my study…." His cell buzzed. There was a disturbance at the café. Headed toward the door, he said, "This won't take me long."

"We're helping Aunt Fran cook supper," Trey called after him.

The call took about ten minutes. A guy had ordered fried chicken, and he didn't like the way it tasted and refused to pay. The problem was, he ate every bit of it, and Carson explained that once he ate it he had to pay for it. The man became belligerent, and Carson told him he could either get out his wallet or be booked into the county jail. He paid but said he was never coming back.

He told Bea she had to do something about the situation. She said she'd hired a new cook, which should solve the problem. Carson wasn't so sure. Everyone's loyalty was to Hilary. The Brooks girls were easy to…

Getting into his car, he paused. Did he love Jena? He wanted to. It was just so complicated, and he didn't want to analyze it much further. They faced insurmountable odds, but if they were meant to be together, they would. He had to believe that.

After supper, he went to his study, and the kids watched a movie with Pa in his room. He was reading through the journal pages he'd scanned when Levi walked in.

"Aunt Fran let me in," Levi said, sinking into a chair.

"Did you get the call?"

"Yeah. The D.A.'s office outlined what they need from me."

"And that would be?"

"Solid evidence to reopen the murder case of Jared Corbett. Seems Jared had a journal. I didn't get to see it because it was locked in the safe, but I got the gist of it."

Carson laid a printed page in front of him. "That's the last entry on the day he died. Why did I never connect the embezzlement with the murder?"

Levi picked up the paper. "Because you were dealing with Jared's murder. You didn't have time to catch your breath before you had to return to duty. At that time you didn't know about the embezzlement. You had your hands full taking care of family. When you came home for good, there was no way to connect the two. Everything pointed to Lamar. There was no evidence otherwise." Levi pointed to the page in his hand. "Now it seems there is."

"Yeah." Carson told him how he'd found the journal. "Pa had that room locked up like a tomb. If he'd just let someone in, this might have been found years ago."

"Have you told Asa about the journal?"

"Not yet. I'm biding my time."

"Might be wise to wait until we have more evidence."

"I was thinking the same thing, but I have to tell Aunt Fran tonight after the kids are in bed."

"Good luck, buddy." Levi pulled out his smartphone. "I spoke with Willie Bass this afternoon and got a signed statement from him, as I did with Mrs. Voltree. I located Curly Sanders in a small town outside of Bastrop. Plan to pay him a visit in the morning."

"You don't let any grass grow under your feet."

"Hell, no. I get paid for being prompt and getting facts that can win cases."

Carson smiled slightly. Levi was a former cop turned private investigator and was well-known for getting the job done—his way. There was no one tougher than Levi, except maybe Ethan. Maybe because they'd all grown up tough.

"What time do you want to leave in the morning?" Carson asked.

"That's what I came over to ask. What time can you get away?"

"Probably around eight. I have to talk to Aunt Fran again about watching the kids. And Jena's coming with us."

Levi frowned. "Is that wise?"

"After what Roland and Curly did to her, she has a right to confront them."

"Carson…"

"Don't start, Levi. And before you ask, yes, I have feelings for her, so that will save you from grilling me. I know it's complicated and…"

Levi held up a hand. "I'm the last person to give advice on affairs of the heart. Go where your heart takes you, buddy, and when it's all said and done we'll still be friends."

"Sorry. I'm a little touchy about the subject."

"It's a touchy situation, so let's move on." Levi looked at his phone. "The D.A. is hiring a handwriting expert to prove the handwriting in the journal is Jared's. I need something with Jared's signature. Maybe his driver's license or something from school that clearly shows it's his."

"I'll get it from his room." It didn't take Carson long to find items in Jared's room: his driver's license, a football sign-up form and one of the other journals that had his name and address written on the inside flap.

Levi left soon after, and they arranged to meet early in the morning. He called Jena to let her know, and then he put his kids to bed. Aunt Fran was getting Asa ready for bed. He waited until she was through.

"Aunt Fran, could we talk for a minute?"

"Sure." She followed him into his study.

"I didn't tell you this morning, but I found Jared's missing journal."

"Oh, my." She sank into a chair.

He told her about the meeting with the sheriff and the D.A. and pushed the last page of the journal toward her. She read it quickly.

"Jared went to meet Roland?"

"Yes."

"What does all this mean?"

"It means that Roland framed Lamar for the murder because Jared found out he was taking money from the Bar C. Roland fooled everyone, including Pa. He spread rumors about Jena and Lamar, and he made it all believable—so believable that Pa wouldn't believe the child Jena was carrying was Jared's." He pushed more of the pages toward his aunt. "Jared wrote about Jena. He slept with her one time. She was a virgin. Lamar had beaten her, and she was bruised and crying. Jared tried to comfort her and one thing led to another. They both regretted it, but then they were faced with a pregnancy—two young kids not knowing what to do and no one to help them."

"I never dreamed it was anything like that. Those poor kids."

Now he had to tell her the hard part, and it took all the courage he had. "I had to tell the D.A. the whole story, and that included Pa's forcefully taking Jena's baby."

"Carson!" Her eyes flew wide with fear.

"I've asked him repeatedly for the truth about the baby, but he refused. That left me no choice. Everything will come out now, and since Roland was Pa's right hand, I'm hoping he knows what happened to the child. Anyway, the next few days will be tense and I wanted you to know in case rumors start to circulate."

"Are you going to tell your father?"

"Eventually, but I want solid evidence in my hand when I do." He ran a hand through his hair. "And I want you to be prepared for the worst. Pa will probably be arrested."

"Oh." The fear was gone from her eyes; they held more of a complacency, an acceptance of the inevitable. "What are we going to do?"

"I'll hire a good lawyer and protect him every way I can. Though I'm not sure he deserves that."

"You're a good son."

As Carson went to bed, he didn't feel like a good son. He felt conflicted and torn, but in his heart he knew he was doing the right thing.

JENA RUSHED TO get out of the house the next morning, which wasn't easy since her sister had taken control of the kitchen. She'd already made the coffee run for the guys, and Jena understood why they liked Hil so much. She made lattes for them and added special ingredients that each liked, such as nutmeg, cinnamon, chocolate or caramel or a dollop of whipped cream.

Jena snatched a muffin and ate as she dressed. She wore capris, a cotton blouse and flats. As she went through the kitchen, Hil was making pie crust and Mama was trying to help.

"I might be late," she called.

Hil followed her to the door. "Just get the evidence you need." They'd talked last night, and she'd told her sister everything, except her feelings for Carson. Those were still very new and personal.

Carson and Levi were ready to go when she reached the office. She liked Levi and she didn't feel awkward around him. Carson drove and Levi complained about that the whole way. They were fun to listen to, and her nerves relaxed as she prepared herself for the day.

They located Curly Sanders without a problem, but once he knew what they wanted, he clammed up and said he wasn't talking to anyone but the D.A. The moment Curly saw her, his ruddy complexion turned a sickly gray, and he probably knew all the lies were about to be revealed.

They followed Curly into San Marcos, and Carson warned him if he tried to get away the highway patrol would pick him up in minutes. Carson and Levi marched him into the D.A.'s office. Levi had called ahead to tell Ms. Stanton they were on their way.

The D.A. was in court, so they had to wait. The room was very quiet as the four of them sat in the outer office.

Curly was restless and couldn't seem to sit still. Finally he looked directly at her. His thinning curly blondish-gray hair hung around his shoulders. His skin was like wrinkled leather from too many cigarettes. A snake tattoo ran up his arm to his neck. He was scary, but Jena's eyes never wavered from his.

"I never meant to hurt you," he said, his voice barely audible.

"But you did," she replied.

Before anything else was said, Riva and her entourage came in. They shook hands. "I think it best if you stay out here," she said to Carson and Jena. "He'll say more without you in the room."

Carson nodded, and Levi, an assistant D.A. and Curly followed Riva into her office.

"You okay?" Carson asked.

"Yes, but I wanted to smash his face in, and I'm not a violent person. Looking at him made me feel like that weak teenage girl who had no way to help herself."

Carson glanced at his watch. "This is going to take a while." He took her hand. "There's a sandwich shop not far from here. Let's get a bite and you can relax."

"I don't need you to protect me. I can handle this." For some reason she wanted him to know she wasn't that weak teenager anymore.

"I know, but I'm hungry."

They walked to the shop. The June day was beautiful with bright sunshine and a clear blue sky. A slight breeze stirred her hair, and birds chirped in the trees. Peaceful. The feeling stayed with her as they ate a sandwich with iced tea. They didn't talk much. That was one of the things she loved about Carson. They didn't need a lot of words. They seemed to understand each other.

They ordered a roast-beef sandwich and iced tea to go for Levi. It had been over an hour and the meeting was still going on. Just as they took their seats, the door opened and Levi came out. A deputy entered and escorted Curly out. Curly glanced at her before he went through the door.

"How did it go?" Carson asked.

"The lady herself will tell you," Levi whispered.

Riva came out as if on cue. "Sorry that took so long, but I wanted to get every detail I could." She took a breath. "He was with Roland Stubbs the day he shot your brother, Mr. Corbett. You were right."

Carson paused before he answered, and she knew the

news was hard for him to hear, even though he'd been expecting it. "What else did he say?"

"He said Roland told him they had to get rid of Jared. He was going to ruin everything. They found Lamar Brooks's truck in a ditch on a county road. He was passed out drunk. Roland stole his shotgun and used it to kill Jared. I asked if Roland also shot Lamar, and he said he wasn't with him if he did and Roland never told him anything about it. We were lucky. We got a man with a conscience and a soul he's trying to save. He found God in prison."

The D.A. turned to Jena. "He seems genuinely contrite for what happened to you, and he gave us an account of everything that happened in the basement of the Corbett home. I emphasized how important it was for him to tell us what happened to the baby, but he said he didn't know, and I'm inclined to believe him."

"Thank you," Jena said.

"He did say, though, that after leaving you with your mother he went to the bunkhouse, threw up and went to bed. Roland apparently went to the house to see Mr. Corbett."

"So Roland might know?"

"Yes. I'm in contact with the warden in Livingston, where Stubbs is housed. As soon as I get an appointment, I'll let you know. I plan to speak to Mr. Stubbs myself."

"Thank you so much." There was hope and that was all Jena could see.

"Mr. Corbett, I'm sorry, but I will be issuing a warrant for your father's arrest. What he did was wrong and criminal, and I can't ignore that. I will honor your request, though, and notify you before that happens."

Carson cleared his throat. "Thank you."

Jena had spent many nights dreaming of revenge. She'd wanted Asa to pay in the worst way. But one look at the expression on Carson's face told her revenge wasn't so sweet. An unexpected pain shot through her. Why did love have to hurt like this?

CHAPTER SIXTEEN

THE RIDE HOME was made in almost complete silence. Even Levi was quiet. There was nothing left to say. Carson's theory about Roland killing Jared was confirmed, but the situation with his father was eating at him. The last thing he said to her was, "I'll call when I hear from the D.A."

They'd just hit a big roadblock and neither knew how to approach it—go around or over it. She'd returned to Willow Creek with one goal: to find her baby. Now it was about so much more. She'd let her heart get involved.

Jena shook the thoughts from her mind and drove home. Hilary was in the kitchen washing the ice-cream maker. A wad of money was on the table.

"Hey, you're back. I'm just finishing up for the day." Hilary set the ice-cream maker on a dish towel to dry. "How did it go?"

Jena told her what had happened.

"So it's true. Roland killed Jared and framed Dad. I'm not sure anyone's going to believe that."

"They will. The story will probably be all over Willow Creek in a week, especially if Roland confesses from jail."

"But you still don't have a clue what happened to the baby?"

"No. But I'm hoping the district attorney can get that information out of Roland."

Hil hugged her. "Keeping my fingers crossed, sis."

"Thanks." Out of the corner of her eye Jena saw paint cans stacked in the utility room. "What's with the cans?"

"Oh. Billy Jack called and said that Lowe's was getting rid of some colors they don't carry anymore. Five dollars a gallon, so I bought enough to paint the inside of the house. I got cranberry-red to paint one wall here in the kitchen. Going to repaint the cabinets white and add red knobs. It'll be so cool."

"I thought we were budgeting our money."

"Come on, sis. We need to freshen up our home. It will help me fight depression when I have to go door to door selling cookies."

It was hard to be upset with Hilary when she was so cheerful about their situation. "How are we going to paint without disturbing Mama?"

"At night, dear sis. In the morning Mama won't know the difference. But I don't plan to do anything to her room. It might be too much."

That night she called Blake and told him the news.

"I guess you didn't need me after all." His voice sounded hurt.

"It's not over yet."

"But you're doing fine on your own. I hope you find your child, Jena. You deserve that."

"Thank you." Blake was complacent, agreeable, and that wasn't like him. "I'm not sure how much longer I'll be here."

"Tianna has taken over your job until you return" was his startling answer.

"Do I still *have* a job?"

"Of course, but after our last talk I've decided to give you your space and stop pressuring you."

She was speechless. "I don't know what to say."

"Just do what you have to do and we'll talk when you return."

"Thank you, Blake." Clicking off, she was glad he was finally getting the message. There was no future for them. And it was a relief to know in spite of that, her job was secure.

Over the next two days she helped Hilary with the house and her cooking adventures. After the paint job and new knobs, the kitchen looked so different, they both agreed they needed new linoleum. So it was another trip to the store. They bought the same linoleum Hil had in the utility room, a white block pattern, and Bruce installed it for a chocolate pie. The price was unbeatable.

The work in the house didn't seem to faze their mother. At times she would say how nice everything looked. Other times she was unaware of what was going on around her. Every day she seemed to sink further and further into herself.

One of Hil's friends came and towed the junk car in the yard away. He gave them a hundred dollars for it, and she and Hil were both pleased. It helped to pay for supplies.

Jena checked her phone so many times she lost track. Carson hadn't called. She knew he had a monumental task ahead of him, but if he didn't call by Friday she would get in touch with him.

But on Friday he called first thing in the morning and came straight to the point. "I heard from Ms. Stanton. She's meeting with Roland at ten this morning at the prison."

"Thank you for letting me know. How long will this take?"

"Depends how it goes. She said she would call as soon as it was over, and then I'll call you."

"I'll wait to hear from you."

And that was the extent of their conversation. Not friendly, as they had been before. They were now on opposite sides, as it should have been from the start. Somehow they'd gotten sidetracked.

The morning seemed to drag. She glanced at the clock constantly. This could be it. Today she might know what had happened to her child. By eleven she could stand it no more. She grabbed her purse and headed for Carson's office. She didn't know if he was even there, but she couldn't sit at home any longer.

As she stopped in front of the building, it reminded her of the day she'd first come here with revenge in her heart. She'd found it wasn't what she'd wanted at all. She had to admit, though, that her emotions were pretty helter-skelter. But she knew she wanted love in her life with a man she could trust. And that man had the face of Carson Corbett. God help her.

CARSON DRUMMED HIS fingers on the desk in frustration. How much longer was it going to take?

Suddenly, the door opened and she stood there looking gorgeous in dark sunglasses. She had a grace and fragility about her that hid enormous strength.

"Sorry, but I couldn't wait at the house any longer. Hilary's like a deranged bee buzzing around doing ten things at once. In case anyone asks, yes, she's selling food out of our home. Mostly baking. Everyone in Willow Creek must have a sweet tooth."

"I'm not worried about Hilary, but if Bea or Mabel

call I'll have to pay her a visit. Tell her to contact the health department. In this rural area, a license shouldn't be too hard to get."

"I will." She removed her glasses and took a seat. "I guess you haven't heard anything."

"No. I'm waiting."

She cleared her throat. "Have you talked to your father?"

"No. I'm waiting for all the facts."

"I…I…"

"It's not your fault." He wanted her to know that and he wanted to take that sad look from her face. "It's a difficult situation, but I don't blame you or…"

His cell buzzed, interrupting him. He glanced at the caller ID. "It's Ms. Stanton." He clicked on and noticed the concern in Jena's eyes. "Ms. Stanton, Jena is here. Do you mind if I put you on speakerphone?"

"No. Not at all."

Jena moved closer and sat on the desk near him.

"I just finished my meeting with Mr. Stubbs, and I must say it went better than I expected. He denied everything at first, saying I couldn't prove a thing. I showed him pages from the journal and Mr. Sanders's testimony. He knew the jig was up, but he still had that you'll-never-convict-me attitude. I informed him he would be arrested for the murder of Jared Corbett and that I was going for the death penalty. That got his attention. I then told him the only way to avoid that was to tell me what happened to Jena Brooks's baby. I gave him thirty minutes to think about it."

"Did he give you the information?" Carson asked, staring into Jena's bright eyes.

"Sadly, no. I'm sorry, Ms. Brooks."

Jena visibly sagged.

"When I went back in, he was willing to make a deal in exchange for information. His story was basically the same as Mr. Sanders's. After they took Ms. Brooks to her mother, they went back to the Bar C. Mr. Sanders was feeling sick and went to the bunkhouse. Mr. Stubbs walked to the house to see what Mr. Corbett wanted him to do. He knocked repeatedly, but no one came to the door. He drove to the Rusty Spur and got drunk. The next day Mr. Corbett told him to burn the bedding and towels from the basement, which he did. There was no mention of the baby and he never asked Mr. Corbett."

"And you believe him?" Carson asked.

"Yes, but I told him if I found any holes in his story, the death penalty would be back on the table."

Jena's face paled and his heart broke for her.

"Ms. Brooks, rest assured this isn't over. I will look into Asa Corbett's involvement."

"Thank you," Jena replied, her voice hoarse.

Carson clicked off and Jena buried her face in her hands. "Roland doesn't know. Asa's the only one who knows what happened to my baby. And he…"

Carson took her into his arms and stroked her hair. "I'll talk to him tonight and tell him everything that's been discovered. Don't give up."

She leaned back and brushed a tear away. "I'll never do that."

Their eyes met and he tucked her hair behind her ears. "When I'm with you, I can't think of anyone but you. I look into your eyes and I see forever. With everything between us, I don't know why that is."

"Me, neither."

"We're wrong for each other."

"Yes."

"Then why does this feel right." He kissed a tear

from her cheek and then gently took her mouth. She moaned and wrapped her arms around his neck as heated emotions took over. Somewhere between paradise and heaven his cell buzzed. Reluctantly, he tore his lips away. "Give me a minute."

He grabbed his phone. "Yes, Mrs. Wesley. I'll be right there." He glanced into her dark eyes, darker now because of the passion they'd shared. "There's a vehicle parked on her road she doesn't recognize. I have to check it out. It won't take long." He reached for his hat. "Wait for me."

Going out the door, he had no idea what he was doing. He only knew he couldn't stop himself from touching her, kissing her.

JENA STOOD IN an aura of warmth. Carson always made her feel that way. She wrapped her arms around her waist. Ms. Stanton's words chilled the warmth to sub-zero. And, like always, the old doubts and fears returned.

Asa was never going to give up his secret. The old man had won. That tore at her like a splinter buried deep into her soul. She would not go down without having her say.

After parking her car on the circular drive of the Bar C, she marched to the front door and rang the bell. It opened quickly.

"Ms. Fran, I'd like to speak to Asa."

The woman's eyes grew wide. "Oh, dear, I don't think that's wise."

"Are the kids here?"

"No."

"Well, then, I think it's very wise." She pushed past her into a large foyer. A dining room was to the right, and she could see a kitchen beyond that. She walked straight ahead into a large den with Ms. Fran right behind her. Asa sat in an electric wheelchair in front of a TV.

"Hello, Asa," she said as she walked closer.

His dull green eyes stared at her. His hands shook on the arms of the chair. The strong, robust man she'd once known was gone; an old, frail man had taken his place. Some of her anger vanished, but her determination hadn't.

He continued to stare at her and she realized he didn't know who she was. That was the last nail driven into her heart. How could he not remember?

"I'm Jena Brooks."

His pale face flushed with anger. "Get…out."

"You would like that, wouldn't you? But I'm not going anywhere until you tell me what happened to my child."

"Bit-ch."

"Bastard," she replied with just as much venom. "You had me kidnapped and forcefully took my child. No woman should have to live through such horror. I was just an innocent teenager. What kind of monster would do that?"

"Go…a-way."

"What did you do with my child?"

"Get…out."

"Where's my child?"

He looked her straight in the eye. "Never…tell."

In that moment she knew that neither arrest, jail nor facing death would ever change his mind. He'd won and there was nothing she could do. But she would have her say.

"Jared and I were the best of friends. We were just

two kids who at times hated our fathers. Yeah." She nodded. "Strange, isn't it? You, with your manipulative and cruel ways, drew us closer together. You've called me a tramp, white trash and many other derogatory names. None of them were true. They were lies fed to you by Roland. Jared and I slept together one time, and I was a virgin. We didn't mean for it to happen, and we both regretted it. When I found out I was pregnant, Jared decided we would get married and give the baby more love than we ever received in our lives from our fathers." She stopped short of telling Asa everything. She'd leave that up to Carson.

"If you feel revenge makes up for your failings as a father, then keep your secret. If you feel that I earned your hatred by being there for your son when you weren't, then by all means take your secret to the grave. Remember all the times you beat Jared with your belt? Your behavior now is just one more lash on his body. But also know that one day you'll have to face Jared and tell him what you did to me and to his child. Are you prepared for that? That day of reckoning is coming, Asa, and you'd better be ready to explain to Jared why you took his child from its mother. All I feel for you is sympathy. You never knew the wonderful son you had or the loving person he was inside. That's your loss. May God have mercy on your evil soul." She turned on her heel and walked out, feeling drained of every emotion she had.

She met Carson in the driveway. "Jena, why did you come here?"

"I had to." Her hands trembled and she clenched them into fists. "I had to face him. He's never going to tell what happened that night and I can't live in this limbo of hate. I'm leaving. I have to go to save my sanity."

"Wait." He caught her arm. "Please, don't go. Give me a chance to try and open his heart."

"There's nothing that will accomplish that. He doesn't have a heart."

"Please."

She sagged at the entreaty in his voice. "Carson."

He stroked her arms. "Give me some time. At least tonight."

His touch was her undoing. "Okay. I don't know how you do that. My mind is all set and you change it so easily."

"We started this together and we have to finish it together."

She grimaced. "It's not so easy."

"I know." He kissed her cheek. "I'll call later."

She drove away and found the angst in her chest wasn't so strong. She'd faced the monster and survived. Maybe all wasn't lost. Maybe a tiny glimmer of remorse lingered in the organ Asa called a heart. He was Carson's father, so there had to be some good in him. If only it hadn't been destroyed by hatred.

CARSON STROLLED INTO the den. His father was sipping a glass of water Aunt Fran was holding. Asa turned the chair to face Carson.

"Kids…with you?"

"No, Pa, I told you they went with Ethan and his family to a Texas Rangers' game. They won't be home until tomorrow."

"Why'd you…do that? They…need to be here."

"We had this conversation this morning. It's summer and they want to have fun."

"Non-sense. They need…to be here. Help me…in bed, Frannie. No reason to live…without the kids."

"Just a minute, Pa. Jena Brooks was just here. What did she want?"

"Nothing," Asa spat.

"That's not true, Asa." Aunt Fran spoke up. "You've hurt that young girl. Couldn't you see it on her face and hear it in her voice? Tell her what happened to her baby. She deserves to know."

Asa's face turned red. "Don't tell me…what to do, Frannie. Ever."

Aunt Fran ran to the kitchen.

"Well, Pa, you just pissed off the last person on your side. Not a wise move."

"Going to…bed." Asa pushed the joystick and buzzed into his room. Carson followed because he knew his father needed help. That blood tie was hard to shake.

Asa stopped the scooter by his bed. Without a word, Carson placed the walker in front of him. Asa shuffled, turned and sat on the bed. Carson lifted his legs into the bed and covered him with a sheet. The bed was adjustable, so Carson handed him the control and also the TV remote.

Asa didn't turn on the TV, so Carson thought it would be a good time for a talk. "Pa, did you know that Jared wrote in a journal about his life?"

"Sissy stuff" was the quick retort. "Told him…he had to learn…to be a man."

"Yeah, Jared and I were both familiar with your outlook on life, especially the belt part."

"Where's the kids?" he shouted.

"Stop asking that," Carson shouted back. "I'm not answering it again. We're talking about Jared and Jena."

His father glared at him. "Don't let them go…anywhere again."

Carson was taken aback at his father's controlling tone. "They're my kids and I make all decisions concerning them. Got it?"

"Stupid."

Carson gritted his teeth. "What did Jena want?"

"She's making a fool…of you."

Carson threw up his hands and walked out, his blood pressure about to explode through the top of his head. Asa was insane—that was the only explanation.

Aunt Fran was in the kitchen slamming cabinet doors and rattling dishes. He caught her in a big hug. "Hey, calm down."

"I'm just mad I was so blind. Jena was sad and strong. I could see she wanted to cry, but she wouldn't in front of Asa. She told him a thing or two, though. I can't believe my brother is that cruel."

"Yeah, and it doesn't seem as if we can change his mind, either." He opened the wine cabinet. "We need something strong."

"Oh, Carson."

"A glass of wine, Aunt Fran, will be good for our spirits."

Carson opened a merlot and poured two glasses. "Oh, yeah, this is what we need." He sipped the wine.

"Not bad." Aunt Fran sat at the table and he joined her.

"I don't understand why Pa's so fixated on the kids being away."

"If you remember, he wouldn't let you or Jared go anywhere when you were little. I think he was afraid you wouldn't come back like your mother."

"I'd forgotten that." He swirled the wine in his glass.

"Talking about my mother was taboo around here, so I never asked about her." He stared into the rich burgundy liquid. "Why did my mother leave two little boys who needed her? I never understood how she could do that."

Aunt Fran took a big swallow. "My husband didn't live long after we married, and I was lonely and came here often to see my nephews. Asa was very controlling of Caroline. He wouldn't let her go anywhere without him. There were a lot of parties here, and if a man looked at Caroline, Asa accused her of flirting and even cheating. I spent the night one time, and I could hear loud voices coming from their room. Caroline had bruises on her arm the next morning. I told Asa later he needed to cool his temper, and you can imagine how well that went over. I guess Caroline couldn't take it anymore."

"How could she leave us, her babies, behind?"

"She didn't voluntarily."

"What do you mean?"

Aunt Fran took another swallow. "I shouldn't be telling you all this. It's over and done."

"But it's not. Asa is still hurting people. What happened?"

"According to Asa, he came home one afternoon and Caroline had the car packed with you and Jared inside ready to leave. He had the ranch hands remove y'all from the car and take y'all into the house. He told her she was free to go, but she would never take his boys. If she attempted it again, he would…"

"What?"

Aunt Fran took a long time inspecting the wine stem. "He would kill both of you."

"He would kill his own sons?" Carson was aghast,

but he was getting the full spectrum of his father's vindictiveness.

"I don't think he meant it," Aunt Fran was quick to add. "It was his sadistic way to get her back. Could we talk about something else? This is too depressing on top of everything else."

But Carson couldn't stop. "So she let Asa have us?"

Aunt Fran nodded. "She was scared of Asa and what he would do to her babies. A month later, she had a nervous breakdown. Her health continued to deteriorate, and her father was taking her to a clinic in Philadelphia when the plane crashed."

"My grandfather died, too?"

"Yes."

"I don't remember that."

"You were too little." She took another swallow of wine. "My brother is one disturbed man, and Jared's death pushed him over the edge."

"Why haven't you told me any of this before now?"

"Asa let me take care of you on the condition that I never mention your mother to you."

"That sorry..." Carson stood and let the anguish and despair sweep through him. He'd figured as much about his mother and Asa, but it was much more difficult to hear it as fact. He sucked in a deep breath and thought it was as good a time as any to tell his aunt the whole story.

"So it's true Roland killed Jared?"

"Yes, the D.A. will present her findings to a grand jury, and once she gets a criminal indictment, arrests will be made, Pa included."

"Asa made it easy for Roland to get away with murder. I don't know how your father is going to take this."

"I was going to tell him tonight, but I could see he's

in no mood to listen. I will tell him in the morning, though. I'm in a mood to tell him a lot of things."

Aunt Fran took a gulp of wine. "We may need a lot of this tomorrow." She got to her feet. "I better check on Asa, though I'd just as soon slap him."

Carson nodded. "I'm going out for a while."

"Okay."

Carson pulled another bottle of wine out of the cabinet. Now if he could talk a pretty lady into sharing it with him, it might ease some of the pain inside him.

"You went to see Asa?" Hilary was astounded.

"I had to face him," Jena replied. "But it didn't do any good. He's a pathetic old man without a heart."

"I don't want to upset you, but for him to remain silent he must have done something horrible and doesn't want the world to know what a monster he really is."

"I've already thought of that. He probably smothered my baby before it could take a good breath." A pain ripped through her, and she had to stop for a moment. "After seeing Asa, I'd made up my mind to leave, but Carson talked me into staying until he had a chance to talk to Asa."

"You can't go," Hil declared, sinking into a kitchen chair and pouting as if she was six years old. "We're still working on the house, and I don't have a job, and you were supposed to go with me to take Mama to the doctor. Now you're just going to leave us again?"

Guilt scraped across her heart. She hugged her sister. "Hil, I have a job in Dallas, and I will eventually go back there. Maybe you and Mama can come with me. I'll get you a job in the law firm."

"In Mama's state of mind, she couldn't handle the move, and I'd feel out of place. I'm not a big-city girl."

Hil wiped away an errant tear. "It was nice to have you home." She swatted at another tear. "I'm being a big baby."

"But I love you anyway, and I'll make sure you and Mama are taken care of. Besides—" she waved at the poster board Hil had on the wall "—look at all the work you have to do tomorrow." On the board Hil had listed pies, cakes and cookies she had to make and for whom. "I'm sure Mabel will be asking you to come back, but in my opinion not unless she's willing to pay you at least twenty bucks an hour."

Hil frowned. "Are you insane? Mabel will never pay me that."

"Learn to negotiate, li'l sis. They can't run that café without you."

Jena's cell buzzed and she went to get her purse, which she'd left in the living room. Her mother was sitting quietly in her chair, watching TV, but Jena wondered if she was really seeing it. Grabbing the phone, she went into the bedroom and clicked it on. It was Carson.

"Are you okay?"

"Yes."

"Are you sure?"

"No, but I'm bracing myself to accept the inevitable."

"Are you busy?"

"Not really. Why?"

"I just had an exhausting talk with my dad and an enlightening one with my aunt. I need a sympathetic ear."

Jena's heart raced. "Did he…?"

"No, that's why I'm restless. I'll be at the picnic spot where we took the kids. I'll leave the gate open if you want to join me."

"Where are the kids?"

"They're with Ethan's family at a Rangers' baseball game. They won't be back until tomorrow. It's just me."

"I don't know. Hil's stressed-out and…"

"I'll be here if you want to spend some time together."

"I'll think about it." As she clicked off she knew this was a big decision. Time together meant sex and the start of a different kind of relationship. With all their complications, she wasn't sure she was ready for that. But in other ways she was more ready than she'd ever been in her life.

The invitation was as tempting as one of her mother's buttermilk biscuits. There was no resisting or quibbling. She wanted it and she had to admit she felt the same way about Carson. She wanted him. Not just for one night but forever. So she must be insane, as Hilary had suggested. Was she willing to settle for one night?

She slipped the phone into her purse and went into the living room. Hil was flipping channels for their mother. Someone knocked at the door and Jena answered it. It was the young girl from the café. Sally or something.

"Hi," the girl said. "Is Hilary here?"

"Hey, Sal, come on in!" Hil shouted.

The two sat at the kitchen table, their heads close together, gossiping. Jena's mind was on one thing, and before she could stop herself, she called, "I'm going out for a while."

"Okay," Hilary answered, but Jena knew her concentration was on Sally and the café.

Jena didn't analyze what she was doing. It wouldn't have helped. The gate was open just like he'd said. She followed the road until her headlights found his truck parked near the creek. He was sitting on a quilt, enjoying the beautiful starlit evening.

Crickets serenaded her as she walked over and sat facing him.

"You came," he said, his voice sounding husky in the silky night.

"Mmm." She pulled up her knees. "What happened with your dad?" Her rattled nerves magnified her senses.

"I tried to talk to him, but it didn't work. He's so damn stubborn, even Aunt Fran is upset with him. He wouldn't say a thing about your visit. He kept changing the subject, and I just got frustrated." He lifted a wine bottle she hadn't noticed in the dark. "How about a drink?" He poured wine into two Solo cups and handed her one.

She stared into her cup, swirling the wine. "I don't drink. When we have parties at the law firm, I just sip it."

"Why?"

"Since my dad was an alcoholic, I was afraid to drink in case I couldn't stop."

"One glass is not going to make you an alcoholic. Trust me, but if it makes you uncomfortable, don't."

She sipped the rich-tasting wine and relaxed.

"I'm so sorry for what my father has done to you. I can't say that enough." And then he went on to tell her about his mother, and she could hear the hurt in his voice.

"I'm so sorry."

"Let's not talk about it and enjoy the beautiful evening."

After a bit more wine her head became fuzzy and her body warm.

"Are you still planning on leaving?" he asked.

"Yes. I have a good job in Dallas."

"Have you thought of staying?"

The crickets seemed to stop chirping; the breeze stilled as the wine mingled with the thoughts in her head, urging her to ignore everything but him. "I can't. There's too much heartache here. I could never live in Willow Creek again, but I have found something wonderful here—you."

"We seem to have a connection."

"Oh." The night swayed, and she handed him the empty cup. "I feel woozy." She lay back on the quilt. "Look at the moonlit sky. It's gorgeous."

He lay beside her. "Just the two of us in this vast universe."

"It feels like it," she breathed, very aware of his strong, lean body next to her.

He propped up on one elbow and looked down at her. "Every time I see you, I want to touch you."

Against every sane thought in her head, she took his hand and brought it to her face. "Touch me."

He stroked the warmth of her cheek. "I didn't invite you here to…"

She kissed his fingers one by one.

A longing sigh escaped him. "Maybe I did." He pulled her on top of him and took her lips in raw hungry need. He tasted of wine, warmth and sex, if that had a taste. It was more of a sinful sensation that obliterated everything but the need to be satisfied.

"Jena," he whispered between drugging kisses. "I want this to be more than a…"

"Shh." Her hand unbuttoned his shirt and caressed his bared chest. As she stroked his firm skin, she knew there was no turning back.

He groaned. "Jena, are you sure?"

She leaned back and whipped her top over her head. "I'm not sure about anything but the way I feel about you."

"Me, neither."

"We don't know what tomorrow's going to bring, but tonight I'd just like to forget and go with everything I'm feeling. And then I might have the strength to face tomorrow."

He unsnapped her bra, and then they were in a frenzy of helping each other remove their clothes. She giggled and felt young as she tugged on his boots. Then they were skin on skin, heart on heart, and their lips were locked in a sensual feast of discovery.

Her curves fitted perfectly into the hard angles of his. Unashamedly, she tempted and teased his body with her fingertips until she knew every part of him. In turn, he worshiped her body with his lips and hands until her breasts were hard and her body moist for him.

Everything seemed natural and right, and when he rolled her onto her back she was eager to experience something she never had: sex with a man she loved. As he entered her, the pain she thought would happen didn't. He was gentle and easy, coaxing every nuance of response from her. It was a coupling of two hearts and two souls who needed each other. The rocking tempo sent them soaring to the heavens. At least it felt that way to her as her body shuddered in delightful spasms.

Carson soon moaned his release into her heated neck, and they lay that way a long time. Eventually he cradled her in his arms, and they lay in the glow of the moon, satisfied, content for now. In this cocoon of darkness they were happy. The real world waited in the light of day. But they were both prepared for whatever came next.

CHAPTER SEVENTEEN

CARSON WOKE UP feeling young and happy. He hadn't felt that way in a very long time. Last night had exceeded his wildest imagination. Jena had been shy and tentative at first, but once she loosened up he couldn't have asked for a better lover. This morning he had no regrets. He just wanted to see her, hold her, touch her and just be with her. He had all the symptoms of a man in love.

He stopped on the way to the shower. He hadn't said the words last night, but neither had she. Under the circumstances, maybe it was best if they didn't. But he couldn't make himself believe that. He needed to say them. He quickly showered and dressed and ran downstairs. The house seemed so quiet without the kids.

"Aunt Fran," he called, walking into the kitchen. "Is Pa up?"

"No." She handed him a cup of coffee. "He was going on and on about the kids last night, so I gave him a sleeping pill to calm him down. He won't be up for a while."

"I needed to talk to him this morning."

"I'm sorry. There's just so much I can deal with."

"Don't worry. I'll talk to him later. He probably won't be in a receptive mood until the kids are home."

"What time are they coming?"

"I talked to Ethan last night and he said around one."

He placed his cup on the table. "I have something I need to do this morning."

"Don't you want some breakfast?"

"No, thanks."

This would give him time to see Jena. He wanted her to know last night wasn't a one-night stand for him. As he drove toward Willow Creek, he tried to picture Beth's face, but he saw only Jena's.

He still loved Beth, but in a different way. She was his past; Jena was his future. Through all the roadblocks and complications he believed there was a future for them. They just had to fight for it.

A little after eight he drove into Jena's driveway. A light was on, so he knew someone was up. The yellow house with the mowed yard and flowers didn't look like the Brookses' house. This was a difference Jena had made.

He could hear voices through the screen door.

"It won't take long," Hilary was saying. "While Mama's sheets are washing let's flip her mattress. That indentation has to be uncomfortable."

"Okay," Jena replied. "We'll stand it up and then turn it."

He knocked on the door, figuring he could help them. Jena came running in shorts, barefoot. His heart leaped in excitement at the sight of her fresh, shining face.

Unlatching the door, she smiled. "Good morning."

"Mornin'." He stole a quick kiss and then another. "I had to see you."

"I miss you," she whispered, and all he wanted to do was take her here on the front porch in broad daylight.

He held up his hands. "It's hard not to touch."

She took his hand. "I'll put those to good use. We need some muscle to flip a mattress."

Mrs. Brooks sat in a chair in the living room, and she looked at him blankly. "What's he doing here?"

"It's okay, Mama," Jena told her. "Everything's fine."

Carson hadn't seen Jena's mother in years. She rarely got out. She'd aged. He wondered if she was even fifty, but she looked eighty. That night nine years ago had affected so many people.

"I brought reinforcements," Jena told Hilary.

"Ah, muscle. That's what we need."

"I'll stand it up and then flip it," he said.

"So easy," Jena teased.

He grabbed the mattress and set it on the floor. A tense silence followed as they stared at the object on the box springs.

"What…what's that doing there?" Hilary choked out.

Carson leaned the mattress against the dresser. "Don't touch it," he said and squatted to get a closer look. "It's a single-barrel shotgun. A very old one."

"How did it get there?" Jena asked, her eyes wide with shock.

"I put it there," Mrs. Brooks said from the doorway.

Hilary ran to her mother. "Mama, don't say things like that."

"It's true."

"No, it isn't," Hilary insisted. "You don't know what you're saying."

Carson got to his feet. "Mrs. Brooks, did you put the shotgun here?"

"Yes." She nodded. "Right after I shot Lamar."

"Mama, don't say that." Hilary took her arm to lead her out of the room, but Mrs. Brooks wouldn't move.

"The sheriff came and told me Lamar had killed Jared Corbett and asked where Lamar was. I told him I didn't know, but I knew one thing—Lamar had hurt my girls for the last time. I stood by for years and watched him beat them because I was weak. Weak!" she yelled in a deranged voice. Jena hurried to her, but Mrs. Brooks pushed her away. "After my girls went to bed, I got my Mama's shotgun out of the closet and put a shell in it just like she taught me. Then I waited on the back stoop for Lamar. When he got out of his truck early that morning, I stood and fired. I went back into the house and put the gun under the mattress. You girls never woke up. Later, I called the sheriff and said someone had shot my husband." She turned and went back to her chair in the living room. Hilary followed her.

His eyes met Jena's, and all her hurt and pain was vivid. "Please don't arrest my mother," she begged. "She talks out of her head."

"It's the last piece of the puzzle and it fits."

"Carson, no, please."

He took her in his arms. "I'm not going to arrest her. I don't know what good that would do."

"Jena!" Hilary screamed.

They ran into the living room.

"She's not responding," Hilary wailed. "Something's wrong."

Carson reached for a pulse in her neck. "It's very weak. I'm calling for an ambulance."

Hilary stayed with Mrs. Brooks while Jena grabbed shoes for her and Hilary and her purse. Carson hurriedly put the mattress back on the bed so the paramedics wouldn't see the gun. As he did that, he knew he was committing a crime. But he'd decided the Brooks family had suffered enough.

The ambulance arrived, and the paramedics quickly checked Mrs. Brooks and then loaded her into the ambulance. Hilary and Jena went with her.

Jena glanced back, her dark eyes sad. "Carson."

"Don't worry. I'll take care of everything."

The ambulance roared away. Carson went to his car for plastic gloves, and then he locked the front door of the house. He found a hammer and a screwdriver in the utility room along with a trash bag. Retrieving the gun from the mattress, he began to take it apart. Screws that were stubborn he broke loose with the hammer. Soon he had it in pieces in the bag.

He took the bag to his car and drove to the Bar C. Stopping at the barn, he got out a shovel. With that in hand, he threw the shovel and bag in the back of his Polaris Ranger ATV. He drove to a brushy, wooded area far from the house and dug two deep holes and dumped parts of the gun into each.

As a constable, he was sworn to uphold the law, but today he'd broken it for the woman he loved. He would do anything to protect her.

JENA AND HILARY SAT, hands clasped together, in the waiting area of an Austin hospital.

"She's going to be okay?" Hilary said more to herself than to Jena. It was like a mantra she seemed to need to keep repeating. Hilary's hand gripped hers. "Do... do you think she really did it?"

Bile rose up in Jena's throat, and it took her a moment to speak. "Yes. It's the reason for her mental decline. She couldn't deal with what she'd done."

"I wish I had just let the damn bed alone," Hil muttered.

"We would have found it eventually."

"But Carson wouldn't have been there. Is he going to arrest her?"

"No," she replied with confidence. She trusted Carson not to hurt her family, and, like he'd said, it would serve no purpose other than to create more gossip.

"I can't believe it." Hilary glanced at a nurse who came in to talk to another waiting family. "Mama's so gentle. She never tried to defend herself against the abuse. She just took it."

"She snapped when she heard about Jared's murder. In her mind she had to do the only thing that would protect us—something she hadn't done before—confront her husband."

"I guess." Hil moved restlessly. "I just want to take her home."

"Brooks family," an E.R. doctor in scrubs called. Jena and Hilary got to their feet, and he walked over.

"Dr. Henderson," he introduced himself, and they shook hands. "Your mother is still not responding. Her blood pressure is low, and her heart rate is dangerously low, too. We have her on an IV and are running tests, but so far nothing is jumping out at us. Did something happen to trigger this?"

"No," Jena replied. "She was sitting in her chair, and my sister couldn't get a response out of her." No way was she telling him otherwise.

"We've ruled out a stroke and a heart attack, and we're waiting on other test results. In the meantime, we're taking her up to a room to monitor her for a few days. She might snap out of it, but please be prepared. I've seen this in nursing homes. Sometimes people just give up."

"Thank you," Jena replied, fearing what he said was true. Her mother had finally admitted what she'd done and now she'd given up.

They got the room number from the nurse, and then they took the elevator. Two nurses were getting their mother settled into a bed when they arrived. An IV was in her arm and she was on a heart monitor. Her skin was pale and her hair seemed grayer. Her eyes stared blankly into space, and Jena felt a catch in her throat.

She and Hilary sat beside the bed, one on each side. Hilary rubbed their mother's arm and couldn't seem to stop talking.

"Are you cold, Mama? I can get you a blanket. Or would you like something to drink? A cup of coffee? Water? Talk to me. Mama, please."

But Norma stared straight ahead as if she couldn't hear or see. She was locked in her own private world or maybe her own private hell. Living all these years with her secret had taken its toll. Jena got up and kissed her mother's forehead. "I love you, Mama. You did what you had to do and I don't blame you."

Hilary kissed her mother's hand. "I don't, either. Please come back to us."

Still there was no response. Jena and Hilary stayed by the bed, waiting. A nurse came in and checked Norma's vitals and said nothing had changed. After a few minutes the heart monitor buzzed loudly. Nurses and doctors rushed in. Hilary began to cry and Jena held her, pulling her out of the way.

The nurse asked them to leave the room, and they waited in the hall. Hilary was crying openly now, and Jena tried to comfort her while dealing with her own emotions.

The doctor came out. "I'm sorry. We did all we could."

"No!" Hilary screamed, and it took a while for Jena to calm her.

The doctor patted Hilary's shoulder. "Your mother is at peace now."

They were allowed to say goodbye. They stared at the mother they loved, the mother who'd raised them through the bad times, and there were plenty of those. But through it all they would remember the little things that made them happy—like the caps and mittens she'd knitted for them for school and the sweaters so they would be warm in the wintertime. They would remember the mother who'd kissed them good-night every night and protected them in her own way, but most of all they would remember the love they'd felt when she hugged them. Their life wasn't perfect but today that didn't matter.

They made arrangements for the body to be taken to the Dripping Springs funeral home, and then they walked out of the hospital. It wasn't until they reached the front doors that they realized they didn't have a vehicle. Jena's phone buzzed at that precise moment.

"Hey, how is your mom?" Carson asked.

Hearing his voice, her emotions snapped and she began to cry. It took a second for her to gain control. "My mom...just passed away."

"I'll be right there."

"We're at..."

"I got the information from the ambulance driver. I'm on my way."

"We'll be at the entrance."

She and Hilary sat side by side in a waiting area, trying to come to grips with everything that had happened today. It would take time. They didn't talk much. Sadness clung to them like a trellis vine binding them in grief, the way only sisters knew. Her nerves were frayed and her insides queasy, but she had to stay strong for Hilary.

She was relieved when Carson walked in with his

long strides. She went into his arms as if she'd been doing it for years. It was that natural.

"I'm so sorry. You okay?" he asked.

"We just want to get out of here."

Soon they were in the car headed for Willow Creek. Jena told Carson what the doctor had said.

"She's finally at peace," Hilary said from the backseat.

They would cling to that thought in the days ahead.

CARSON HURT FOR JENA. He just wanted to protect her from the pain, but he knew he couldn't. She had to process her mother's death in her own way. He went with her and Hilary to plan the service. They opted for a private one, figuring the people of Willow Creek had forgotten Norma Brooks a long time ago.

A misty rain filled the morning when he picked them up for the service. Mrs. Brooks would be buried in the Willow Creek Cemetery next to her husband. Ethan, Abby and Walt, along with Levi and Mr. Henry, showed up. Before the preacher could start a short sermon, trucks and cars began to pull into the cemetery. A lot of them were Hilary's friends from the café, and the others were people of Willow Creek who remembered Norma Brooks and wanted to pay their respects. Even Mabel and Bea came. Carson was happy for the show of support for the Brooks sisters. They needed it.

When he took them home, he and Jena sat on the stoop and Hilary went inside.

"What did you do with the gun?" she asked.

"Don't worry. It will never be found."

"Thank you. It seems unreal. I still can't believe my gentle mother would do that."

"The abuse finally got to her."

"Mmm." She tucked her hair behind her ears. "I'm glad I got to spend some time with her. I took her walking one day." A tear slipped from her eye and she quickly brushed it away. "I came home to find information about my child, but that didn't happen. We found other answers, which I'm happy about. But none of that changed anything. Asa has truly won." She clasped her hands together. "I'll be leaving soon."

His stomach gave way at the thought. "What about Hilary?"

"I want her to come with me to find a life she deserves."

He rubbed his hands together. "What about me?"

She touched his face, and he caught her hand and kissed it.

"I feel more for you than I've felt for anyone in my life. I love everything about you—your sweet smile, your gorgeous eyes, your compassionate nature, your love for your kids. But you're Asa's son and that will always cause problems between us."

She was right and that wasn't easy to admit.

She stroked his face. "I'll always remember our night together, but I have to go where I'm just Jena without a past."

"What about this Blake guy?" He had to know.

"He's my boss. That's it," she replied. "Please understand I have to go."

He wanted to ask if he could come see her in Dallas, but that wouldn't solve anything. And he couldn't leave his kids for long periods of time.

He looked into her soulful eyes. "I understand, but it hurts."

"I know."

"I'm not saying goodbye."

"Okay."

He pushed to his feet. "But let me know when you leave."

"I will."

He walked away to his truck, his heart breaking. He had one thing to do before he said goodbye—talk to his father.

When he reached home, the kids were playing in the den. Trey was gently throwing the baseball he'd gotten at the Rangers' game, which several baseball players had signed. He was throwing it to Claire, who never caught it. She'd squeal and chase after it. Pa watched with a contented look on his face. He was happy; the kids were home.

There was no way he could talk to his dad with the kids around. He stormed into his study, frustrated. He had to find a way. Pulling out his cell, he called Ethan. Within minutes he'd arranged for a playdate for the next day. Walt would take Kelsey and Trey fishing and Claire would stay with Chloe. He hated to impose on his friends, but this was important.

All night he wanted to pick up the phone to call Jena and beg her not to go, beg her to stay, beg her to give them a chance. But they still had the same problem: Asa knew where her child was and he refused to tell. There was no way around that. But tomorrow morning he was telling his father everything, and if there was a God in heaven, Pa would give him the information he wanted.

The next morning the kids were excited. They packed their things and were eager to go. He dropped them at Ethan's and hurried home. Pa had had breakfast and he seemed in a good mood sitting in the den in his chair.

Carson hurried to his study to get copies from Jared's journal. As he went back into the den, he saw Aunt Fran watching from the kitchen. She was worried, but she didn't try to stop him. They both knew it had to be done.

He sat in a straight-backed chair facing his father. Asa had Trey's baseball in his hand, trying to grip his fingers around it.

"Pa, could we talk?"

"Why?"

"Because it's important."

Asa looked around. "Where…the kids?"

"At Ethan's, playing."

"But…they're coming home?"

"Yes." Carson scooted forward. "Pa, I need you to listen to me. Some things are not going to be easy to hear, but I want you to listen."

Asa frowned at him.

Carson held up the papers. "These are pages from Jared's journal."

"Sissy stuff."

Carson ignored the response and started reading the notes about Jena, and then he read the last entry—the day Jared died. "Jared went to meet Roland because he discovered he was stealing from the Bar C. Roland shot him, not Lamar."

"No," Asa said, his voice gravelly. "Not true."

"It is. Curly admitted it and so did Roland. The D.A. will present her findings to a grand jury in two weeks. She's planning to prosecute them both for murder— Jared's murder. You believed Roland, but he lied to you about everything, especially Jena."

"Roland killed…my boy?"

"Yes, Pa."

"Bastard! Bastard!" Asa banged a fist on the arm of his chair.

Carson gave him a moment. "The D.A. knows you

had them kidnap Jena and that you took her baby. She's going to prosecute you, too."

"Don't care."

"Help me, Pa. Help me to help you. Tell me what happened to Jena's baby."

Asa leaned his head back against the headrest. "I'm tired."

"Me, too, Pa. I'm tired of all the lies. For Jared, tell me what happened to his child."

"I can't" came out low, but Carson heard it. It was the first time his father had said anything besides "never." He had to keep pushing.

"Why not?"

"Hurt…too many people."

"Too many people have already been hurt. It's time to tell the truth."

Pa didn't say anything and just hung his head as if he couldn't take any more.

"Pa, tell me."

"You'll…regret it."

That threw him, and for a moment he was hesitant. "Tell me. Where's Jared and Jena's baby?"

Suddenly, Asa raised his head and flung the ball at him. He caught it before it blasted into his chest. "You want to know so bad…I'll tell you. Maybe…I can die in peace."

Carson placed the ball on an end table. "Where's the baby?"

Asa's mouth worked, but no words came out.

"Where's the baby?" he kept on.

A diabolical expression spread across his father's face. "He sleeps upstairs every night. You call him… son."

A shiver of alarm shot through Carson "That's not funny, Pa."

"No, it isn't."

He took a controlling breath. "Trey is my and Beth's son."

"Trey is Jared's and...her son. You wanted to know. There it is."

He stood because he could no longer sit still. "I was at the hospital with Beth when Trey was born. I was the first one to hold him."

"Yes, you were."

"Then how can you say he's not mine?" Carson could feel his control slipping.

"Because...he's not."

Carson gulped in air and sat again. "What happened the night you had Jena kidnapped?"

His father was calm and his speech was better. "I did everything Minnie told you. I wasn't going to let her pass that baby off as a Corbett. As soon as it came out I pushed Minnie aside and bundled it in a big towel. Minnie cut the cord, and I took it upstairs to my room. I wrapped the towel tight, hoping it would suffocate. She took my son. I'd take her child."

"She didn't take your son. You never had him." His voice was angry and he couldn't help that. "Oh." Suddenly, he remembered Jared's keys and wallet lying on his dresser. He had to have had them with him when he was murdered. Pa had returned them to his room after they were released by the authorities. The diabolical pieces of the puzzle fitted together in his head. "After the murder, you found the marriage license and the receipt for an apartment in Jared's room, didn't you? You knew Jared was leaving you and the Bar C behind, just like everyone else has left you. That's why you wanted no one in his room. That's why you hate Jena."

"Yeah." For a moment Asa looked contrite. "She filled his head with…nonsense. She made him turn his back…on his birthright."

"No, Pa. You did that all by yourself."

"She…she…"

"What happened next?" he asked, refusing to listen to any more hatred of Jena.

"When Roland and Curly left with her, I had to decide what to do with…the baby. As I was going up the stairs, I heard…Beth scream. I found her on the floor and I put her back in bed. She said something was wrong with the baby. The baby wasn't…breathing, but I told her Trey was fine. I picked him up and told her to rest…and I'd take care of him."

"Where was the nurse I hired?" Beth had to have a C-section with Trey, and she'd lost a lot of blood before they finally delivered the baby. She was so weak she could barely hold her son. He was scheduled to leave for Afghanistan in three days. It was hard to go, but he made sure his wife had round-the-clock nurses.

"I sent her home early because…"

"Yeah, I know why. What happened next?"

"I took Trey to my room and…laid him beside the other baby. I blew in his mouth and pressed gently on… his chest, but he was dead."

"No." Carson held his face in his hands. "No!"

"Beth called for me to bring the baby back, and I knew I couldn't…tell her. She couldn't take it. I unwrapped the other baby and saw it was a boy. The babies were the same size despite the fact that Beth's was two weeks old and…hers just a newborn. They even looked alike. And…I knew…it was Jared's son. I took him into the bathroom and cleaned him up and then…I put Trey's clothes on him. I wrapped him in Trey's blanket and took him back to Beth. Only the night-light was on, so she couldn't see very well."

"But she would have known the next morning. The nurse would have known."

"I fired the nurses and I took care of the baby. Beth had been so weak and slept so much in those early days, she was really only able to hold and feed it before she needed to rest again. I made sure she never…saw the umbilical cord. The new baby had no problem taking the bottle…and he filled out fast. By the time we took him to be circumcised, he was Beth's baby. She grew stronger and stronger and never suspected a thing. Nei-ther…did you."

He stood in an angry movement. "Who gave you the right to play God?"

"I did what…any father would do."

"You took a woman's baby from her."

"And saved your wife's sanity. Besides…what kind of life could Jena Brooks have given him?"

"You…you…" He couldn't even put his emotions into words. "You had no right."

"Beth was like a daughter to me. I did what I had to for her…and for you."

"Wait a minute." Carson's head pounded from all the lies. "You've known since Trey was born that he was Jared's son, yet you've continually denied that Jena's baby was Jared's. Why?"

"I didn't want anyone to get…suspicious. I had to keep up the act to protect…you and Beth. You can't let…that woman take your son."

"You're insane." Carson ran his hands over his face. Trey was Jena's baby. When Trey was born, he had sandy-blond hair like him, but as he got older Trey's hair had grown darker. Since his and Beth's families were basically blonds, they wondered where he'd gotten the dark hair. From his mother. *Jena*.

Oh, my God!

"What are you going to do?" Asa asked. "The truth… isn't so easy to swallow…is it?"

Carson stared at this man who was his father, and in that moment he hated him more than he'd hated anyone in his life. The hate seemed to boil through his system like acid eating away at his control.

"If you tell her…she will take your son from you. From us. Use your head…and forget the whole thing. It will do no one…any good now."

"She has a right to know."

"And she has rights…as a mother. Think about that."

Carson couldn't take any more. He turned toward the kitchen and swung back. "What did you do with *my* son?"

Asa looked down at his hands, and Carson noticed how haggard his father's face looked. "After Trey was fed and asleep and Beth was, too, I found a box with a lid in the garage. I layered the box with white towels…and then I wrapped him in a white satin blanket…and put him inside. At two that morning I buried him…beside Jared. I placed a big rock at the site…so I'd always know where he was."

A choked sob left Carson's throat, and he ran for the back door. Aunt Fran tried to stop him, but he had to get away. The Corbett cemetery was two miles from the house and he started walking, trying not to let his thoughts get the best of him. He felt the sun on his head and the wind against his face, but all he really felt was the pain in his heart.

When he reached the chain link fence that enclosed

the cemetery, he was winded. He opened the gate and went inside. Corbetts were one of the first families to settle Willow Creek. Most of his ancestors were buried here. He walked to his brother's grave and saw the stone Asa had talked about. Seeing it somehow made it real. His knees gave way and he sank to the ground.

Before he could stop them, tears rolled from his eyes, and he cried for a little boy whom he'd loved and would never know. How did he accept this?

Trey was his son. Trey would always be his son, but he was Jena's son, too. What could he do? He had to protect Trey...from his mother? As the thought ran through his mind he knew it was wrong. But could he risk losing his son?

CHAPTER EIGHTEEN

JENA AND HILARY spent the morning at the funeral home, setting up a payment schedule for their mother's funeral. They also picked out a headstone for both their parents. Jena would make the payments until Hilary found a job. On the way home they went to the grave site for another goodbye. Jena planned to leave the next day.

Hilary went to meet with Mabel and Bea, and Jena packed her few things. Her cell buzzed. Blake. She'd been meaning to call him.

"I'm sorry to hear about your mother."

"Blake, I'm sorry. I should have called you. It's been a very emotional time. I'll explain when I get to Dallas. I plan to leave tomorrow."

"I'm glad you're coming back. Any news about the baby?"

"No. I'll tell you about it later."

"You sound stressed." As usual, Blake couldn't let it go.

"I hate leaving my sister. I'll see you tomorrow." She quickly clicked off. The last time she'd talked to him she thought he understood she didn't have those kinds of feelings for him. Today he was all concerned again. She might have to quit her job. The thought didn't send her into a panic. She'd survive.

Her thoughts turned to packing. She'd been home only a short time, but she felt as if she'd been here forever, and it was hard to leave. It was hard to leave Carson. Their love wasn't meant to be but that didn't stop the ache in her heart.

Now she had to focus on saying goodbye without bawling her eyes out.

The front door opened and she heard singing. Hilary slid across the hardwood floor. "R.E.S.P.E.C.T." She sang an old Aretha Franklin song. "Oh, yeah, I finally got me some respect." She swung around and clapped her hands. "Oh, yeah."

"You're in a good mood."

"Wait till you hear." Hilary's face was beaming.

"What?"

"You're looking at the new manager of the café. I have free rein to do whatever I want."

"Not at minimum wage, I hope."

"Hell, no. Bea said she's tired of the stress and wants to spend more time with her grandchildren. Mabel likes coming in, sitting at the cash register and passing out candy to the kids. And she likes to visit with everyone. So I'm taking over. Asked for a monthly salary that would blow your socks off, and they gave it to me. You know what?" Hil was thoughtful for a moment. "I'm going to buy a new vehicle with Italian leather I can smell."

"Take it slow," Jena advised.

"I don't have a slow button today. I'm going to make changes to the decor. It hasn't changed in fifty years, except for my mural." Hilary's expression saddened. "I wish you could stay longer."

"I wish you'd come to Dallas with me."

Hilary frowned. "I told you, I'm not a city girl. I'd hate it, but I promise to visit in my new vehicle and wear your clothes and shoes and pretend to be a city girl."

Jena pointed a finger at her sister. "I'm holding you to that."

Later that night they sat on the floor in the bedroom staring at Hilary's mural on the ceiling.

"We'll never know what's at the end of that rainbow," Hil said. "We're not fairy-tale type girls."

"No," Jena replied.

"We're hardworking, kick-butt survivors."

"Oh, yeah."

She would never find her child or know anything about its life, but in her heart her baby was with a wonderful family who loved it, and her child would grow up to be a stellar human being surrounded by loved ones. That was her fairy tale.

The other fairy tale included a man with green eyes—but as Hil had said, they weren't fairy-tale types.

CARSON SPENT THE day with his kids. He needed to be with them, hold them and touch them. He took them to the movies in Austin and then to a park that had cool stuff, as Trey had put it. As his son played, he watched for signs of Jena in him, and he saw them constantly: the way he turned his head, the way he smiled sometimes, or sometimes when he was thinking, Carson saw Jena in his expression.

He had to tell her and he had to do it soon. He finally realized he couldn't keep that kind of secret from her. But the truth left a bitter taste in his mouth.

Claire fell asleep on the way home. Trey chatted on and on about summer, fishing, Kelsey and baseball. He was a happy little boy. He always had been—like Jared. Carson wasn't sure how to tell Trey or if he even needed to. Jena needed to know first.

When he arrived home, he got a call. He left the kids

with Aunt Fran. The call didn't take long. As he got out of his car, he heard loud wails. *Trey!* He ran into the house. Aunt Fran was trying to comfort him. His face was red and blotchy, and he sobbed uncontrollably. The moment he saw Carson he flew into his arms.

He picked him up as if he weighed no more than Claire and held him. "What's wrong, buddy?"

Aunt Fran was wringing her hands and he knew it was bad. "I'm sorry, Carson. I was upstairs with Claire and..."

Out of the corner of his eye, he saw Claire coming down the stairs. Aunt Fran ran to meet her and hurried her back up the stairs.

He sat on the sofa, cradling his son. "Calm down and talk to me."

"Grandpa...Grandpa said...I'm not your son." Sobs racked his body, and he buried his face against Carson.

That sorry son of a bitch!

"Shh. I am your father."

"He said...Jena's my mother...and she's gonna take me from you. I don't want to go, Daddy." Carson held him tighter as the sobs continued.

Fury like he'd never known before gripped him, and he wanted to hurt someone—his father. The man was a monster, as Jena had called him. He'd done this to bend Carson to his will. He had used an innocent child as a pawn to stop him from telling Jena.

He wiped tears from his son's face, and Trey looked at him with watery eyes. "It's not true, is it, Daddy?"

He'd have to tell a nine-year-old boy a story that was hard for a grown man to handle. "I love you and you're my son. Remember that."

"Okay," he muttered, scrubbing his face with both fists.

Carson told him the story as it had been told to him. Trey listened closely, getting as close to Carson as he could. "I don't want to be that boy. I want to be your boy."

"You are my boy." He kissed his forehead. "Nothing will ever change that."

"But…is she gonna try and take me? I hate her."

"Trust me. Daddy will handle it."

"I don't want her to be my mommy. I have a mommy. She's in that photo upstairs."

"I know, son."

It took two hours to calm Trey enough to get him to go to bed. Once Trey and Claire were asleep he went downstairs and stormed into his father's bedroom.

"How dare you! I thought you loved Trey."

"I do, but…you can't tell her…. Had to stop you. She'll take him. He had to be told. You don't have the guts to do it…. I had to."

"You bastard! How could you hurt him like that?"

"He has to be strong. He's a Corbett."

"Like that counts for something, huh? As of this day forward, you will have no contact with my kids."

"You can't…do that."

"Watch me, old man." He turned and swung back. "You may have broken my mother's spirit, but you will never break mine." He walked out, feeling no victory at having to talk to his father as if he was scum of the earth.

Trey woke up and Carson finally let him sleep in his bed. Claire soon joined them. "Trey sad, Daddy," she whispered in his ear. She had no idea of what was going on, but she knew her brother was hurting.

He held her in one arm, Trey in the other. He went to sleep with his kids near his heart.

THE NEXT MORNING he was up early and got the kids dressed for the day. He'd talked to Ethan and told him the whole story. Levi, too. They were his support system, and he would need them in the days ahead. They were shocked, as he'd been. He'd arranged to leave the kids at Ethan's so he could talk to Jena.

He'd also called Jena to meet him at nine in his office. He'd hung up quickly. Hearing her voice hurt too much. They would now face the final roadblock, and he had no idea what she was going to say or do. His gut instinct told him she wouldn't hurt Trey.

He'd been in Afghanistan, lost his brother, lost his wife and dealt with his father's insanity, but he'd never been as afraid as he was now. He felt he was about to lose everything he loved.

Trey balked at being left, but Carson explained he had to talk to Jena, and that seemed to do the trick. Trey was counting on Carson to make all the pain go away.

If only it were that easy.

JENA HAD A bad feeling in her stomach. Last night Carson's voice was different, sharp and defeated almost. Seeing him would be difficult, but she couldn't leave without talking to him one more time.

She parked in front of his office and went inside. He sat at his desk, looking as if he had the weight of the world on his broad shoulders. Her heart went out to him.

"Have a seat," he said in a voice that sounded like a stranger's.

"What's wrong?" she asked because she knew something was.

He leaned back in his chair, his eyes troubled. "I spoke with my father."

"And?" She held her breath.

He swallowed visibly. "He told me what happened."

"Oh." Her purse hit the floor with a thud, and she covered her mouth with both hands. "What...what did he say?"

"I don't know how to tell you this."

"Did he kill my baby?" Her whole body began to shake.

"No" was the quick answer.

"Then...then you know where my child is?"

"Yes." He ran a hand over his face and started to tell a story that curdled her insides. Tears filled his eyes, and she went around the desk and slipped onto his lap. He gripped her around the waist, and she pressed her face against his as he told her the horrible truth. "You see, once my son was dead, he switched the babies. He didn't plan it. It just happened."

"Trey is my son?" she whispered.

"Yes. Please don't take him from me."

An eerie feeling came over her, and she slipped from his lap. "You want me to walk away, don't you? I've just been given my son, and you want to take him again."

"I didn't say that. Trey is upset and confused and..."

"He knows?"

"My father told him while I was out, and I had to tell Trey the truth. He's cried so much his voice is hoarse. He's afraid you'll take him away from the family he loves."

"Do you believe that?"

"What?"

"Do you believe I would hurt him like that? Do you believe I'd hurt *you* like that?"

"I don't know. I'm barely holding it together here."

"If you loved me, you would know."

"Jena..."

Suddenly, everything came crashing down around her. The man she loved didn't trust her. She swallowed the sob in her throat. "I want to see my son."

He ran both hands through his hair. "I don't think that's wise. Right now he hates you. Are you prepared for that?"

"I've waited nine years and I'm not going to wait any longer."

"Jena, he's a little boy and he's hurting."

"I understand that. And you have to understand I'm his mother and I need to see him. I will not do anything to cause him any more pain."

Carson threw up his hands. "Okay. We'll meet you in thirty minutes at the picnic spot. He should be comfortable there."

"Fine."

His eyes caught hers. "I'm trying to protect you, too."

"But you're worried I'll fight you for custody. You're worried I'll take him from you."

"Yes. It has crossed my mind."

"Then you never knew me at all." She picked up her purse and walked to her car. Carson followed her and drove away.

She sat numb, fighting tears. She'd just been given the most wonderful gift—her son, but with that came a monumental price. She'd lost the man she loved. But she never really had him. She knew he was the one, the one who'd captured her heart, the one she'd dream about, the one she yearned to be with. And he'd believed horrible things about her.

She watched the clock in the car, each minute feeling as long as all the years she'd wondered about her baby. She was waiting for that euphoric feeling to take over, but that would only happen after she saw her baby's face.

Thirty minutes later she drove to the Bar C and followed the road to the creek. She parked behind Carson's car. He and Trey were at the water throwing rocks. She took a long breath and got out. Her legs were shaky but she walked to meet them. Carson stepped away to his car and then she was alone with her son.

"Hi, Trey."

He didn't say anything, just kept throwing rocks in the water.

"Would you look at me, please?"

He raised his head and stared at her with defiant eyes. "My daddy said I had to talk to you, but I don't want to. You're not my mother. I hate you."

His words hit her like a fist to her stomach. She gasped for breath. "But I am your mother, and I've waited nine years to see your beautiful face."

"Please don't take me from my daddy," he blurted out. "Go away and leave me alone."

She bit her lip to keep from crying out. "Is that what you really want?"

"Yes," he answered without hesitation.

All the years of dreaming came down to this. What would she give up for her child? Her rights? Her heart? Her very life? Nothing was too big for his happiness.

She managed a breath out of lungs that were locked in pain. "Okay. On one condition."

"What?"

"That you let me hug you."

He thought about it for a second. "Okay."

She wrapped her arms around her son and held him tight. He remained stiff as a board, but it didn't matter. She kissed the top of his head, and the world seemed to right itself. She'd found her son and now she had to have the strength to let him go.

Releasing him, she said, "All I ever wanted was for you to be happy and healthy and with people who love you. And you are. I wish I could be a small part of your life, but you've made it plain you don't want me to be. I would never do anything to hurt you. I've loved you from the first moment I felt you in my stomach. Goodbye, Trey."

She managed to walk to her car on trembling limbs. Carson stopped her.

"Give him time."

Her throat muscles wouldn't work. She couldn't form one syllable, and it was just as well. Words at this point would not ease her heartache. She got in her car and drove away. She had to stop before she reached the gate. Tears blinded her. Leaning her head on the steering wheel, she cried for Carson, Trey and herself. She cried for everything she'd lost. And she cried for the cruel irony of finding her son and then having to say goodbye.

With the back of her hand, she wiped away the tears. She finally knew where her son was and that would sustain her in the days, months and years ahead.

THE FOLLOWING DAYS were hard for Carson. Jena was hurting and he couldn't help her. His concentration now had to be on Trey, but Jena was never far from his mind.

Trey, who had always been independent, was now clingy and needy. He didn't want Carson out of his sight, so he took the kids with him when he went to work. It wasn't ideal, but it was all he could handle at the moment. If he got a call he considered violent, he'd drop them at Abby's.

Asa was causing a scene every day because he

couldn't see the kids, but Carson refused to give in. Whenever the back door would open, Asa would shout for Trey. Today was no exception. They were learning to ignore Asa. But then Trey surprised him.

"I'll see Grandpa, Daddy."

"Are you sure?"

"Yeah." But he wasn't going alone. He took Carson's hand and Claire took the other one as they walked into Asa's room.

"Trey, my boy." Asa patted the arm of the wheelchair where Trey often sat. "Come talk to Grandpa."

"No," Trey replied.

Asa nodded his head. "Okay. I'm sorry. I am old and sometimes…I don't think things through, but I want you to know…I love you. No matter what anyone tells you…you remember that."

"Okay."

Asa looked at Claire. "Princess, come sit on Grandpa's lap."

"No." Claire almost spat the word. "You make Trey cry." Saying that, she ran from the room and Trey followed her.

Carson looked at his father and wondered how one man could cause so much misery. "All Jared and I ever wanted from you was love. You never showed us any. Then you opened your heart to Trey and Claire and they worshiped you. Yet, without a second thought you crushed Trey's heart as if it was no more than a paper cup. You'll never be able to get that back—that grandpa love."

Asa's face creased into a haggard expression. "I… screwed up, son."

A moment of sympathy touched Carson's heart, but only briefly. He cleared his throat. "I spoke with the

D.A. She got an indictment against Roland and Curly. They will be tried for Jared's murder."

"Good. I hope they…hang 'em."

"She also got an indictment against you for kidnapping Jena and Trey."

Asa stared at him with tired green eyes that had seen too much and now would pay the price. "Am I supposed to…beg for mercy?"

"No. I just wanted you to know what's going to happen."

"Think what you want…but you have a son…because of me."

"Is that supposed to make it right?"

Asa waved a hand. "Go away. Sometimes…you make me tired."

Carson did as asked and joined his children in the den. Yes, he had a son. But at what price?

JENA SETTLED BACK into her apartment and job as if she'd never been gone. Blake bombarded her with questions and was insistent she file for partial custody. She had to remind him it was her life and she would never put that much stress on Trey or Carson.

For years she'd sidestepped Blake's advances in a number of ways, but she decided she wasn't going to do that anymore even if it cost her her job. And it did, sort of. Once she told Blake there was no future for them she was transferred to another attorney, who was in his sixties and had grandchildren. They worked well together, and she at least had some peace in the workplace.

She couldn't wait for the evenings when she could talk to Hilary. Sometimes Hil sent pictures of Trey or of Trey and Carson. She lived for those moments. They were all she had.

AUGUST WAS A month of change. Asa was arrested on two counts of kidnapping and endangering the life of a child. Because of his health, he was allowed to stay home, but the sheriff had to be notified if he left the premises. It didn't faze Asa. He actually laughed at the sheriff, knowing there was nothing much they could do to him. The trial date hadn't been set yet, but if convicted he was facing the rest of his life in an institution.

August also brought a change in Trey. Levi asked him to go fishing and they stayed all day. Trey didn't call once. Abby took them to a theme park in Austin, another all-day event, and Trey was not anxious to get back to him. Trey was becoming Trey again. And he started asking questions about his mother, which Carson saw as a good sign.

One night as they were watching TV, Trey lay on the floor, his chin in his hands. Claire lay beside him. Suddenly, Trey sat up. "Daddy, did you know that Kelsey didn't know her daddy until she was twelve years old?"

"Yeah, buddy, I knew that." Ethan had gotten a woman pregnant while he was in the service, and she'd never told Ethan until she tried to extort money from him in exchange for Kelsey.

"Kelsey said she told her daddy to go away and he wouldn't. He took Kelsey's mom to court and got full custody. Is Jena gonna do that?"

Trey was trying to make sense of everything. "Do you want her to?"

"I don't know. Kelsey says I should talk to Jena because kids are kids and they don't know anything. But I don't want to leave you, Claire and Aunt Fran."

"You don't have to, son. Even though it hurt her, she walked away and let me have you. She could have filed for custody, but she loves you too much to put you through that."

"Oh." He picked at the hem of his shorts. "Did Grandpa hurt her?"

"Yes, son, Grandpa hurt her."

He turned and lay by Claire, who was asleep, but Carson could almost see the little wheels in his head turning. He was thinking about his mother.

The next day they went into Austin to buy clothes for school and school supplies. For a treat he stopped at the café to buy one of Hilary's special sundaes for them. Carson had a plan. He wasn't sure Trey had made the connection that Hilary was his aunt. Being a smart kid, he would figure it out, and today could be a good day for that.

Trey gobbled up his sundae without any mention of Hilary, even though she'd put extra cherries on his. While Carson was paying, Trey and Claire looked through the glass of a bakery case Hilary had installed. All kind of goodies that caught a kid's eye were inside.

Two couples sat in a booth not far from it and their voices could be clearly heard.

"Ella at the convenience store said Jena Brooks was back in town last spring and she didn't have her kid with her," Nancy Foley said.

"Probably got rid of it or gave it away," Lois Bayfield responded. "I mean, how was she going to raise a kid?"

"Young girls these days think nothing of giving away their babies," Ed Foley added.

"It happens more than we think," was Clyde Bayfield's opinion.

Before Carson could stop him, Trey walked over to them. "Why are you talking about Jena?"

"Hey, Trey," Clyde said. "Didn't see you there."

"Why are you talking about Jena?" Trey asked again, sticking out his little chest.

"It was nothing." Ed tried to brush it off.

Carson could have stopped Trey, but his son wanted answers and he had a right to hear them.

"She didn't give me away," Trey told them. "Grandpa took me from her and made her leave town. So, you see, you don't know nothing. You're just gossiping."

"Trey, we don't know what you're talking about," Lois said.

"I'm Jena's son." He walked back to Carson, and Carson was so proud of him, he wanted to shout it to the rooftops.

Hilary stood there with a shocked look on her face.

"Are you my aunt?" Trey asked.

Hilary beamed a smile. "You bet I am, and if I don't hug you I'm going to explode." She came around the counter and gave him a bear hug. Trey hugged her back.

"Carson," Ed called. "We're sorry. We didn't know."

"Don't worry about it." He wanted to thank the man. Their gossip had opened a little boy's heart.

AUNT FRAN WOKE Carson at midnight. "Come quick. It's Asa."

He slipped into jeans and ran down the stairs to Asa's room. He was gasping for breath.

"It's...time...son."

"I called 911," Aunt Fran said. "An ambulance is on the way."

"Daddy." Trey and Claire stood in the doorway.

"Tr-cy," Asa gasped.

Carson let them in, for he knew it might be their last chance to talk to their grandfather.

"For-give...me."

Trey and Claire huddled close to the bed, and Carson helped to lift his father's hand to touch them.

"'Bye" was all he could manage.

"'Bye," Trey and Claire echoed.

Paramedics rushed in with a gurney, and Carson got his kids out of the way. He ran upstairs to get his boots.

"I'll follow the ambulance in my truck. Aunt Fran, please stay with the kids."

Carson stayed as close as he could to the ambulance, but at times he got behind. He rushed into the E.R. and found his dad. He was pale and still gasping for air. Asa tried to reach for his hand, and Carson touched him to calm him.

"I…sor-ry."

"I know Pa. Just relax." Asa closed his eyes and his body went limp.

"I'm sorry," the E.R. doctor said.

"Thank you." Carson walked out, feeling drained and sad. After all, Asa was his father.

"THEY BURIED ASA TODAY," Hilary said. "Carson, Trey and Claire looked so sad. You have to come home. They need you."

"I can't do that," Jena told her. "I promised Trey I wouldn't."

"If you had seen him that day in the café, you would know he's changing his mind."

"I want to believe that."

"Then do. The monster is dead. There's nothing standing in the way of you two being together."

"It's not that simple. Carson doesn't trust me not to take Trey from him. If he really loved me, he would know I would never do that."

"Oh. You are so stubborn."

"But I don't know if I can stay away much longer. I miss Carson. I never knew love happened that fast."

"Now we're talking. Just hang on to those feelings."

Jena had a restless night as her head and her heart fought for dominance. In the morning she had no answers, but she knew she couldn't go on like she was.

As she drank her morning coffee, she flipped through the Dallas paper. A Texas Family caught her eye and she read on.

"No!" She couldn't believe what she was reading. The murders and everything that had happened were there, even Asa taking her child. No secret was left out. Willow Creek, the murders—the Brooks and Corbett families were headline news.

She felt her privacy had been violated. But oddly that lasted only a minute. It was time for the truth to be known.

She wondered how Carson was taking it. It had to be hard after losing his father.

Carson. She wanted to hold him.

Ms. Stanton had called Carson to let him know a reporter had broken the story. It was all over Willow Creek, and he had to talk to his kids because they were back in school. He didn't know if they could handle anything else. He himself grew weary from the scandal. But he'd underestimated the resilience of children.

"Don't worry, Dad. If anyone says anything to me, Kelsey will kick their butt. She's tough. I'm tough, too, and I'll watch out for Claire."

"Thank you, son." Maybe he was the only one feeling the strain.

One evening Trey sat at the kitchen table doing his

homework. Suddenly, he said, "Daddy, I want to see my mother."

He froze. "Do you mean you want to visit her?"

"No. I want to talk to her and tell her I'm sorry I hurt her feelings. Grandpa was mean and I don't want to be like him."

"Okay." He was so proud of his son. He'd worked it out on his own. Maybe there was an end to this nightmare. "I'll give her a call."

"Can she come to the house?"

"Of course."

"Can you call her now?"

Carson wanted to do that in private, but it was important to Trey, so he reached for his cell.

She answered immediately. "Carson?" He soaked up the sound of her voice.

"Yes. Trey would like to see you."

"Oh. When?"

"Whenever you can make it."

"I'll leave now."

"You don't have to rush."

"I'll be there before morning."

"Jena…"

"What?"

"Have a safe drive." He clicked off and voiced in his head what he couldn't on the phone.

I love you.

JENA DROVE THROUGH the night and arrived at Hilary's in the wee hours of the morning. She slept for a few hours and got up when Hilary had to go to work. Her nerves were about to get the best of her. At eight she called Carson and he said it was okay to come.

When she arrived, she took a deep breath and prepared to see her baby. This time without all the heart-ache. Just nerves. Carson answered the door and she found she couldn't look away from all the pain in his green eyes.

"How are you?" he asked.

"I'm okay."

"You look great. Your hair is longer."

"Yes." She self-consciously touched it.

"Come in." He stepped aside and they walked into the den. Trey and Claire were on the floor playing a board game.

Trey jumped to his feet. "Hi." He shoved his hands into his jeans.

"Hi, Trey."

There was an awkward moment until Carson said, "You had something you wanted to say to your mother?"

"Yeah." Trey twisted on his bare feet. "I—I'm sorry I hurt your feelings."

"Thank you, Trey." Her heart was about to pound out of her chest.

"I'm playing Candy Land with Claire. It's her game. Wanna play with us?"

"I'd love to." She sank to the floor and engrossed herself in child's play. The day passed too quickly. Aunt Fran fixed lunch and asked Jena to stay. Afterward, she played with Trey on his Xbox. By the time she left, she'd made a connection with her son. And Claire. Somehow she'd inherited an extra child and she didn't mind.

As she was leaving she asked Carson if she could take Trey for an outing. The next day was Sunday, so she thought it would work.

But he was clearly thrown and hesitated.

"Are you afraid I won't bring him back?"

"No."

"You are. I can see it on your face."

"I'm feeling my way here."

"I want to take my son out for the day. Yes or no?"

"Yes, but…what about Claire?"

"I wouldn't leave her behind."

"Then the answer's yes."

She drove away wondering if he was ever going to trust her again.

THE NEXT FEW days were hard for Carson. Jena spent every moment with the kids when they weren't in school. She took them to school and picked them up. He no longer had to worry about Claire's hair. Braids, bows, curls, Jena could do it all, to Claire's delight. Jena helped with their homework, played games with them and took them fishing and to the movies. Every morning they jumped out of bed and got dressed. "Jena's coming," they'd shout, running about.

Not once did Jena ask him to participate and neither did the kids. He was a grown man and he was feeling left out. Terribly. The worst part was he and Jena didn't talk like they used to. He missed that. He missed her.

Trey's birthday arrived and Jena planned his party. It wasn't his real birthday, but Jena didn't seem to mind and Trey didn't question it. Balloons and streamers were all over the house, along with a large banner that read Happy Birthday, Trey. The James family, Levi and Mr. Henry came, as well as Hilary, who'd outdone herself on the cake. The top looked like water and a small boy was fishing beneath a willow tree.

Trey stood at the head of the table, getting ready to blow out his candles. But he paused. "This is the best birthday ever. Thank you, Mama."

Complete silence filled the room. Tears filled Jena's eyes and she hugged Trey.

"She's my mama, too," Claire announced.

"No, she's not," Trey told her.

Claire's bottom lip trembled and Jena looked at him. He nodded. It was the first communication they'd had since she'd returned. Squatting, she pulled Claire into her arms. "I'm happy to be your mother, too."

"See?" Claire said to her brother.

"You're such a girl."

Everyone laughed and Jena cut the cake. Aunt Fran served ice cream. He never realized how much his kids had missed having a mother.

He stood with Levi, eating cake. Bits and pieces of conversation filtered through the crowd.

"I'm leaving on Monday." That was Jena.

"The kids will miss you," Abby said.

"I'll miss them, too."

She was leaving and she hadn't said a word. He turned and walked into the kitchen. Levi followed.

"Hey, I was talking to you."

"She's leaving."

"What?" Levi looked confused.

"Jena's leaving and she hasn't said a word to me."

"Doesn't she have a job in Dallas?"

"Yeah."

"Did you think she'd stay forever?" Levi laid his plate on the counter. "Oh, I can see you did."

"I don't know, man. I fought for her to find her child. Now I feel as if I'm losing both of them."

"Talk to her" was Levi's advice.

"I screwed up."

"What do you mean?

"When I found out Trey was her son, I didn't trust

her not to take him from me. I didn't trust my feelings for her."

"Well, then, you need to talk to her as soon as you can."

"Yeah." Carson had figured that out for himself.

After everyone had left, Jena put the kids to bed and he helped Aunt Fran with the last of the cleanup.

Aunt Fran wiped her hands on a dish towel. "Do you mind if I turn Asa's old room into my room? Those stairs are hard on my aging knees."

"No. Do whatever you want. We can paint it."

"I'm thinking something fresh and bright." Laughter could be heard from upstairs. "It's nice to have a little happiness in this house for a change."

"Yes, it is."

Aunt Fran kissed his cheek. "Night."

"Night."

Carson walked into the den. Barbie dolls and their clothes were strewn on the floor. He picked up one of the dolls and Jena walked in.

"They're out for the night," she said, bending to gather Barbie clothes.

Carson wasn't sure how to start the conversation so, of course, he blurted out, "You're leaving?"

She straightened. "Yes."

"Does Trey know?"

"Yes. He knows I'm a part of his life now. He trusts me to never hurt him." Her eyes narrowed. "Unlike his father."

"Oh, God." He jammed a hand through his hair. "Jena, it's just I don't know what you're thinking or feeling. We don't talk like we used to."

"You want to know what I'm thinking. I have a job and an apartment in Dallas. I'm returning to give my boss notice I'm quitting, but he's probably figured that out since I've been gone so long. He's a nice man and I'm hoping he'll just let me go instead of working two more weeks. I also have to let the apartment manager know I'm leaving and I have to pack everything. But I'm coming home to Willow Creek for good. Hilary said she'd give me a job at the café if I need one."

The pain around his heart eased. "I'm sorry. I just had this sense I was losing my kid and you."

She shook her head. "Carson, when I take him out, do you want to know what he talks about? Daddy. Daddy this and Daddy that. He has you on a pedestal. I just want to share a little part of that pedestal. Can you trust me enough to believe that?"

"Yes," he replied without having to think about it. "The logical answer is for us to get married and raise him together."

She frowned. "Did a buzzer go off in your head when you said that? Marriage is about two people in love who can't live without each other. It's not a logical answer."

He ran a hand through his hair again. "I'm getting this all wrong. I'm tired of arguing when all I want to do is this." Dropping the doll, he stepped closer to her and cupped her face with both hands and kissed her with a fierce need. She moaned and wrapped her arms around his neck. The kiss went on and on and all the confusion and mistrust seemed to disappear.

He leaned his forehead against hers. "I've wanted to do that for days."

"Why didn't you?"

"Scared." He took her lips briefly. "I'm doing it right this time. Jena Brooks, will you marry me? I love you. And I really can't live without you. I actually become an idiot when you're not around."

She laughed, a warm bubbly sound that chased away all his fears. "I love you, too."

Wrapping his arms tighter around her, he kissed the warm hollow of her neck. "Ah. What's that fragrance on your skin? It drives me crazy."

"Sweet pea. It's a body lotion," she murmured.

"Spend the night with me."

"Carson..."

"Shh." He ran his hand beneath her knit top, stroking her warm, unbelievable smooth skin. "Let's just think about us. We have the den to ourselves. We'll turn out the light and..."

"O-kay." Her breath was urgent against his skin.

Her fingers unbuttoned his shirt and he sighed as they tumbled onto the sofa. Wrapped in her arms, there was no doubt happiness had finally found a home on the Bar C.

EPILOGUE

One year later...

"ARE YOU WATCHING ME, Mama?" Trey called, casting his line into the water.

"Yes, sweetie, I'm watching you," she called back. It was hard to take her eyes off him. Sometimes at night she'd go into his room just to make sure he was there.

Jena sat on a quilt beneath a large live oak. Carson lay with his head in her lap. As she ran her fingers through his hair, he opened his eyes and looked at her with a content expression.

"Happy?" he asked.

"Yes, and I know what that feels like now. After everything that happened in this small town, I never dreamed happiness would be waiting for me here."

"It is." He stroked her cheek. "After what you've been through, you deserve it."

She caught his fingers and kissed each one. "A whole year and I'm still so in love with you."

He scooted to sit beside her. "When Claire had the flu you sat up with her all night, I knew I'd never love anyone the way I love you."

She brushed away a tear. "We're getting maudlin."

He was picking up rocks and she was getting

too far away to suit Jena. "Claire, baby, come back this way."

"Where did she get that floppy hat and old Easter basket?"

"When we cleaned out Aunt Fran's room for her to move downstairs, Claire latched on to them and Aunt Fran gave them to her."

He entwined the fingers of one hand with hers. "I like what we did with Jared's old room."

"Me, too." When they'd cleaned out the room, they'd decided to repaint and to make the room bright and sunny. They were big on diminishing depressing memories. They'd cleaned out the basement, too, and Hilary had painted colorful murals all over it. The kids used it as a playroom.

Trey never talked about his biological father and Jena knew he didn't want to be disloyal to Carson. But someday he would ask and they would be there to love and support him.

Claire came running and plopped onto Jena's lap. "I'm tired."

Jena removed Claire's hat, lifting the braided pigtails from her damp neck. "You're sweating."

Claire nuzzled against her and Jena loved the child as if she were her own. She had two kids and she loved them dearly.

The past year had been replete with happiness from the start. They were married in the small church Jena and Hilary had attended with their mother as kids. Trey stood up for his father, Hilary was Jena's bridesmaid and Claire a flower girl. It was a private ceremony with their closest friends. But as they said their vows the small church began to fill up with the people from Willow Creek. As they walked out, everyone clapped. The support and friendly faces were a sign of good things to come. The truth had truly set everyone free.

Jena was a full-time mother now and she loved it. She helped out at the school and had been elected to the school board. Her heart was full.

"Mama, Daddy," Trey screamed.

They were on their feet in a heartbeat and running to the water.

"I think I got Ol' Big. He's pulling me in. Daddy!" Trey kept screaming.

Carson kicked off his sandals and hurried into the water. "Hold on, son."

Jena did the same with her sandals and rushed to help. That fish was not getting her son.

Reaching for the rod, Carson caught it and pulled it up. "Reel, son, reel."

Jena wrapped her arms around Trey's waist. "I got you."

Claire, not wanting to be left out, tromped into the water and held on to Jena.

Trey kept reeling, his little chest pounding.

Carson grabbed the line with one hand. "Back up," he said, and they slowly inched out of the water.

The fish fought vigorously, the big splashes giving them a bath, but Carson and Trey finally maneuvered the fish onto the bank.

Trey knelt by it. "Look at him, Daddy. Look how big he is!"

"Is it a whale?" Claire asked, kneeling by her brother.

Carson squatted. "No, baby, it's a yellow cat. Probably about thirty pounds."

"It can't breathe, Daddy." Claire pointed to the fish's gills, which were working feverishly.

"What do you want to do, son?"

Trey touched the wet fish. "Ol' Big's a legend in Willow Creek. We have to let him go."

"Are you sure?"

"Yeah," Trey nodded.

"I'll get my phone," Jena said. "I want a picture to put up in school and in Trey's room."

She snapped several with Trey and Claire by the fish, and then they all pushed it back into the water. It kicked and splashed and swam away.

They sat on the bank. Carson put his arm around her. Claire sat on his lap and Trey scooted close to her.

"Honey, did your phone get wet?" Jena asked.

"No," Carson answered. "It's in my shirt pocket."

"We don't want to miss the call." Abby was about to give birth at any minute and they wanted to be there for the James family as they'd been there for them.

Claire sat up straight. "Are we getting a baby, too?"

Carson rubbed her shoulder as she sought for a response.

"No," Trey replied before she or Carson could. "Mama has us. We don't need another baby."

It was as if he knew there wouldn't be any more children. The thought didn't sting as before. She had all she ever wanted and more.

"We're wet again," Trey commented.

"Thank God I didn't have on my boots," Carson said.

"We should get cleaned up," she remarked, but no one seemed inclined to move. The wind played with the willow branches hanging in the water. Peace settled in her heart. Trey rested against her and she hugged him. Claire wiggled onto her lap and laid her head on Jena's chest. Kissing the child's soft cheek, Jena lifted her head to gaze into Carson's warm green eyes and saw her future filled with love—his love. She'd found heaven.

Maybe she was a fairy-tale type of girl, after all.

* * * * *

Watch for Levi's story in the next book from Linda Warren's WILLOW CREEK, TEXAS *series,* A TEXAS CHILD, *coming December 2013, only from Harlequin Superromance.*

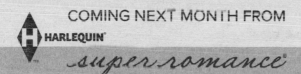
Available November 5, 2013

#1884 BRINGING MADDIE HOME
The Mysteries of Angel Butte • by Janice Kay Johnson

Colin McAllister always believed he would bring Maddie Dubeau home. Then he finds her. Except she's now Nell Smith and has little memory of her past. He must find her abductor, keep her safe...and not fall for her!

#1885 ADVENTURES IN PARENTHOOD
by Dawn Atkins

Aubrey Hanson is an ordinary woman trying extraordinary adventures. But she's unprepared for helping raise her orphaned twin nieces. Luckily she's not alone. Dixon Carter seems to have it all under control—except their attraction!

#1886 NOW YOU SEE ME • by Kris Fletcher

Lydia Brewster longs to shake her "poor widow" image. But reputations die hard in Comeback Cove. No one understands that better than J. T. Delaney. Suddenly Lyddie's ticket to reclaiming her life has appeared in a tempting package....

#1887 THAT RECKLESS NIGHT
The Sinclairs of Alaska • by Kimberly Van Meter

Miranda Sinclair, reeling on the anniversary of her sister's death, has a passionate night with a stranger. The next day she's shocked to discover the man is her new boss, Jeremiah Burke!

#1888 BETTER THAN GOLD
The Legend of Bailey's Cove • by Mary Brady

In Bailey's Cove, Maine, restaurateur Mia Parker and anthropologist Daniel MacLarey discover each other while dealing with a two-hundred-year-old skeleton found in her wall. Their attraction is irresistible, but his past stands between them and love.

#1889 THE MOMENT OF TRUTH
Shelter Valley Stories • by Tara Taylor Quinn

When Dana discovers that her whole life has been based on a lie, she escapes by accepting an opportunity in Shelter Valley. When Josh realizes that *his* whole life has been a selfish pursuit of pleasure, he wants to change—and comes to this town to do it. And when they meet, both their lives are transformed....

On the anniversary of her sister's death, things
aren't going well for Miranda Sinclair—especially
after losing out on a big promotion. So she's
determined to forget about it all tonight. But the
stranger who walks into the bar might not be a
stranger for long....

Read on for an exciting excerpt of
the upcoming book

That Reckless Night
By **Kimberly Van Meter**

"You're as stubborn as your old man and just as mean," Russ,
the bartender, said, setting up her drink. "Why do you do this
to yourself, girl? It ain't gonna bring Simone back."

Miranda stilled. "Not allowed, Russ," she warned him
quietly. "Not allowed." Today was the anniversary of her
youngest sister's death. And most people knew better than to
bring up Simone's name.

This, Miranda thought as she stared at the glass, was how
she chose to cope with Simone's death, and no one would
convince her otherwise. What did they know anyway? They
didn't know of the bone-crushing guilt that Miranda carried

every day, or the pain of regret and loss that dogged her nights and chased her days. Nobody knew. Nobody understood. And that was just fine. Miranda wasn't inviting anyone to offer their opinion.

Russ sighed. "One of these days you're going to realize this isn't helping."

"Maybe. But not today." She tossed the shot down her throat. The sudden blast of arctic air chilled the closed-in heat of The Anchor, and Miranda gave a cursory glance at who had walked through the front door.

And suddenly her mood took a turn for the better.

A curve settled on her mouth as she appraised the newcomer. The liquor coursing through her system made her feel loose and wild, and that broad-shouldered specimen shaking the snow from his jacket and stamping his booted feet was going to serve her needs perfectly.

"Hey, Russ…who's he?" she asked.

Russ shrugged. "Never seen him before. By the looks of him, probably a tourist who got lost on his way to Anchorage."

A tourist? Here today, gone tomorrow. "He'll do," she murmured.

But what if the stranger is not a tourist?
Find out in THAT RECKLESS NIGHT
by Kimberly Van Meter, available November 2013
from Harlequin® Superromance®.
And be sure to look for the other books in
Kimberly's The Sinclairs of Alaska series.

HSREXP1013

REQUEST YOUR FREE BOOKS!
2 FREE NOVELS PLUS 2 FREE GIFTS!

HARLEQUIN®

super romance®

More Story...More Romance